IT'S ALL CHAOS

IT'S ALL CHAOS

IT'S ALL CHAOS

IT'S ALL CHAOS

IT'S ALL CHAOS

IT'S ALL CHAOS

IT'S ALL CHAOS

IT'S ALL CHAOS

IT'S ALL CHAOS

IT'S ALL CHAOS

IT'S ALL CHAOS

Also by HUGH AARON

Essays
Business Not As Usual

A Novel
When Wars Were Won

ABOUT THE AUTHOR

For the past fifty years Hugh Aaron has been writing constantly: letters, plays, movie reviews, essays, short stories and novels. Nineteen of his articles, mostly on business management, have appeared in *The Wall Street Journal*, but only two of his short stories have seen print. In addition to the books listed on the previous page, he has published a business novel, his second, under a pseudonym. A travel journal, and a collection of his war letters are being readied for publication in the near future.

A graduate of The University of Chicago, he was CEO of his own plastics materials company for twenty years, selling it in 1985 to write full time.

He resides by the sea in mid-coast Maine with his artist wife.

IT'S ALL CHAOS

Tales of the Young, the Old,
and the Middle Aged

Hugh Aaron

STONES POINT PRESS
P.O. Box 384
Belfast, ME 04915

COVER by Imageset Design
EDITED by Barbara Feller-Roth

FIRST EDITION

Aaron, Hugh
It's All Chaos: Tales of the Young, the Old, and the Middle Aged
Library of Congress Catalog Card Number: 95-72363
ISBN 1-882521-10-2

$15.00 Softcover
Printed in the United States of America

Grateful acknowledgement is made to the following for permission to reprint from previously published stories:

SAIL magazine: *Old Hands Don't Need Motors* originally published as *"I'll let her go . . ."* copyright © 1987 Sail Publications, Inc.

Preview: *Sailing Free*, copyright © 1991 Timber Publishing Co., Inc.

Epigraph is excerpt from *THE CALL OF STORIES* by Robert Coles. Copyright © 1989 by Robert Coles. Reprinted by permission of Houghton Mifflin Co. All rights reserved.

To

*my wife, Ann,
whose belief in me
gave me the courage to
assemble this book.*

Their story, yours, mine—it's what we all carry with us on this trip we take, and we owe it to each other to respect our stories and learn from them.

William Carlos Williams

Contents

FOREWORD

Life is ten percent of what happens to us and ninety percent of how we respond to it. Aging and its unstoppable passages eat at our thoughts, memories and worries, often causing us to respond in both predictable and very odd ways. As we grow older, passing from the innocence and arrogance of youth, through the blender of middle age, to the creative melancholy of old age, we can't stop thinking about the passing of our lives and the changes that it imposes on us.

Hugh Aaron's short story fiction captures many of the thoughts and worries that plague us all, no matter what age we are. We may not admit it, but most of us, at some time, will reach an age when we reflect and examine our lives, often concluding, "If I had to do it all over again, I'd do it sooner, longer and more often!" A few others may try to seize the lofty high ground, grandly proclaiming that age is not important, unless you are a cheese. Don't believe it. Age is important, but how we respond to aging changes is far more important than merely counting wrinkles or fondling the cheddar.

Since ninety percent of our lives is spent responding to the ten percent of what really happens to us, Aaron has created twenty-three tales that illuminate the human condition of how we deal with life's events. One of his stories is non-fiction and you will have to figure out why he put it in this collection. All ages and predicaments are fair game for Aaron's characters, most of whom you will recognize as being part of our own lives. Tales of marriage, business, friendship, tragedy, lost love, unfulfilled dreams and personal uncertainty all flow from Aaron's pen with masterful delivery, sensitive and poignant.

When you have finished reading, you will feel that several of these stories are too painfully real. The beauty of Aaron's stories is that we see ourselves in them. We can pretend otherwise, but we are there nonetheless. And sometimes that hurts. But take heart! We cannot stop the clock, but we can change the way we respond to life. As for me, the only thing worse than having another birthday is not having one.

WILLIAM D. BUSHNELL

PREFACE

Not until I had assembled this collection of short stories did I have a clue as to what they signified. Although they were written during a period of about thirteen years, they cover roughly the middle fifty years of the twentieth century.

Their characters range in age from five to eighty-five and include both men and women. As I underwent the process of deciding in which order to present the stories, I suddenly realized that they constitute a recapitulation of the post World War II experience in middle class America. They are about the generations that fought and lived through that war and went on to become the most materially successful in our history.

The stories develop many themes, among them loss, courage, trust, friendship, and love. Taking the book as a whole, however, I discovered a common theme that runs through most of them. It's that life is essentially unpredictable, chaotic. The characters I portray are usually in a predicament of their own making. They cope in a variety of ways, some not always successful.

Of course, this revelation says much about myself. The world I seek is one in which I can depend on the predictability of events and the loyalty of others. But this sort of world can exist in twentieth century America only in the imagination.

HUGH AARON

EARLY MANHOOD

Doctor Banner's Garden

The woman's voice issuing from the darkness was frail, yet its tone was commanding.

"Before I would consider employing you, I must have your assurance that you respect plants," said the woman. It was a voice in possession of itself, accustomed to being heeded and certain of its intention.

As I peered into the room and my eyes adjusted to the dimness, for the window shades were drawn against the September afternoon light, I could make out the source, a small, longish, web-lined face framed in a scant wreath of stark white hair supported on a white pillow. The rest of the person disappeared into the bed's blanket folds on which books were scattered, some still open.

"Do you meet that qualification, young man?" She sighed wearily, as if the episode were an effort.

"Well, I used to work in a nursery, ma'am."

"That hardly answers my question. Can you distinguish the weeds from the cultivars? That is what I must know, young man. Your name?"

"Pete—Pete Albert."

"Two good first names. Do you have a last name?"

"No, ma'am. Only first names."

"Well, at least you have a sense of humor. Now I shall see whether you have common sense. One dollar and a half an hour—is that satisfactory?"

"Yes," I said. It was a generous wage for 1947.

"I think twelve hours a week will be sufficient."

"That's okay with me, ma'am."

"When can you start?"

"Tomorrow afternoon, ma'am."

"I'm not a 'ma'am,' Mr. Albert. I'm Doctor Banner."

"Yes, ma'am—Doctor Banner."

"Show him the garden, Justine. I'm tired now and wish to rest," the doctor said, dismissing me with a wave of her spindly arm.

Justine Faray, the doctor's live-in companion, was a tiny, bedraggled, bent woman in her mid-sixties. She stood tentatively in the doorway of the bedroom smoking a cigarette during the interview as if anticipating its early termination. She led me out the rear entrance of the old house to a tiny wooden porch that overlooked a small corral surrounded by a rusty wire fence. Inside the corral sat a large, old, white-haired, sad-eyed dog.

"That's the White Princess," said Justine in a singing Southern accent. "Hello, sweet Princess. Yes, Clarissa will see you again soon, deah."

We stepped off the porch onto a soft, damp dirt path that led into the garden. It was a large triangular plot of tangled growth bordered on one side by a parking lot that belonged to the university hospital. On the second side a thick, high privet hedge shielded the jungle from the street, which was walled with an endless string of low apartment buildings. On the third side stood the doctor's house itself, a two-story twenty-foot-wide Victorian affair with an ornate sandstone face. Many such houses once filled Chicago's South Side grid, but now only a few unappreciated specimens remained.

The university allowed Doctor Banner, a professor emeritus, and her assistant to use the house rent free for as long as the doctor lived. Although Doctor Banner, then in her eighties, hadn't formally taught at the university for more than ten years, she was still conducting biological research in the cellar of the old house. Scores of cages full of peeping mice were stacked there.

After we explored the garden Justine led me back to the house.

"Before we proceed any farther, young man," Justine said apologetically, "Ah must make one thing cleah. The cellah is off-limits, most definitely. Nothing must be disturbed theah."

Dr. Banner's Garden

Justine lit another cigarette and beckoned me to sit down at a large, worn oak table in the center of what was ostensibly the dining room. A pool table-style light fixture hung from the ceiling. On the table books were strewn helter-skelter—books by E.M. Forster, Einstein, Myrdal, Hemingway, books on a bewildering variety of subjects. The room was chaotic, except for a prim, elegant corner in which stood, to my amazement, a massive mahogany cabinet that housed a state-of-the-art Capehart phonograph and amplifier. It was enveloped in dust.

"Ah presume, Mr. Albert, you are a man of yoah word and you will show up when you say you will. Please understand, suh, next to the White Princess, yes, even before mahself, good ol' dependahble Justine, the garden is the most impoatant thing in Clarissa's life. Its curative powah surpasses any of the medicine those quacks have prescribed."

Being a compulsively dependable person, I did of course show up on schedule. Moreover, I liked gardening; I enjoyed feeling cool soil in my hands. It was a welcome reprieve from the daily grind of books and lectures at the university. The unruly garden—a riot of excess growth, weeds ensconced in the perennial beds, lilies of the valley running rampant, masses of roses in unshaped thickets—was to me no less exciting than a lump of clay to a sculptor. I found it especially appealing that by restoring the garden to its former splendor, I might also help restore the doctor's flagging health.

Through the month of September I worked three afternoons a week bringing order to the morass. My relationship with the old women remained on a professionally distant plane. Justine greeted me at the door each time, a cigarette drooping from her pale lips.

"Hush, Pete, walk tippy-toe," she would inevitably say. "Clarissa had a most difficult night and is resting."

The first time I walked through the house to the porch, I saw two sliding paneled doors that closed off another room.

Weeks later when, as was rare, the doors happened to be open, I observed that the room was the parlor. Its space was overwhelmed by a concert grand piano and a large, old Victorian settee.

During my early visits Justine stuck to garden matters, and I hardly saw the doctor even though I had to pass by her room on my way through the house to the rear entrance and the garden.

In early October after I had labored for an afternoon, Justine invited me to sit at the oak dining room table and join her for a cup of tea. I had just cleaned out the weed-choked chrysanthemum bed, which was in abundant flower.

"Ah decleah, Pete, the garden is becoming a mahvelous sight to behold."

"It's shaping up, isn't it?"

"You have been most diligent, and on behalf of mahself, ah do wish to reward you with something extrah." She handed me a small book entitled *A Room With a View*. "Are you familiar with Forstah? No? Well, you certainly should be. Please take this mahvelous gem as a token of mah regard." Inside she had inscribed: "To Pete, the ultimate gardener, for providing my room with a most gracious view. J. Faray."

By the end of October I had completed preparing the garden for the harsh Chicago winter, tying up the shrubs to protect them against fracturing under the weight of the heavy snow that was sure to come, and mulching the flowers with fallen leaves that I hauled from beneath the trees on the street.

On my last afternoon, an unusually mild one for so late in the season, Doctor Banner appeared on the garden path. Her rippling, silky white hair was now neatly contained and her pale, leathery complexion was disguised with rouge. She wore a heavy wool scarf about her neck. Justine supported her by one arm.

"Here, take my other arm, Mr. Albert; let's walk through our little paradise. It pleases me to look out my bedroom window again. You have brought order to chaos—the very noblest of human endeavor. Don't you think that lily bed would look better over there? I think so. Let's do that in the spring. May we expect you in the spring? Yes, it will be something to look forward to, won't it? It will make the winter more endurable."

"Clarissa, don't ovahdo it, now," warned Justine. "Don't you think you've had enough?"

"Perhaps you can return in early March, Mr. Albert."

"Let's go back to the house, Clarissa."

"Shut up!" Clarissa exploded. "I don't need you to tell me what I should or should not do. Now, if you wish to leave the garden, then go. Mr. Albert and I are having a conference."

Justine, her eyes brimming with tears of hurt, released Dr. Banner's arm and headed back toward the house.

"Let's continue, Mr. Albert. Show me everything you have done—everything. I want to miss nothing."

We toured the remainder of the garden, and as the doctor wished, we discussed its every detail, missing nothing.

Returning to the house, I said good-bye. As I headed for the door, the women withdrew to their respective bedrooms—Justine's was off the dining room—stewing in acrimony.

Renting an apartment room near the university from a congenial family, I passed that first winter in Chicago concentrating on my undergraduate studies and making new friends among my fellow students. I met Vicki, who dreamed of someday becoming a concert pianist, and I fell in love with her. Vicki had wide, gentle, dark eyes and a beguiling fragility.

I also formed a happy friendship with a devoted and complicated young man who lived at home with his affluent parents. Good-looking, blond, and pixyish, Lenny dreamed of someday vanquishing the mysterious unhappiness within himself, which he hid under a happy-go-lucky manner.

It was a winter of deep snow and long weeks of subzero cold, more severe than any I had known in my native New England. In January I dropped by to see Doctor Banner and

Justine to find out how the doctor was feeling and to reassure them that I hadn't forgotten the garden. Justine greeted me with her usual exuberance, reeking of cigarette smoke as she embraced me.

"Why, Pete, how nice of you to think of us. What a sweet boy you ah. Shall we have some tea? Please sit down, mah boy."

"How have you been, Justine?"

"Well, you know Justine just goes on and on—Justine the dependahble."

"And Doctor Banner? How is she?"

"She has good days and bad ones. At eighty-five that's how it is." Justine squashed a spent cigarette into a butt-crammed ashtray, then nervously lit another. "Clarissa," she shouted, "you must see who has come to visit."

"You know I'm busy. I have no time for nonsense," the doctor shouted back from the cellar.

"Ah hope you'll excuse her, Pete. Clarissa is in the midst of some very impoatant work, perhaps as momentous as the work that had won her the Nobel."

"Doctor Banner won the—?"

"You didn't know, deah boy?"

"I had no idea. What was her work in?"

"Cansah research. She had discovahed that the propensity for cansah is carried in the genes—that theah's a hereditary factor. Indeed, we traced the disease through thousands of generations of mah lovely mice. But just as impoatant, Clarissa is convinced that a virus is a contributing cause."

"Possibly, possibly," Doctor Banner said as she shuffled into the room out of breath from climbing the cellar stairs. "The early results are pointing in that direction."

The White Princess had straggled feebly behind the doctor, then plopped down at her feet. Clarissa bent over and stroked the dog empathetically. The two, the old woman and the aged dog had reached a similar stage in their biological lives.

"Clarissa, do you know whethah anyone has evah received a second Nobel?"

Doctor Banner laughed; it was a wild cackle, unrestrained and primordial. "Dear lady," she said, "you know as well as I do, I shall be gone long before my work on the virus is completed. And so will you with your stubborn addiction to cigarettes."

"But aren't ah a statistic in the great national experiment? Mah raison d'etre, really. Ah'm a mouse, a most mousy mouse. See, see mah beady eyes," said Justine, pulling her eyelids into slits with her fingers.

"No, you are more stupid than the mice. You are at least aware of the consequences," said the doctor, bitterly. "An experiment on a grand scale is presently in progress, Mr. Albert. Because of our changing social mores, smoking is increasingly prevalent among women. In twenty years, as the incidence of lung cancer in women increases, we shall have statistical proof that smoking is a major cause."

"Peep, peep," said Justine. "Don't ah sound like a mouse? If only ah were as pretty." As Doctor Banner stared contemptuously at her, Justine popped a cigarette between her lips, then struck a match with an exaggerated flourish. "Clarissa, how could ah dayah outlive you?" Abruptly she turned to me. "Well, Pete, have you read the Fostah?" I nodded I had. "And how did you like it? Let's talk about it."

"What Forster?" Doctor Banner inquired.

"The authah, Clarissa. Not in your field. This is between mah friend and ah, if you don't mind." I realized the war between them hadn't abated.

As planned, I resumed working in the garden in early spring. It provided me the extra money, beyond my government stipend under the GI Bill, to take Vicki to concerts and movies and to keep up with my rich friend, Lenny. He called for me in his father's long gray Cadillac, and we glided luxuriously the eight or so miles north along the

Outer Drive that bordered Lake Michigan to expensive restaurants on the near North Side. I was too proud to let him treat despite his insistence. Inevitably he drank too much and lapsed into a tirade against his wealthy and too-generous father.

My girl, lovely Vicki, the daughter of equally affluent parents, saw me regularly in spite of her parents' objections on religious grounds. She was Catholic and I Jewish. On Sunday afternoons we took the IC commuter line downtown to Orchestra Hall where in the uppermost balcony we sat enthralled with both the music and each other. We met weekdays in the library to study together and afternoons we relaxed in the student lounge, where Vicki practiced on the grand piano. Playing Mozart and Beethoven, she always attracted a crowd of admiring listeners. We talked mostly of ourselves, of our future together, and about our mutual problem: her parents.

I told Vicki and Lenny, who had not yet met each other, of the garden, Doctor Banner, and Justine.

"Exactly what is their relationship?" Lenny asked suspiciously.

"What do you mean by 'their relationship'?" I asked. "Justine came up from New Orleans; she had been one of the Doctor's students. They have been doing this research together for more than forty years."

"Probably lesbians," Lenny said.

"I—I don't know," I stammered, puzzled. "I never thought about it."

If they were, I realized somehow it would seem perfectly understandable.

"Someday I'd like to meet them," Lenny added.

"I doubt if that would be possible."

"Just because I said they're lesbians? C'mon, Pete."

"Of course not. It's just that they lead a kind of self-enclosed existence. They seem to shield themselves from the world. Nothing personal, but I don't think they'd welcome you; you'd be intruding."

"Why not ask? Tell them I'm a good friend who'd like to see their garden."

Lenny's motive was suspect, but he did propose an intriguing possibility that aroused my curiosity. What were the two women really to each other? I had to admit there was a chance that Justine and Lenny would hit it off. A common theme pervaded their personalities: Each had a tragic, self-destructive nature.

Through that spring of '48 I worked not only the prescribed twelve hours per week in the garden, but often, at Doctor Banner's request, an additional eight hours on Saturdays. She supervised me closely, showing me how to identify the weeds from the flowers, instructing me to move certain plants from one spot to another, and so on. She was like an inspired artist obsessed with her creation.

"Oh, how wonderful to be young and strong," she exclaimed in admiration as I lifted the heavy rootball of a shrub to transplant it. Actually the doctor had regained some of her waning physical strength. Justine no longer had to support her, and although Clarissa carried a cane, she used it mostly to point at things.

"The gahden has done wondahs for her," Justine said during one of our teatime talks after work. "She hasn't had to stay in bed foah weeks."

Justine, often cynical and self-deprecating, also seemed more pleased with herself lately. Our friendship warmed so that I began confiding in her, telling her of my friends and of my conflict with Vicki's parents. Justine listened, always sympathetically, commenting without pressing advice upon me. When I had a complaint against some injustice, whether real or imagined, she always took my side like a doting parent. She also asked to hear in detail about the concerts, movies, art exhibits, and plays I attended.

"You're so interested. Why don't you go?" I asked.

"Me? Don't be silly, mah boy."

"I'll take you."

"And have you be seen with an ugly, beady-eyed old hag? Why, Pete, you'd be the laughingstock of yoah friends. No, this house is enough foah me; this house and mah mice and literature and Clarissa ah all ah need."

Realizing Justine was most definite, I pressed my suggestion no farther.

By the end of April the taming of the garden was complete and only routine maintenance was necessary, requiring no more than one or two afternoons a week. Having become accustomed to my presence however, Justine pointed out that I needn't wait for my garden chores to have an excuse to visit.

One evening, several weeks later, my landlady knocked on the bedroom door to inform me that I had a phone call. Expecting the caller to be either Lenny or Vicki, I was astonished to hear Doctor Banner's voice.

"I understand you are a frequent concertgoer, Mr. Albert," she said in a most businesslike tone.

"Well, I wouldn't say 'frequent,' Doctor. I go maybe once a month because that's all I can afford."

"How would you like to escort me to the concert as my guest this Thursday night? I have two of the very best box seats in the house."

Hastily I considered the logistics of getting us to the concert hall. Certainly not by commuter IC.

"As you know, I don't have a car," I said bewildered by the invitation.

"We'll use a cab, Mr. Albert. I always do."

When I called at the house on the evening of the concert, the cab was already waiting. Justine was as excited as a mother seeing off her children to their first prom. She kissed us both on the cheek. Even the usually lethargic White Princess barked and licked the Doctor's hand.

"Stop it, stop all this silly emotion," the Doctor protested, but the tone of her voice belied her delight, and she hugged the White Princess. She was glamorous—old fashioned, ornate, overdone glamorous. Her makeup was thick and garish, her brassy dress fitted too loosely, and she was bedecked with sparkling necklaces and bracelets and oversize pendant earrings.

The seats were indeed the best to the left of and overlooking the string section, then located so that we could see the conductor's profile and watch his expressions during the performance. I learned they had been the Doctor's seats for the past fifty years. My seat had been occupied by many a distinguished guest—famous scientists, politicians, and artists from around the world—who came to visit the Doctor during her active years at the university.

As we were led to the box, I sensed that the entire audience was watching us as if royalty were arriving. Many reached for the doctor's hand or waved and said, "How nice to see you. How well you look." Smiling and nodding, Dr. Banner acknowledged their greetings. She was back in the throbbing world again.

Gazing up toward the lofty balcony where Vicki and I always sat, I was surprised at how far away it was. From Dr. Banner's spot the music was all-enveloping. I was immersed in sound as I had never been before.

Concentrating her gaze on the orchestra, closing her eyes from time to time as if in a reverie, Dr. Banner said nothing throughout the entire performance. Learning how deeply she loved music, I wondered why there was none in her home. Why was the Capehart allowed to gather dust, and the piano's keyboard always closed?

During our cab ride back home to the South Side Dr. Banner raved about the new conductor. I reminded her that he had already been the orchestra's leader for more than two years. "My lord, has it been that long since I went to my last concert?" she exclaimed. "What splendid direction. How expressive, how imaginative he was, not like the stiff old German they used to have."

"What German was that?" I asked.

"Never mind. It was before you arrived here."

I wondered why she had refused to explain. What was there about the German conductor that she avoided talking about him?

"Thank you most kindly, Mr. Albert, for a rewarding evening," she said as I helped her to her door. She kissed me lightly on my forehead. "Shall we do it again next Thursday?"

Unaccustomed to such luxurious entertainment, which was, of course, far beyond my means, I was only too eager to accept her offer. Through the rest of the season I escorted the doctor, and on each occasion she was no less enthusiastic than on our first outing. Indeed, I began to suspect the concert was the highlight of her week.

Gradually she dropped her formal ways with me. I became "Peter", and she inquired subtly about my personal life.

"And this girl of yours, how good is she at the piano?"

"You should hear her play. Her teacher tells her she could someday become a concert artist."

"Maybe so. But does she have the dedication?"

"She practices constantly."

"Good. A good sign."

"Would you like to meet her?"

"I'm not sure. I'll think about it."

Dr. Banner's reply surprised me. What could possibly be the harm in meeting Vicki, in talking to her or in listening to her play? But I knew the doctor was not one to be pressed. I brought up the subject of Lenny, of his brilliant mind and his puzzling inner turmoil and his enormous record collection.

"Maybe someday, with your permission of course, I'll bring him to visit."

"Perhaps someday."

"We could listen to his wonderful records on the Capehart."

"We'll see."

Doctor Banner's transformation from the irritable, distant, demanding, bedridden old woman who interviewed me nine months earlier, to the presently involved, expansive, more giving spirit that was revealing itself, was miraculous. Justine attributed the change mostly to my zealous restoration of the garden. She said it had taken her out of a boring rut, too. Then inhaling a cigarette deeply, Justine lapsed into a coughing fit.

"I wish to hell you'd listen to Dr. Banner and quit," I said.

"Ah appreciate yoah concern, mah boy, but ah've gone beyond the point of redemption. Heah we ah, three old hags, with nothing but ouahselves to live foah. You've brought us beauty and young strength and yoahself. Now we have somebody moah than ouahselves to worry about. It's about time."

As my familiarity with Dr. Banner increased, I noticed the reverse was happening in my relationship with Justine. It was as if she purposely drew away in order not to dilute or distract the other developing closeness. At times she exhibited a new brusqueness. Had I said or done something that hurt her?

I conceived an ingenious proposal. "Could I bring Lenny over?" I asked Justine one afternoon. Lenny was so well read. And were he to play his records on the Capehart, it would be like bringing a concert hall into the room. He also drank too much; Justine was naturally drawn to anyone who indulged in some excess. "We would have Dr. Banner's permission of course," I reassured her.

"Clarissa's permission be damned," Justine shrieked. "This place is as much mine as hers — hah, it belongs to neithah of us. Ah'd be pleased to meet yoah friend. Perhaps we'll get drunk together."

She and Lenny were symbiotic from the very first. Justine embraced him as if their meeting were a loving reunion. She patted his back.

Although it was only two in the afternoon on the day of our visit, a large bottle of white wine stood on the oak table which was tidier than usual: The books, instead of being strewn about and open, were stacked closed along the far edge. Justine's short, straight hair had been neatly combed; uncharacteristically, she wore lipstick.

"You poah boy," she said. "A fellow smokah and a drinkah too."

Lenny grinned, joyous at finding another renegade. "You? Suicidal too?" he said.

"Of course, mah boy, but moah impoatant, ah'm statistical — hah, mah death will have meaning. But what is yoah unhappiness about? Let's begin with some wine and a cigarette and a discussion on Forstah. Pete has informed me of yoah appreciation of mah favorite authah."

Excusing myself to take up my chores in the garden, I overheard Lenny say as I left the room: "Forster reaches me like no one else. I suppose it's because he and I have something in common — personally, I mean."

Later in the afternoon when I returned from my gardening labors for the traditional teatime, Justine and Lenny were still at it, a bit more boisterous from the wine, and by then declaring themselves old friends in spirit. They were joined by Dr. Banner, who, although not having imbibed, was thickly engaged in the repartee.

"I'll put on some tea," said Justine, rising to go to the kitchen as I entered the smoke-fogged dining room.

"I must say, Peter," said Dr. Banner, "I like your friend."

"I think the Bach did it," said Lenny. "Right, Clarissa?"

Had he called her Clarissa? Audacity was part of Lenny's charm.

"Well, of course, one can never hate a lover of Bach," said Dr. Banner.

"We're going to have a concert on the Capehart next Saturday evening," said Lenny triumphantly.

"I trust you'll join us, Peter," Dr. Banner announced as if it were mandatory.

Justine returned with teacups and a steaming decanter and began to pour.

"Could I bring a friend?" I asked. "I mean Vicki."

"Certainly, mah boy," Justine piped up. "It's about time we met her."

"Is that okay with you, Doctor?" I pursued cautiously.

"I suppose so," she said indifferently.

"In fact, we could have a live concert, too. I'm sure Vicki would be willing to play for us," I added.

"Say, what a wondahful ideah," Justine exclaimed. "But of coahse we wouldn't want to impose. Clarissa, we must have the piano tuned. It has been so long since you've played, deah."

"Because they no longer obey, my sweet," the doctor said, spreading her gnarled arthritic fingers before her on the table.

"But aren't we lucky? Suddenly we ah surrounded by new, fresh lives," said Justine ecstatically. "It's fah from ovah, Clarissa."

"Why, yes, I agree."

"Then you'll try again. As we used to."

"Oh, I'll see."

"Try what, may I ask?" I queried.

"To shake the world, mah boy," said Justine.

"Terrific, Clarissa, shake it," said Lenny.

For some time, Vicki had wanted to meet the "old ladies." When she and I were together, which was three or four times a week, I rarely failed to refer to something Justine had said, or to Dr. Banner's opinion on a musical performance or to the new blossoms in the garden. Although I believed I did this in all innocence, it was unthinking of me. My allusions only whetted Vicki's desire to meet them all the more, but I had to stall and make phony excuses because of Dr. Banner's curious aversion to meeting my girl.

Now, at last, Vicki would meet them. We were going to a musical party at the "old ladies'" on Saturday night. Vicki said she could hardly wait. It would also be her first chance to meet Lenny, whom I often mentioned admiringly. But when I suggested that she plan to play a piece on the piano that evening, she vehemently rebelled.

"I don't understand your objection," I said. "You play in the student lounge all the time where anyone can listen."

"That's not the same as giving a performance," she responded.

"You wouldn't be performing, Vicki."

"Of course, I would."

"Christ, I told them you'd be willing—"

"Without consulting me?" she interrupted, anger flashing.

"Doctor Banner should hear you play, Vicki. She'd appreciate you more than anyone I know."

"Well, I'm sorry," Vicki said, calming down. "But I don't want to be judged."

"Okay, okay, if that's the way you feel."

"It is, Pete. Please try to understand."

That cool May Saturday evening, Lenny fetched me in his father's Cadillac, then we drove to Vicki's home. Lenny called at the door so that I wouldn't have to deal with her parents and risk a scene.

"They think I'm going out with Lenny," Vicki said, giggling. "And were they impressed when they saw the Cadillac."

"Yeah," said Lenny. "Hell, they wanted to know which model it was and how I liked it. I played right along. Was that okay, Vicki?"

"Perfect."

"I told them it was the best Caddy I'd driven in years."

We laughed until tears came.

On the way over to the doctor's house, Lenny, outgoing and always appealing, informed Vicki of the program he had planned on the Capehart. They were her favorites, too, she said. Beyond their common love of music, their personalities seemed to simply mesh.

"At first, you'll probably take Clarissa for a sourpuss, but don't be fooled," Lenny said, proud of his insight. "She's got a real funny bone. Right, Pete? And Justine's the opposite; she acts like she doesn't give a damn about anything, but she cares about everything."

Justine greeted us at the door. "Yoah here! Owah stahs ah here, Clarissa," she shouted, as if amazed that we showed up. She drew Lenny to her, pulling him through the doorway. "Come in, come in, you lovely boy. And this is Vicki, is it? Come in, come in, sweet girl. Immensely delighted to meet you."

As she embraced me, she said softly near my ear, "Ah must say, yoah taste is impeccahble."

As Lenny warned, Clarissa greeted Vicki with a cool "How do."

Glancing at the Capehart, I noted that it was now free of dust, its mahogany grain shimmering under the floor lamp setting beside it. Turning to the parlor, I observed that the piano too was now shiny, the keyboard exposed, the cover raised.

We sat around the oak table as Justine asked Vicki about herself, about her music and her ambitions. Dr. Banner merely listened without comment, without displaying any interest.

"Would you kindly play something for us, deah girl?" Justine said, smiling tenderly.

"I thought—I mean, didn't Pete explain—I'm sorry, really sorry, but—"

"Oh, yes, Pete explained yoah reluctance— yoah understandahble reluctance—but mah deah, you needn't be nervous. It's all in fun and you ah among friends."

"I know quite how you feel," Dr. Banner said suddenly. "When I was young I hated it when my parents asked me to play for their guests. After all, they weren't my guests. I wished to play only for my own pleasure and for the pleasure of others of my own choosing. Yes, I quite understand how you feel."

"Thank you for being so understanding, Doctor Banner. Do you still play?" Vicki looked toward the parlor to scrutinize the piano, an old Steinway, older than any she had ever seen.

"Sadly, my playing days are over."

"Your piano is beautiful."

"Yes, fifty years ago it stood on the stage at Orchestra Hall. A gift from the conductor."

"Hah, yoah boyfriend, the conductah," Justine interjected, referring to a romantic liaison of Clarissa's youth.

"But why did you stop playing?" Vicki asked.

Dr. Banner rose, walked to the piano, and sat on the bench. She placed her hands on the keyboard and played a chord.

"See, my fingers are like the twigs of a petrified tree, not like yours. Let me see them." Vicki moved toward her. "Here, sit beside me. What glorious fingers; how slender and supple they are. I would give years of my life to have such hands now."

Ever so lightly, Doctor Banner positioned her twisted fingers on the keys, pressed them down slowly, then moved them over to a new position. We heard an exquisite melody issue forth, the first chords of Mozart's Sonata in A Major—the eleventh. Then her fingers stumbled and stopped.

She closed her eyes as if imagining that her fingers had resumed their tripping course across the keys, as if the melody were still magically filling the room. But it was not a fantasy after all; the music was impossibly real, marvelously lovely. The sonata was alive. Vicki had taken up where Dr. Banner, who gently removed herself from the bench, had left off.

For the next fifteen minutes Vicki played the piece flawlessly to its triumphant end, pouring herself into it with relentless intensity. Her world was entirely circumscribed by the keyboard and somehow this frightened me. It crossed my mind, as she became lost in a distant glowing trance, that I was witnessing an overwhelming adversary.

When she was done, we clapped until our hands ached; we shouted bravo, and I kissed her and said, "Thank you, thank you, I love you," and Lenny kissed her and Justine embraced her and Dr. Banner held her hand and said, "Well done, young lady, very well done, I must say."

"It's time to celebrate, mah deah friends. Let's all have some wine," said an elated Justine.

After the wine, which enhanced our exuberance, Lenny loaded the records in the Capehart. Lenny was adept at this complicated process, which was typical of the early automatic players. The impossible complexity, I learned, was the reason that Doctor Banner had given up trying to use it.

When the music began, Vicki and I withdrew to the Victorian couch in the now darkened parlor while the others remained seated around the oak table in the dining room. Invisible in the gloom, Vicki and I held each other and kissed, urged on by the tremendous tension of Sibelius's Second Symphony, which amplified our emotions. Later, during the playing of *El Amor Brujo — Love the Magician*, and inspired by its raw, erotic power, we made love.

Soon the evening disappeared and we slept until the glint of a rosy dawn penetrated the parlor. In the dining room Lenny was lying spread-eagle across the oak table, a pillow under his head. The ladies had retired to their own rooms.

"Oh, my God, Pete," Vicki said, leaping from my arms, "my parents must be going crazy with worry."

"They'll blame Lenny," I said gleefully. "Maybe now they'll appreciate me more."

That summer I remained in Chicago working the night shift at a gas station on 51st Street. At least once a week I spent a few hours working in Doctor Banner's garden. Vicki went off to a music camp in Vermont, much to her parents' relief—anything to keep us apart—and Lenny aimlessly hung around the city, bored and gradually destroying himself with alcohol. He must have spent a good deal of time visiting

Justine, however, for whenever I showed up for work in the garden, I usually found him sitting at the oak table in lively conversation with her. Justine, a natural if not a passive listener, thrived on being needed. She, better than anyone I knew, could relieve, at least for a while, Lenny's torment.

On occasion I was baffled by Lenny's apparent disinterest in women, except as asexual friends, but I shrugged it off as a meaningless and temporary aberration. Often I worried aloud to Justine about Lenny, both before and after she became his confidante.

"If he'd find the right girl, I know he'd find himself," I suggested.

Justine squinted at me to ascertain whether I was really serious. "Ah see you have a very limited understanding of yoah friend's problem," she said with a certain sting.

"It's his parents," I said unequivocally.

"No, mah boy, it's ouah society, but ah have said all ah intend to say, and ah wish to discuss the mattah no futhah."

Months later, prompted by a tragic event that would befall us both, Lenny confessed that he was homosexual. In 1948 such an orientation was devastating. It was a frustrating, agonizing existence in which he was torn between his desire, the shame of it and the self-hate it generated, and the wish to be otherwise.

During my weekly work visits to the garden, I rarely saw Doctor Banner. She was hardly ever home those days, Justine said, because "She's busy out theah doing her patriotic duty." I interpreted that to mean the doctor was actively espousing her anti-cancer crusade against cigarette smoking. Not until the doctor joined me one afternoon in the garden did I discover that I was mistaken.

By the end of that summer her metamorphosis from an irascible, discouraged, incapacitated shadow to a vital, enthusiastic person was complete. Throughout the concert season when I was her escort, she still had her bad days and often had to cancel our plans, but now she was routinely up and about, no longer needing a cane, taking in the fragrance of the flowers and their parade of colors as if she had discovered sensation for the first time. In fact one afternoon she had knelt down on the damp ground and began assisting me in weeding. We worked side by side for an hour, sometimes talking, sometimes lapsing into an easy silence.

"This fall, Peter, I think I shall have you plant some flowering shrubs and shorten the flower beds. It will reduce the maintenance."

"Okay, if you want, but I can keep up with it as it is now."

"Ah, I see. Then you plan to stay with me forever."

"Well, I'm only in my second year."

"Of course, I shall have you awhile longer then."

"Absolutely."

"And have you decided on a career? I gather you are still in the general undergraduate program."

"I haven't the faintest idea what I want to do, Doctor."

"I presume you know I wanted to be a concert artist, and look what happened." She chuckled. "Few of us become what we dream of in our immaturity. All my life I have been frustrated over how little I've accomplished."

"But the Nobel—"

"An accolade representative merely of world opinion. What I wish for myself is far more important. It was never the prize; still I suppose I'm pleased with the quality of what I have achieved. And now—have you considered politics, Peter?"

"No, never have."

"Our country is in such dire need of good leaders."

Mentioning the national elections coming up in November, she asked which presidential candidate I favored. It wasn't Henry Wallace, her choice.

"More than anyone else, I assure you, Henry knows what ails our country and what medicine to apply. More than anyone else, I assure you."

"But he's surrounded by fellow travelers. Aren't the Communists behind him?"

"Nonsense. That's the ultimate absurdity, Peter—propaganda spread by his enemies. There will be a giant rally at Soldiers Field next week. You must come and listen to him."

One hundred thousand souls thronged the rally. Clarissa stood on the rostrum, paused momentarily before the microphone awaiting silence then in her aged, cracking, imperative voice introduced Henry Wallace. One hundred thousand adulating souls roared their approval. Henry raised Dr. Banner's tiny arm with his. It was Henry and Clarissa, Henry and Clarissa. I could hardly believe my eyes; I could hardly believe my ears.

September. More than plants had flourished in Doctor Banner's pleasing and peaceful oasis plunked in the middle of that South Side brick and asphalt desert. Our lives, too, intermingled and grew together, flowering no less dazzlingly than the cultivars that Dr. Banner coaxed and treasured. But nothing endures, neither the ugly nor the beautiful.

And then I turned down Dr. Banner's invitation to escort her to the concert hall that first Thursday of the new fall series. I had promised to take Vicki. Dame Myra Hess, Vicki's idol, was to be the soloist playing the hauntingly melodic Rachmaninoff Second Piano Concerto.

"You could ask Lenny," I suggested to Dr. Banner.

"Are you telling me whom I should ask? Your audacity, young man, is boundless." Dr. Banner picked up one of Justine's books and slammed it down on the oak table. "I believe I've made my preference clear."

"There will be other concerts," I said. My statement had a familiar quality. Hadn't my mother spoken to me in the same manner when I was a child?

"She is not good for you, Peter. Let me warn you, she will yet break your heart." Dr. Banner's tone was sardonic.

"Vicki?" I said. She remained silent. "You resent her," I went on.

"Certainly not. I fear for you. She is good, very good at her art, Peter. I perceive that her music is all consuming.

Someday, and very soon, there will be no room for anything else."

"We love each other," I exclaimed.

"Of course you do. But do you want a life languishing in her shadow, taking a back seat to her music? As certain as I know the results of my mice experiments, I predict she will someday appear on the stage at Orchestra Hall. You have much to offer, son; make a mark for yourself. She can never help you become somebody."

Dr. Banner was a woman mad with resentment, mouthing total nonsense, I felt. Hadn't she herself said being somebody wasn't important? Refusing to listen to more, taut with rage, I stomped from the house, passing Justine returning from the market with a bag of groceries in her arms.

"What's the mattah, mah boy?" she said, alarmed.

"She's a jealous, domineering witch," I shouted and ran on.

October passed, then November. Henry Wallace lost. The garden went untended. Without preparation for the coming winter, some of the plants were bound not to survive. I hadn't shown up once; I never called. I was more involved with myself, less aware of the implications of my actions. My inattention was painfully cruel and unforgiving. My reaction was unpardonable.

Lenny had continued to drop in to see Justine from time to time. He told me that she was hurt by my behavior, that she now realized I added up to less than I seemed to be. But Lenny, too, began seeing the ladies less often as his drinking increased. Soon he hardly saw them at all. He was thinking of committing himself to a mental hospital to dry out. He was drunk when he called one evening to tell me that Dr. Banner was not well. The White Princess had died.

"My God, the poor woman," I said, stricken with sorrow at her loss.

I was at their door the following afternoon after class. Justine answered my knock.

"I just heard about Clarissa—and the White Princess," I said.

"And what do you want?" Justine said coldly.

"May I see her?" I shifted uncomfortably from one foot to the other.

"She's sleeping. And if she weren't ah don't think she would be pleased to see you."

"May I come in at least?" I begged. She hesitated. "I'm sorry, Justine. I'm sorry for the way—"

"All right, come in, if you wish, but only for a short while."

I followed her into the dining room and we sat as we used to at the oak table. The room was chaotic as never before: newspapers, books, soiled dishes lying about on the table, on chairs, on the Capehart, dust laden again. Through the window the garden appeared brown, dead, wild, pockets of leaves covering the flower beds, scraps of paper, having blown in from the street, strewn here and there. Even an occasional tin can and a soda bottle were visible.

"She's dying, mah boy," Justine said, suddenly abandoning her earlier rancor towards me. "Ah'm afraid she's lost her will to go on. She won't cooperate with the doctah. Nothing ah do pleases her. The White Princess is the only creature that has ever truly made her happy. Not me. Never me."

"Sure you have, Justine."

"No, nevah." She shook her head emphatically. "Nevah enough."

"No one could be a more dedicated companion than you, Justine."

"You pleased her, mah boy. You made her happy again. She became the way she used to be. It was truly remahkable."

"If I could see her—maybe it would help."

"Perhaps. Yoah absence saddened her—moah than you realize."

"Then I'll come by tomorrow. Okay?"

Dr. Banner's Garden

She rose to accompany me to the door. "If tomorrow comes, if it comes." We embraced. "Good boy." She smiled sweetly. "How nice to have you back. Aftah Clarissa you are the only family ah have left."

The following afternoon there was no answer to my knock on the front door. I climbed through the privet hedge on the street bordering the garden and banged on the back door. Again no response. After dragging an old iron garden bench to Dr. Banner's bedroom window, I could make out her bed and lying on it in the gloom a wraith of her person.

The police had little trouble forcing open the front door. In the dining room Justine was bent over the table, her face lying sideways in her arms as if she were sleeping. The policeman, feeling for her pulse, said she was dead. Clarissa too was gone.

Dr. Banner's lengthy obituary, which stated that she died of natural causes, made the first page of the three major Chicago newspapers and the *New York Times*. It listed her remarkable achievements in science and her many activities "dedicated to advancing the democratic principles of our free society."

A small, routine notice on Justine's death appeared among a long roster of similar notices on the obituary page. There was no mention that she died of an overdose of sleeping pills, no mention of her contribution to science or of her long association with Doctor Banner. Neither had surviving relatives.

But they did have survivors. A few retired colleagues showed up at Dr. Banner's funeral, so Lenny and I appointed ourselves the ladies' survivors. We would keep their memory alive and pass it on to anyone who cared to listen.

On the drive back from the cemetery in Lenny's father's Cadillac, I reproached myself for having severed my ties with Doctor Banner and Justine.

"I deserted them," I said. "Actually they depended on me for more — for more than just the garden."

"You couldn't have known," Lenny said.

"But I should have. I should have been more aware."

It was then that Lenny spoke of his own misery, of his homosexuality.

I had missed seeing so much.

Natural Friends

The professor and the German were sitting in the lounge at Ida Noyes Hall when I arrived.

"Ben, this is Sigmund," said the professor.

Rising from the chair, bowing stiffly at the waist, the German clicked his heels, extended his hand, and smiled.

"Hans Sigmund Wolff at your pleasure," he said with barely a trace of an accent.

Only the Nazi salute was missing. I knew his sort. Only four years earlier (when I was 19) I had entered the concentration camp with my platoon and witnessed the horror.

"I hope I won't cause you any inconvenience," he went on. "Professor Herzog has explained everything."

The left arm of his threadbare blue blazer was folded and pinned to his shoulder. A camera hung on a leather strap from his other shoulder.

The professor was Jewish. Why would he tolerate a Nazi? Wolff was thin, pale, even emaciated. His cheeks were sunken. A shock of sandy hair fell over his forehead Hitler style.

"Thank you, Ben, for hosting Sigmund," the professor said.

"No trouble at all," I responded.

"You know that his father, the judge, was my closest friend when I lived in Munich."

"I know, Professor."

"You do?"

"When are you leaving for Baton Rouge?" I asked.

"Tonight, the eight o'clock train. I ask myself, why go south in the summer? Ah, the life of a teacher. When did I last see your father, Sigmund? Maybe eleven years ago?"

"I was only a child, Professor."

"Yes, so you were, and look at you now with a wife and child in Germany." The professor's eyes moved from

Sigmund's face to his empty sleeve. "Stay at my place as long as you wish. I'll be back in late August. Did I tell you that Ben will then take a room elsewhere?"

"Yes, I know—thank you for your offer," Sigmund said, "but I must leave by the first of September. I miss my wife and child even now."

"Sigmund is an executive with Kodak back in Munich, Ben."

"Yes, you told me, Professor."

"You know that his company has sent him here to attend the university's business school."

"I do, Professor," I said.

"Ah, me. Am I repeating myself?"

Sigmund's eyes met mine and we smiled, amused at the professor's forgetfulness.

"I wish to learn of your remarkable American management methods," said Sigmund. "By the way, are you interested in photography? No?" He laughed. "I confess, next to my wife and my child, I love my Zeiss most." He paused. "I hope we shall be good friends."

"I hope so."

"Call me Siggy, eh?"

"My name's Ben, an old Jewish name."

"A good name," he said, grinning.

Siggy attended class at the University of Chicago and I pumped gas. In the evening he studied in the professor's large, airy bedroom. I read novels in my cubicle off the kitchen. One of them was Orwell's *1984* which I planned to give him when I knew him better.

"I'm crazy about America," Siggy said one evening. "I inhale democracy with every breath, eh? Your country is my country's model, and you are mine, Ben."

On Sunday afternoons I drove him around Chicago and the prairie countryside.

"Everything is so big here," he said. "In my country the world is smaller. Someday you must visit. My wife would like you, Ben, just as I do."

Siggy was indeed irresistible. A natural good feeling arose between us, and our compatibility gave me great pleasure.

I took him to a party of mostly university students at a friend's sparsely furnished apartment. Everyone sat on the floor.

"This is my friend Siggy from Munich," I said. "He's at the B School for the summer learning how America works."

Siggy pumped hands and bowed. "Delighted, delighted," he said.

I had warned him not to click his heels.

"I was Hitler Youth, Ben," he had explained. "It is hard to forget the habits of the past. I want to be American. Thank you for advising me. This is good."

Siggy's easy nature instantly captivated the students at the party. He was the center of a huddle most of the evening.

"Why have you kept him to yourself?" my friends asked.

Someone turned on the phonograph. Edward R. Murrow's solemn voice commanded us to silence. It was his new recording: "Hear It Now," a series of speech excerpts by the world's great political leaders just before and during World War II. We heard Roosevelt's compelling voice, Churchill's venerable words, and Mussolini's bombast. When Hitler came on spouting frenzied German, we ignored him and began a free-for-all conversation.

"Quiet! Quiet!" Siggy shouted. "The Fuhrer is speaking. Listen to what he is saying. It is important."

Our eyes fastened on Siggy. He seemed bewitched by Hitler's screeching. As the dictator reached a crescendo, his audience thundered, "Sig Heil, Sig Heil, Sig Heil." Siggy's eyes glistened. He rose and made the Nazi salute at each shout. He was transported back in time to the glory days of Nazi hegemony.

Everyone fell silent. I wanted to disappear. When the speech was over Siggy turned to us. "Thank you for your attention. I hope I caused you no inconvenience."

"Let's get out of here, Siggy," I said annoyed, and rushed him from the room.

On the walk to our apartment, he said, "I like your friends. You Americans are so, so,—what should I say—so loose. But you aren't very political. I mean, you have a limited view, no ambitions for your country. You are too self-involved. But I like you all the same. It was a most stimulating evening, Ben. Thank you."

I was angry at myself for trusting him. I should have realized that a leopard doesn't change its spots. "You're a goddamn Nazi, Siggy," I said.

"No, Ben. I told you before. I was never one of them."

We walked on in silence. When we arrived at the apartment we went to our rooms without saying good-night.

After that evening I made a point of avoiding him. When I couldn't, feeling uncomfortable in his presence, I kept conversation to a minimum.

Siggy's nights grew troubled. His screams and moans often awakened me. His face had become even more wan than when I first met him and his eyes were bloodshot.

One evening he knocked on my door while I lay on my cot reading.

"What do you want?" I shouted.

"Let's talk, Ben."

"I have nothing to say."

"Ben, I want to know. Why have you stopped having dinner with me?"

"Don't bother me, Siggy."

"Why do you shut your door? You never used to. What have I done, Ben?"

I opened the door.

"It's what you are," I said.

"Ben, I'm an ordinary man. I feel only goodwill."

"I don't like your beliefs."

"My friend, my dear friend, our beliefs are the same. I believe in democracy, peace, the basic goodness of people everywhere."

"Like hell you do," I exploded. "You're a goddamn Nazi. You have no concept of what makes America tick. You haven't accepted your country's defeat. You still think you were right."

"Please, please, Ben, you misjudge me," Siggy begged, his voice cracking. "I admire you, I admire America. I worship your freedom. It is a model for the world."

"Words, Siggy, goddamn words."

"Please, please hear me out," he said, raising his finger to his lips. "As I have said, I have never been a member of the Nazi party. How can I prove this to you?"

"But you were sympathetic. All of you were."

"Not all. No, not all. I agree, most went along. We had no choice. But my family was apolitical. You served in the American army, a draftee. Like you, I fought for my country as a conscript in the Wehrmacht."

"But you—you were an officer, a captain, a leader," I said venomously.

"Yes, of course. I had the education. I was qualified. Would you hold that against me?" He was perspiring and his hands trembled as he swept the lock of hair from his forehead.

"I suppose you deny knowing about the concentration camps."

He raised his eyes to the ceiling, and when he lowered them they were brimming with tears.

"How could I know? I was only a soldier on the Russian front. You can't imagine how terrible it was. A rout, Ben. My arm is still there. In the mud. Crushed under the tread of a Russian tank. I am ashamed of what my people have done. But I personally didn't know. How could I? I swear. The shame. The shame."

He sat on my cot covering his face with his one hand. Tears coursed down his sunken cheeks and dripped from his chin onto his trousers.

We began spending time together again. We resumed the weekend drives into the countryside, visited the Morton

Arboretum, basked in the sun at the Indiana Dunes, and sailed a rented boat on Lake Geneva in Wisconsin. But I avoided having him meet my friends again.

One friend who witnessed Siggy's behavior at the party said later, "I know his type. He's programmed. He thinks he's a superman and that Jews are dirt. How can you live with him?"

"He's not that way," I said.

"After what he did at the party? Christ, Ben. He's a robot."

"No, he isn't. He suffers for what his people have done."

"He's sucked you in," my friend said.

The professor was due back in a few days. The late summer winds whipped up the lake. Siggy and I stood fascinated as we watched the waves smash against the rocky revetment.

"I think I'll take up the professor's offer and stay awhile longer," he said. "Until my money runs out."

"I'll be staying at the Rheinsteins," I said. "Let's keep in touch."

"Definitely, Ben. You are the main reason I'm prolonging my visit." We sat on the sea wall. "You see, Ben, I'm quite happy here. I like your country. It is like—well, like this lake: enormous, beautiful, pulsating. It excites me."

"But your country is beautiful, too. The loveliest in Europe. And Germans have cause to be proud; once you were the world's leaders in science and technology."

"But it is all over, lost," he said forlornly. "I never understood. With all our brilliance we should have won. We almost did. Do you realize, Ben, that had our factories not been in ruins from your bombings we would have made the first A-bomb?"

"That's crap. Nazi propaganda," I said.

He smiled condescendingly. "You admit that we had the world's best scientists. Why not accept that we also led in nuclear physics?"

"Because the best brains fled your country and all of Nazi Europe. Don't you know what happened? Einstein went to Princeton. Fermi came here to Chicago."

"Einstein? Fermi? Who are they? I don't know them."

"What? Are you kidding me?"

"Certainly not."

"Szilard? Von Neumann?"

"I've never heard of them."

I jumped to the sidewalk, yanking Siggy with me. "Freud. What about Freud?" Siggy shook his head. "Ever hear of Kafka?"

"Who are they, Ben?" he asked bewildered.

"Brilliant scientists, writers. Mostly Jews."

"Ah, I see."

"I'm not so sure. We're going for a walk. I'm going to show you where it all began."

He laughed. "Now you are absurd, Ben. You Americans exaggerate so. You are always the biggest, the best, the first—just like children."

"You blind sonofabitch," I said.

Pulling him by the arm, I raced across the Outer Drive, dodging the speeding traffic. We fast-walked almost two miles along the grassy Midway until Siggy begged me to stop for a rest. I refused.

"Are you coming or not?"

"Please, Ben, I'm not as young as you."

"What happened to all your Wehrmacht training?"

"Ben . . ."

I dragged him on. I was releasing all the years of accumulated rage I had felt against the Nazis, against all Germans, for what they had done to the Jews, my people.

We reached the rear of the football field stands and stared at a brass plaque mounted on the sidewalk. I read aloud, "On December 2, 1942, Man achieved here the first self-sustaining chain reaction and thereby initiated the controlled release of nuclear energy."

Siggy shook his head. "This proves nothing, Ben. Anyone can cast words in bronze."

"Under those bleachers in the squash court Fermi built the first atomic pile," I said.

"In a squash court? Ridiculous. A fairy tale. Someone has a wild imagination. Let's go home. You have worn me out."

I had nothing left to say.

After the professor returned I reclaimed my old room at the Rheinsteins, a German refugee couple in their early sixties. Mrs. Rheinstein, a large motherly woman, enjoyed doting on me. She left a snack in my room each evening to "nache" on.

"We had a son," she said with tear-filled eyes. "He would have been your age but . . ." She was unable to complete the sentence.

Her husband, Willy—round, bald and impish—spoke in guttural English about his department store in Danzig. He found it hard to adjust to the life of a menial factory worker in Chicago.

Siggy and I saw little of each other after I moved. My quarter at the university had begun and I pumped gas at night. The episode at the stands nagged at me. I couldn't abide Siggy's distorted view of history. We may have been natural friends but ideologically we were strangers.

After a month he appeared at the door of the Rheinstein apartment. It was late—almost eleven. I had just changed into my pajamas. Mrs. Rheinstein pounded on my bedroom door, shouting excitedly, "A man is here to see you." Opening the door, I saw she was terror stricken.

"What's wrong, Mrs. Rheinstein?"

"He's in the hallway," she said and walked away, wringing her hands.

Siggy was standing in the apartment entry. He seemed upset.

"What's the matter?" I asked.

"It's your landlady."

"What about her?"

"She said she knows me."

"Does she?"

"I have never seen her before."

"Then what's the problem?"

"I frighten her. Am I so terrible?"

"Forget it, Siggy. She's high-strung. Life has been hard for her. Come in. Take off your coat. Let's go into my room and talk."

He wanted to return to Germany, he said, but he had run out of money. "I don't have enough for airfare. I've thought of asking the professor for a loan, but he has been so generous already." He reached into his coat pocket and withdrew his Zeiss camera. "Would you accept this as security against a loan, Ben?"

Receiving only a small stipend under the GI Bill and pumping gas to supplement it, my savings were small. The professor would have been a better touch. But this was an opportunity to prove something to Siggy.

"I don't need a camera, Siggy."

"I see. I remember. You don't take pictures. Forgive me." He slumped forward on the bed and stared at the floor, dejected.

"I'll give you the money," I said. He raised his head. "Not a loan. A gift. How much is the fare?"

Tears started down his cheeks and he embraced me. "My good friend, how can I thank you? I'll pay you back someday when the mark is worth something."

"Don't worry about it. But promise me one thing."

"Anything, Ben. Just ask."

"Read this. Read it on the plane." I handed him my copy of *1984*.

"I will, I will," he said with joy and gratitude. We embraced and said good-bye.

Immediately after Siggy departed, Mrs. Rheinstein knocked on my door.

"May I speak with you, Ben?"

Her voice was shaking. "That man must never enter my home again. Do you understand? You must tell him he cannot come here. How can you associate with him? I am surprised at you, Ben. A Jewish boy."

"But, Mrs. Rheinstein, what has he done?"

"What has he done? You don't know? He was there on Krystallnacht. He knocked on thousands of Jewish doors. He led us to the ovens. I know him. What is he doing here in America? He soils the air."

"You're wrong, Mrs. Rheinstein. You're lumping him in with the Nazis. He wasn't one of them. He's a decent man."

"So, he has won you over. We used to believe what they said, too. We thought they had accepted us. We were all Germans together. But we were wrong. Don't let him fool you, Ben. They are all the same."

I realized that nothing I could say would change her mind.

"You are like a son to me," she went on. "But if you invite this man into my home again, I must ask you to leave. I am sorry. I would have no choice."

"He's on his way back to Germany," I said.

"Good. That's where he belongs. May he stay there and rot. Now, let me bring you something to nache."

"Not tonight, thank you, Mrs. Rheinstein. I'm going to bed."

"Then sleep well, my boy. Good-night."

As I lay back on my pillow, I felt a lump under it. From beneath it I withdrew an object. It was Siggy's Zeiss.

All That Glitters

His first summer at college, Jimmy operated a candy route on the south side of Chicago.

"I'd like to make one thing clear," said the boss the day he hired Jimmy. "If you extend credit to anyone, it's your responsibility, your neck. We'll take any delinquencies out of your bond, see?"

The customers were small mom and pop neighborhood stores and an occasional supermarket. Most were poor credit risks, only marginally profitable at best.

At 7:00 A.M. Jimmy stocked the shelves of his rattly company van with a variety of candy bars—coconut, peanut, peppermint—both chewy and soft. The rule was that he'd be stuck with what didn't sell unless he traded it with another driver.

In a few weeks, several store owners had befriended Jimmy and favored him with the bulk of their candy business. Among them was Gus Fantas, a small, beaming, friendly man in his early forties who owned a tiny, sparsely stocked, rinky-dink convenience store in the middle of the "black belt." Gus was one of those who let Jimmy make up his orders for him.

"Whatever you think I need is okay with me," he'd say. "How much do I owe?"

Gus would push the NO SALE key on the cash register, withdraw a fistful of cash, and count out the desired amount of bills with a flourish, making sure that Jimmy saw how flush he was.

Gus's store, which Jimmy visited every Thursday, was his favorite stop. He and Gus had such congenial talks he found it hard to tear himself away for the next call. They talked about a range of subjects: the economy, Gus's war experiences, Jimmy's long-range plans and women. Gus was a true man of experience, informed and wise.

"I've got to go, Gus," Jimmy would say, still lingering. "I've got to go."

"Jimmy, you got it made," Gus said.

"What do you mean?" Jimmy asked.

"The niggers go crazy over your peanut bars. 'Course it's junk but it fills 'em up."

"Are you saying the *customers* are eating candy instead of real food?" Jimmy asked. He emphasized *customer* because the word *nigger* bothered him.

"Hey, Jimmy, where you been? The niggers don't have enough money for real food. See the dust on those cans of vegetables? Your candy moves ten times as fast which is okay with me. I make more money on the candy anyway."

"That's not right, Gus. You shouldn't encourage them to eat so much of my stuff."

"You want to sell, don't you? Get wise Jimmy, unless you want to finish last."

On the second Thursday in August, Jimmy made up Gus's order as usual. Gus pushed the NO SALE key on the cash register but this time the bill sections were empty.

"Christ, Jimmy, I forgot to go to the bank for cash this morning. How about a check this time?"

"I'm sorry, Gus, but checks are against the rules. The company won't take them."

"Well, that's too bad. I s'pose you'll just have to take back the candy."

"I don't want to do that, Gus."

"I know you don't, Jimmy. You're a real friend. But I wouldn't expect you to break company rules."

"Well, I could take your check but I'd have to cover it personally."

"You mean you'd do that, Jimmy?"

"If it bounced I'd be responsible."

"You have my word. My check's as strong as steel. You've got nothing to worry about."

"I know that, Gus. I'm not really worried."

Gus made out a check for fifty dollars and handed it to him.

"You've got all my candy business from now on. I owe it to you," Gus said.

"I appreciate that."

"You mean much more to me than just a candy salesman, Jimmy."

Jimmy departed glowing. He thrived on the trust and friendship that had ripened between him and his customers. Though he was eager to return to college, he felt a certain regret that his job would soon end. He would miss the everyday banter with the customers, especially the talks with Gus.

A week after he turned in Gus's check to the company, his boss informed him the check had bounced.

"It's all rubber," said the boss. "I warned you. Give no credit, take no checks. You didn't listen."

"Gus Fantas is a friend," Jimmy retorted. "I'm sure it's a mistake. I know he'll stand behind it."

"I hope you're right, kid, but don't count on it. The company's taking the money out of your bond. Sorry."

"That's okay. I'm not worried," Jimmy said.

On Wednesday, the day before Jimmy normally called on Gus, he visited Gus's store. Though on a hot summer day Gus's door was usually open, that day it was closed. A sign was affixed to its window. In large red letters it read: SHERIFF'S NOTICE. Smaller print explained that the store was closed for non-payment of debts and that any unpaid creditors should file a complaint with the local police.

Jimmy was in a daze as he drove to the neighborhood police station. He hadn't figured Gus to be a deadbeat. There had to be an explanation that would exonerate his friend.

Detective Sullivan, a brash, middle-aged man, was in charge of the case. He directed Jimmy to the chair beside his desk.

"Fill out this complaint form and join the crowd," Sullivan said.

"I don't understand," Jimmy responded, stunned. "Gus was so friendly and considerate. He seemed like a real nice guy."

The detective laughed. "Looks like a lot of others thought so too. He sure knew how to play people for suckers."

"I still can't believe he won't make good."

"Wise up, fella. You've been taken. Let's have the check. We'll need it as evidence. It's a felony, y'know."

"Maybe I ought to wait."

"Look, fella, do you want your money or not?"

"Maybe if I talked to him —"

The detective roared with laughter. "Talk to him? Where do you expect to find him?"

"You mean you don't know where he is?"

"Someplace on the moon, I suspect."

"I see."

"The guy's a con artist. I hate seeing a decent fella like you get hurt. It's a tough world. So now you're damned pissed, right?"

"Yeah, I'm real sore."

"Good, you stay that way. You've been conned and you've got a right."

"I suppose so," said Jimmy. It sure was a tough world.

Jimmy's candy route had surpassed the aimed-for $500 mark. In early September Jimmy quit after giving fair notice and breaking in a new man. Back in college he took up his studies with the same conscientious and determined attitude he had demonstrated on the candy route. Submerged in college life, he had, by December, relegated the incident with Gus to the almost-forgotten past.

During the Christmas break Detective Sullivan phoned.

"We've got him," Sullivan gloated.

"Who?" asked Jimmy.

"Whaddya mean 'who'? You forgot already, fella?"

"You mean I'll get my fifty dollars?"

"Is that all you care about?"

"Well, sure. I mean—"

"Don't worry, you'll get your money. They've set a court date for next Wednesday morning. I'd like you to be there."

"Next Wednesday? Let me see."

"I thought you were pissed off."

"I was."

"Christ. I don't know why I stay in this lousy business," said Sullivan.

"Well, I am sore," Jimmy said, summoning up a remnant of his old rage.

"If you want your money, you'd better be there, or you can forget it."

"I'll be there."

"Be in the lobby outside Courtroom B of the county courthouse at 9:30. I'll tell you what to say. Look, I've been working damned hard on this case, so I expect you to show up, okay?"

"I said I'll be there."

Jimmy admired Sullivan's perseverance. Clearly he was a fine cop. Never having been in court before, he was glad that the detective would be at his side.

Though Jimmy arrived at the appointed location on time, Sullivan was late. But Gus was there, hardly recognizable in a smart blue business suit and a white shirt with a red tie. Jimmy was used to seeing him wearing a soiled white apron over a T-shirt and trousers that were too long.

Grinning like a Halloween pumpkin, Gus approached Jimmy, his hand extended.

"Jimmy, Jimmy. Gee, it's good to see you. I've been looking everywhere. Where you been hiding?"

"That's baloney, Gus."

Gus took Jimmy's limp hand and shook it firmly. "I've been looking for you so I can pay you back the fifty bucks I borrowed."

"Borrowed? Don't give me that, Gus. Your check bounced."

"Hey, I'm sorry. You can't imagine how sorry I am. D'you think I'd leave you holding the bag? A decent kid and a good friend like you? Not on your life. When I gave you that check there was enough to cover it. But some jerk attached the account for no good reason. I feel terrible about what happened."

"What about the others?"

"What others?"

"The other creditors."

"Who cares? They're not my friends." Gus pressed six crisp bills into Jimmy's hand. "Here's the full amount and ten more for your troubles."

As Jimmy was about to insert the bills into his wallet, Detective Sullivan appeared.

"Don't take his money, fella," he said. Jimmy turned as Sullivan reached for his arm and pulled him away from Gus. "He's buying you off. Let's you and me talk privately for a minute." With lightning motion he slapped Jimmy's hand, causing the bills to flutter to the marble floor. "Leave them," he ordered as Jimmy bent down to collect them. Gus stared at the bills strewn at his feet.

"He's paying back everything he owes me," Jimmy protested.

"Sure, and something for your trouble, too, I suppose," Sullivan retorted.

"The money's all that matters."

"What about justice? Don't you care about that?" Jimmy flinched. "How do you expect us to put criminals behind bars—protect society—if the public don't complain? How do you expect us to do that, huh? Don't you think it's your duty as a patriotic, public-spirited citizen to help stop crime? We bust our goddamn humps for you and is this all we get? As long as you get yours. Is that all that counts? Huh?"

"No, sir, but Gus isn't a criminal. He just explained—"

"Explained what? That ten rubber checks is an accident? Say, you gonna let him twist you around his little finger again?" Jimmy looked toward Gus, who stood ten feet away staring at the floor, undecided whether or not to retrieve the bills. "Listen fella, if you drop the complaint, I won't have a case, see, and that sonofabitch knows it."

"How about the others, the other complainants?"

"They've settled for fifty cents on the dollar, the bastards. Do what I'm asking and you'll get yours, all of it, and he'll get what he deserves. On my word of honor as a cop."

Jimmy strode over to Gus, picked up the bills, and handed them to him. "I don't want your money, Gus."

"So you'd rather take the word of that cop sonofabitch? Well, I'm disappointed in you, Jimmy; I'm hurt and very disappointed."

Gus's lawyer appeared. "You'd better get your ass into the courtroom, Gus, unless you want the judge to declare you in contempt." A sheen of sweat covered Gus's face.

Sullivan and Jimmy sat on a bench at the rear of the courtroom. After a bailiff introduced the case, Gus's lawyer spoke. He depicted Gus as a responsible family man. He had five children and a wife in Kansas City.

"Why," the judge asked, "weren't they living with the defendant at the time of the alleged crime?"

"Because," the lawyer explained, "my client couldn't afford to move them here."

"Bull," Sullivan muttered, "Gus was living with some floozy in a crummy walk-up right here on 63rd Street."

Gus's lawyer continued. "My client is also a highly educated man; he attended Illinois State. He's a reputable businessman with a record of success in St. Louis."

"Bull again," said Sullivan. "He dropped out of State in his first year, and the business in St. Louis was a Mafia-financed setup."

Jimmy was confused. Who was telling the truth: Gus's lawyer or Sullivan? Which was the real Gus: the man he came to know as a friend or the one who welshed on his debts?

"Furthermore," Gus's attorney continued, "my client has settled with all his creditors. He's made good on all his debts. Under the circumstances, I urge your honor to dismiss the case."

Jimmy nudged Sullivan. "What about me?"

"Relax, fella. Just relax. It's not over yet," Sullivan said.

"Certainly it would appear a dismissal is in order," the judge said.

The state's attorney protested. "Just a minute, Your Honor. If I may enlighten you concerning this man's record?"

"He has a record?" the judge said, astonished, looking at an impeccably dressed Gus Fantas, who had put on his most innocent demeanor.

"Five years in Leavenworth, your honor: robbery, three years: passing bad checks, two years—"

"What?" Jimmy whispered to a grinning Sullivan. "It's hard to believe."

"Surprised, are you?" Sullivan said.

"I've got the picture, Counselor," said the judge, raising his hand.

"Yes, Your Honor, I'm sure you have."

The judge motioned the two lawyers to approach the bench. While they huddled the bailiff removed Gus from the courtroom through a door at the side of the room.

"Stay here, fella. I'll call you in a few minutes," Sullivan said, heading for the same door.

Ten minutes later Sullivan showed up and led Jimmy through the door into a small room. It was bare and windowless. A detective was bent over a table counting out stacks of bills. Gus sat stark naked on a wooden chair in the center of the room, staring at the floor. He seemed in a trance, oblivious to anyone's presence. Gus's blue suit, shirt, underwear, and red tie lay crumpled in a pile on the floor beside him. Picking up the trousers, Sullivan pulled the pockets inside out.

"We got it all," he said to the detective.

"I wonder what bank he robbed this time?" the other detective said.

"Yeah, Gus, what job was it," Sullivan cracked as he hovered over Gus's nude figure. He struck a stiff blow to the side of Gus's head with the palm of his hand. Gus remained unresponsive. "Help yourself, fella," Sullivan said, directing Jimmy to the stacks of bills.

Jimmy felt pity for Gus. How could this likable, supportive man, a seemingly sincere friend who had always been so wise, how could this man now reduced to a zombie have failed him? How could he be the opposite of what he had seemed? Sitting in the middle of the room, he appeared so harmless, so innocent.

"Go ahead, help yourself," Sullivan repeated. Jimmy picked up a stack and counted out fifty dollars. "Take the whole damned thing," Sullivan said.

"This is all he owes me," Jimmy said.

"He's a crook, fella. Take more. He doesn't rate any consideration."

Jimmy gazed at Gus, whose eyes never left the floor.

"Everybody deserves some dignity," Jimmy said.

"When are you gonna wise up, fella?" asked Sullivan.

"You're no better than he is," Jimmy retorted.

"You crazy? You can say that after what I just done for you?"

Jimmy returned the fifty dollars to the stack.

"What in hell you doing?" Sullivan demanded.

Ignoring Sullivan, Jimmy strode from the room. Too bad they caught Gus, he thought. Too bad he himself had cooperated with Sullivan. The old friend he knew remained branded in his mind. He forgave Gus. As Sullivan said, the world was tough. Jimmy refused to reciprocate in kind.

It's All Chaos

Dear, dear Julian,

You will find Allan Ackerman, the bearer of this note, intelligent, trustworthy and hardworking, the sort of young man who would be of immeasurable value to you in your thriving enterprise. Having just returned from the war, he's had his fill of horror and man's inhumanity. You know how impossible it all is, dear, even without war. Now he wants to build a future for himself in a secure and challenging organization. Poor searching boy. I know you'll give him your utmost consideration.

Love to Carol and a double portion to you,
Bessie

Julian Martin Brodsky tossed the letter on his vast, bare mahogany desk, whose top resembled an airport runway. He tilted back in his soft-cushioned, high-backed, black velvet executive chair.

"What are you good at Mr. Ackerman?" he asked, making a tent of his hands. He wore a white shirt with gold cuff links; his shaven face was powdered, pocked, and pasty.

"A lot of things," I replied, seated stiffly across the runway. Behind him was a large factory window that looked across the Illinois Central tracks to the busy highway beyond that bordered a length of Chicago along Lake Michigan.

"That's not what I asked," he said gruffly, raising his bushy eyebrows and staring into my face with watery eyes. "How much do you know about business?"

"Nothing, I'm afraid," I said meekly.

"Good. You have no preconceived notions. Then I take it you're prepared to start at the bottom?"

"I think so, sir."

"You think so? Either you are or you aren't. Which is it?"

"Just so long as I have an opportunity to advance," I said, shifting awkwardly in my chair.

"The goddamn trouble with your generation is that you expect to start at the top. You think in a year you'll be ready to move into my job. Ain't that right? Do you have any idea what it took to get to where I am? Hell, you don't have the vaguest notion. Of course you don't."

He rose and walked to a bar along the wall behind me. The ice cubes clinked as he poured a glass of scotch on the rocks even though it was only ten in the morning.

"Well, whaddya say? How'd you like to sit where I am?"

I studied the thick beige wall-to-wall carpet at my feet searching the pile for the safe answer. The office was quiet, save for the dull background rumbling of machines on the floor above.

"Someday, Mr. Brodsky, I think I'd like that."

After quaffing his drink as if it were Chicago's chlorinated water, he poured another.

"Then be my guest," he said, crinkling his face into a smile and extending both arms from his sides, palms up. "We'll find out how good a judge of character Bessie is, won't we? Okay, seven tomorrow morning, report to the fifth floor. You'll start as a stock boy."

Bessie was the kind-hearted, wacky wife of the director of the boys' camp where, only a few months after my discharge from the army, I was a counselor during the summer of 1946. She and an older fellow counselor, Kirk, a social studies instructor at the Laboratory School of the University of Chicago, took a special interest in my then-uncertain future. I returned from the war in a quandary and bitter over three "wasted" years. I felt "old." Should I enroll in college or immediately take up a career.

"I feel in a hurry," I had told Kirk. "I've got to get started at something—stand on my own feet. I'm almost twenty-two, just when most kids are graduating college."

"Look, I'm twenty years older than you," Kirk had said. "From where I stand, two or three years one way or the other don't matter. Sure, many of your classmates may be kids, but because of your maturity and experience you're bound to get more out of your studies. You'll be a model for them."

Kirk's advice notwithstanding, I had my fill of discipline in the army; college seemed to be only more of the same. Bessie's advice had impressed me: "Dear boy, taste the bitterness and sweetness of life first before deciding on a direction. Few of us end up doing what we studied for in college. Life is a constant muddle, don't you know. It's all chaos."

The stockroom filled an entire factory floor, a maze of shelves brimming with an endless variety of lampshades in all shapes, sizes, and materials—from paper to silk. Jerry, a vigorous, tall, rod-shaped man in his thirties, was in charge. He screamed orders and rushed from one place to another as if attached to a rubber band.

"Who says you're a stock boy? JB? What does he know? You're an order picker, see. Stocking the shelves is only a minor part of your job. Homing pigeon, that's you; after you know where things are, you'll go after 'em without even thinking. See that stack of shades there? Learn where each item belongs. Don't waste time. Go to it."

In a few weeks I became top man in the department. I planned my itinerary up and down the rows in advance and never backtracked.

"You're a fuckin' homing pigeon all right," Jerry said, giving me a raise. "I'll scream if they take you away from me."

I knew that Mr. Brodsky had other plans. After three months he made me manager of the silk lampshade division on the fourth floor, which produced five thousand of the company's daily total of thirty-five thousand lampshades.

"Now don't let this go to your head," Mr. Brodsky cautioned. "This is just a trial to see how well you handle responsibility. I'm appointing you against Jim's advice; he doesn't think you're ready. Says you're still a kid, which you are, but . . . Well, just don't let me down."

He sauntered to the bar and poured a scotch on the rocks. It was only eleven in the morning.

Jerry had no use for Big Jim, the plant superintendent and number two man after Mr. Brodsky. "He's all for himself, bad for everybody else," he warned. Big Jim's hulking body was shaped like a watermelon, with a small cantaloupe for a head perched on top. When puzzled, he had the habit of squinting his tiny birdlike eyes into the distance.

The silk lampshade department manufactured the Rolls Royce's of the entire line. The department, taking up half a factory floor, was bright and colorful. Eighty women worked there. They cut the fabric from patterns on vast tables, stitched it together on a battery of sewing machines, fitted it onto steel frames, applied the trimming, and finally wrapped the completed shades with strips of shiny cellophane.

The women were proud of their department. They hummed the popular songs that blared from the plant-wide PA system. The women were supervised by two competent foreladies—Helga, a sour old-timer, and Jan, a young, dark, green-eyed beauty with high cheekbones and a rousing figure. Since neither had a family, their work was the most important thing in their lives. I was lucky to have them.

September 1947 was a heady time to be in Chicago, especially on the South Side around the university where I lived. There was a freshness and excitement everywhere. It emanated from the trees along the streets. Gusting breezes, still tinged with the warmth of summer, tore at the leaves that had begun to turn yellow and brown. Streams of students making their way to class, their arms laden with books, jammed the sidewalks.

Kirk found a room for me with the Kilbourn family on 57th Street near Kimbark. Mrs. Kilbourn was delicate, in her mid-fifties. Mr. Kilbourn, a tall, slender man, smiled but rarely spoke. Kirk himself lived in an airy old-fashioned apartment nearby on 59th. The building was an elegant, imposing three-story Victorian affair.

Filled to the brim with low apartment buildings yet quiet and peaceful most of the time, the neighborhood was an island of affluence and primness extending from 57th Street to the Midway north and south and to Cottage Grove and Lake Michigan east and west. Beyond, Chicago roiled and pounded. Well to the north, off Michigan Avenue, was the lampshade factory.

"Dear boy," Bessie Lightman had said, "there's too little time for formalities and pretense. I am what you see. Just call me Bessie." Though some counselors took her for a "screwball," Kirk, the camp's tennis counselor for six years, said she was "really all heart."

I wrote Bess Lightman.

Dear Bessie, I want to thank you for recommending me to Mr. Brodsky. In less than three months, I've been made manager of a small division in the factory. Despite his bluntness, I like him. But I do have a few reservations. He tends to drink too much. I suspect he has some personal problems. Should I be concerned about these matters? I know you'll level with me.

Soon after I took over the department I began dating Jan, the forelady with the comely figure. We'd go dancing at the Trianon on Saturday nights to the rich, full sound of big bands. Later in the evening a hush would fall on the hall as the music softened. We could hear only the shuffle of the dancers passing by. It was like gliding across smooth water as we danced into the early morning. I was enraptured. Jan's shapely form melded into my body. I became confused. Was this love?

Jan and I talked mostly about the department. She complained about her women. One popped bubble gum. Another was malodorous. Jan's complaints bored me. But her beauty overshadowed her shallowness. When we danced on the crowded floor in muffled silence, she was all I wanted.

Hoping to broaden Jan's interests, I took her to a symphony concert at Orchestra Hall. We sat in the uppermost tier, where the stage seemed miniature but the music was clear and strong.

Fidgeting, she whispered in my ear, "The band's too far away."

"Good seats are hard to get," I said. "Shush."

"This is my last time unless . . ."

"We can hear perfectly from here. Quiet."

"But we can't see. They all look like tiny dolls."

"Damnit, Jan, we came here to listen. So listen."

She sulked. At the end I stood up and shouted "bravo" and applauded until my hands hurt. That was our first and last concert together.

It became apparent that our department couldn't keep up with the demand for silk lampshades. Big Jim said we weren't doing our job. I pointed out that our daily production figures exceeded those of my predecessor.

"If he was competent, you wouldn't be here," he said. "You've got to do better."

The previous manager had quit after five years, sick of putting up with Big Jim's demands. "You'll never make Big Jim happy," he had told me while cleaning out his desk the day I took over.

I met with the foreladies in my small office at the edge of the production floor to discuss what we could do to increase production.

"The girls are doing their very best," said Jan. "We don't have a single slacker."

"Don't pay any attention to Big Jim," advised Helga. "He's impossible to please. He'll make your life miserable if you don't ignore him."

I was challenged by the task despite Big Jim. Either I could hire more workers, which probably would hurt the bottom line, or I could devise a more efficient system. Over the next month I secluded myself at a table behind some stacks of lampshades. By relocating cardboard scale models of equipment and work stations, I simulated a floor plan that would improve the flow of goods through the manufacturing process.

During lunch and coffee breaks, the women would wander to my corner and study the plan and make suggestions. One suggestion, a simple but revolutionary way of transferring the shades in their various stages of manufacture from one operation to another, was brilliant.

One day while cruising through the department, Big Jim discovered my project.

"What's this?" he demanded, glancing at a replica of the department lying on the table.

"A flow plan," I replied.

"I didn't authorize any changes."

"It's only a proposal, Jim."

"Just stick to managing. Don't try to be an engineer."

"You asked for more production, didn't you?"

"Sure I did," he said, his voice rising. "And if you'd keep your girls from screwing off . . . They're always combing their hair or manicuring their nails. Your department has become a goddamn beauty shop."

"I've told you before, Jim," I said as my voice neared falsetto, "they're waiting because of a bottleneck up the line. This new layout will solve the problem."

"Hell it will," he shouted. "If you managed your people better . . ."

"Let's let JB decide."

"You report to me, not JB."

"Maybe, but he picked me."

"Okay, kid, you asked for it. It'll be either me or you."

As Big Jim stormed off, Jan offered support. "I know Mr. Brodsky will back you, Allan. Don't worry about a thing."

"I'm not so sure," I said.

"I just know," she said as she kissed me lightly on the lips.

I was puzzled by her confidence but I was too upset to think about it. I told Kirk about my difficulties with Big Jim. He was always a sympathetic listener.

"Sounds like Big Jim is out to prove that JB was wrong about you," said Kirk.

"Maybe I made a mistake not going to college," I said. Kirk always raved about the university and the exciting innovations that Chancellor Hutchins had introduced.

"What happened at Jefferson Industries could happen anywhere," Kirk said. "If you were in college, some professor could be giving you just as hard a time. Anyway, I suspect that Brodsky has too much of his ego invested in you to let Big Jim have his way. I think your job is safe."

Kirk calmed me. He was immensely popular among his students. He looked ordinary—a thin frame and a small face with a receding chin, wavy gray hair neatly parted in the middle. But his brown eyes revealed a humanity and generosity. Never when I needed him did he deny me an ear.

That evening after dinner at a restaurant on 57th Street, dejected, I trudged up the stairs to the Kilbourn apartment. Passing through the worn living room to my cubicle, I found Mr. Kilbourn seated, still in his business suit and tie, perusing the newspaper. Mrs. Kilbourn, nearby in an upright chair reading Emily Dickinson, looked up and said, "Good evening, Allan. I hope your day was fulfilling."

"Oh, sure," I said wearily.

"Would you care to join us for dinner tomorrow evening?"

"I'd be glad to," I said, happy at the prospect of a home-cooked meal. Having been exposed to the enticing aromas that often wafted in from the kitchen when I came home from work, I knew that Mrs. Kilbourn was an outstanding cook. Her invitation, added to Kirk's encouragement, restored my spirits.

Jan had her own apartment on the North Side. After the Saturday night dances I would stay over at her place. In 1947 an illicit liaison was kept secret, mostly because it sullied the reputation of the woman involved. But Jan didn't care who knew. She admitted having been with other men, and I was no virgin either. While we dated steadily, I demanded sexual commitment. But her tight sweaters and slacks troubled me and I thought that she was too cordial toward other men. When I complained she feigned innocence saying that she didn't really mean anything by it: It was simply her natural way. My jealousy delighted her.

On the job Jan was all seriousness. She was as dedicated and conscientious as I was. Furthermore, she disliked Big Jim as much as I, but for a different reason. Shortly after she had joined the department, he made advances. She resisted, objecting that he was married. He persisted. When she said she wouldn't have anything to do with him even if he weren't married, he fired her. But in a week, she was mysteriously rehired.

Big Jim and I reported to Julian Brodsky promptly at 8:00 A.M. the Monday after our altercation. Seated behind his desk on his throne, sipping a drink, Mr. Brodsky motioned us to a long couch to his left. Behind us were two wide, grimy factory windows with chicken wire embedded in the glass.

"Okay, Jim, tell your story again."

"JB, the kid's got to understand he can't change things without my okay."

"Would you say that's an unreasonable request, Allan?" Brodsky asked as he swirled his drink into a whirlpool.

"No, but I intended to show him my plan before I did anything with it."

"He has a point, Jim."

"The kid goes off half-cocked on his own when he's supposed to be running the department. I didn't ask him to make any changes."

"Excuse me, Jim. I'm Allan, not 'the kid', okay?"

After downing the rest of his drink, Brodsky leaned back, pondered momentarily, then said, "This flow plan of yours—I understand it has some clever, maybe revolutionary, ideas. Are you sure it'll work?"

"I'm damned sure, Mr. Brodsky."

How did Brodsky know the details of the plan? Certainly Big Jim wasn't the source.

"Then you can guarantee an increase in production, right?"

"Yes, I can."

"His girls aren't doing their job," Big Jim interjected. "He has to get them to work harder. We don't need his new-fangled ideas."

Brodsky waved his words aside. "By how much can you increase production?"

"I can't say," I replied.

"What if you're wrong."

"I won't be."

"Are you willing to put your job on the line?"

"Yes, sir," I said promptly.

"What more could you ask for, Jim? You have my permission to fire him if he doesn't deliver."

"But that's not the issue here, JB. He's defied my authority."

"The issue is, do you want to increase production or don't you? You've got someone with fresh ideas. We should encourage him, not beat him down."

Brodsky walked to the bar and scooped some ice cubes into his glass. "Let's give the kid—that is, Allan—a chance. If he doesn't make it, you win; if he does, you still win: His production will be better."

Big Jim clenched his jaw and squinted his eyes. He was now a hardened enemy. But I had a new appreciation for

Brodsky. He believed in me and my morale soared. I blessed Bessie. She knew that the man to whom she had consigned my future was a man of quality after all.

Early spring arrived. Kirk and I took long walks on the Midway, through Jackson Park and along the wall that bordered the lake shore. I yearned for the open fields and woods of my native New England. Kirk sold me his '39 Ford, a jewel of a car that I planned to keep polished and garaged in an alley off Drexel Avenue. The car would enable me to visit the nearby Wisconsin countryside to assuage my homesickness.

I had the car for only a day when I let Jan drive it. An oncoming car hit us broadside in the rear quarter when she went through a stoplight. Mortified, I screamed at her: "How could you be so stupid?" She sat paralyzed behind the wheel and wept.

She wanted to pay for the damage. I refused, grateful for her offer. I cared for her. But did I love her? Certainly I valued her more than my precious Ford. Someday I suppose I would ask her to marry me. But I wasn't ready yet. Something indefinable held me back.

One morning about a week after the meeting in Brodsky's office, Julian Brodsky in a wrinkled business suit, his tie slightly askew, strode in. It was 10:00 A.M. and the department had developed a smooth pace. As they worked the girls hummed to the popular ballad bleating from the PA; I was bent over the table in my corner finishing up the flow plan. Brodsky stood inside the entrance to our floor, hands on his hips, surveying the busy scene. Suddenly he pointed to one of the women. "You're fired," he shouted. Flustered, the woman burst into tears. I rushed down the aisle between the stacks of lampshades to see what had happened. Jan was there trying to comfort the helpless victim.

"What did she do?" I asked Brodsky.

"Nothing," he replied.

"Then why—? I don't understand." Jan led the tearful woman away from her workplace.

"Why? You're asking me why? 'Cause she's doing nothing. Not a fuckin' thing, see. Tha'sh why."

He reeked of whisky. Jan glared at him. He leered back, challenging her. Their silent exchange was oddly personal, as if it were part of a pre-existing private battle.

"See tha'sh she leaves the building now or elsh," he warned, then turned and left.

Or else what? Or else he'd fire me too?

Bessie's letter, which arrived soon after the episode, elucidated in part JB's behavior.

Now I'm not one to indulge in gossip, dear boy, and I don't want you to think ill of Julian. But I suspect he's beyond saving after what you tell me. Surely, my dear, you deserve to be enlightened.

In his defense, I must tell you that Julian's marriage has been stormy to say the least. Yes, it's not surprising that he's drinking. Gladys, his wife, is one of my favorite people, and taken separately I love them both. But they aren't for each other. They never were, dear boy.

Twenty years ago when they were first married, she was crazily in love with him. But he, an irrepressible philanderer—I know from experience—married her only for money. Everyone knew what Julian was except Gladys, who didn't want to know.

Despite becoming the manager of her father's business, Julian soon reverted to his wicked ways. Of course, that Gladys is willful, yes, even spoiled, didn't help him reform. At her father's death, Gladys inherited the business and unfortunately never lets Julian forget it.

The lesson to be learned, my dear Allan, is that whatever you do, do it yourself. Don't owe anyone except a bank. And, dear boy, never marry a rich girl, for you may never have the opportunity to know your true potential. She may someday wonder whether you married her for money, and the pity is, you may wonder so yourself.

I needn't worry about her last admonition, at least not with Jan.

Now I understood JB's misery. I could sympathize. But his problem didn't justify what he had done. His arbitrariness and frequent bouts of drunkenness were getting to me. Still, I admired him for his decisiveness, his willingness to innovate, and of course his desire to bring me along. Perhaps he was grooming me for his chair, after all. But I was paying for it. The question was, was it worth it?

I thought Jan overreacted to Brodsky.

"He's so vile; I hate him," she said.

"You'd think you were the victim, the way you talk," I responded.

"Not a chance," she said as she slammed the door behind her.

We implemented the new layout gradually, and the women fine-tuned it to suit their needs. Within a month production increased 25 percent. Meanwhile Big Jim boycotted us. JB responded: "I knew you'd do it, son. Congratulations." He gave me a substantial raise.

I then committed myself to a future at Jefferson Industries. JB became more and more solicitous. He called me "son." He urged me to familiarize myself with the design department. He encouraged me to take night courses in accounting and marketing at company expense. More pay raises followed.

I was accumulating savings, so I consulted with Kirk, an expert on investments. We discussed my financial future during our Friday evening ritual dinner at Ida Noyes Hall on campus. His financial advice soon led to advice about my career.

"I take it, you've decided to stick with Jefferson Industries."

"That's right."

"What about your education? Is that out the window?"

"Why go to college? I'd be no better off than I am now."

"Of course. One doesn't have to be educated, to be a man trained to think broadly and deeply, trained to enjoy the fruits of our civilization, to make money." His eyes sparkled with irony.

"I can go to school anytime."

"Yes, you can."

"Maybe I'll go—but later."

"Now is better than later; now is certain."

"I'll think about it," I said.

"Good. That's all I ask."

"I'd like to show you the factory. Interested?"

"Why, Allan, I thought you'd never ask."

After taking the IC commuter train to the Loop, we walked the mile south on Michigan Avenue to the plant.

"It's the largest lampshade factory in the world," I crowed.

"Really?"

"Too bad everything's shut down for the weekend."

To visit the plant at night was a novelty. I was anxious to show Kirk my department's new layout. I bragged about how we boosted production beyond expectations, about Brodsky's increasing support and about his hints of bigger things to come.

"God bless Bessie," I said. "I owe it all to her."

We entered a narrow corridor of the building, a six-story structure built in the twenties. A network of pipes and electric wires crisscrossed its high ceilings. The closet-sized elevator lifted us jerkily to my department on the fourth floor. An accordion-type gate clanked when it closed behind us.

"It's an old-fashioned building," I said, "but you should see JB's office."

Kirk stood in the darkness at the entrance to my department while I switched on the lights section by section.

"Wonderful. So many colors," he said, dazzled. "It's like an impressionistic painting."

"It is a sight," I said. "You know, I've been too busy to notice."

We took the elevator up one more floor to the executive offices where I showed him our new mechanical office machines and an array of private modern offices of the administrative staff: the accountant's, the personnel manager's, the design engineer's, Big Jim's. Then I led him down a corridor toward the most impressive of all, JB's office with its ankle-deep carpeting, runway desk, and shiny bar.

"The place is enormous," Kirk remarked.

"The biggest in the world," I exclaimed again.

A slot of light shone from JB's doorway. Was JB working long hours? Or were the lights left on accidentally?

I asked Kirk to stay behind while I investigated. I heard a woman's voice.

"Julian, you promised me," said the voice.

"What's wrong with the coat I bought you last winter?"

"That was a winter coat. I need one for the spring."

"For chrissake, what do you do with the money I pay you? I'm already covering your rent."

The woman's voice was familiar. I was trembling.

"I pay plenty for what you give me," the woman said. "No one could give you as good a time as I do."

Crouching, I peered into the doorway. JB and Jan, their backs to the door, both naked, were sitting side by side on the couch, sipping highballs. My heart pounding, I slinked away and joined Kirk.

"We'd better leave," I said. "JB's in there with someone."

"Your face is ashen," Kirk said. "Are you okay?"

"Let's get out of here."

"You saw something?"

"Nothing, not a thing. I'm okay."

I was humiliated, too humiliated to confide my pain to my friend and mentor. Had I been alone, I would have wept.

I was in turmoil. Jan, the one I loved, and JB, the one I depended on, had betrayed me. The pain was enormous. The future I had expected with each was no longer possible. They were dead to me.

Over the next few days Jan noticed the change.

"What's wrong?" she asked, closing my office door behind her. "You don't call. You hardly talk to me."

I feared I'd crumple into tears or scream in anger. My office was the wrong place for a confrontation.

"I'm busy," I said.

She must beg, she must hurt.

Bessie once wrote in her didactic manner, "Dear boy, talk doesn't hold a candle to action. Only action is unequivocal."

Forget words; I would act instead. It was April; the Chicago air had softened. In the evening people sauntered along the sidewalks under the budding trees. On sunny afternoons, the students, pale from the winter, lay about the campus lawn soaking in the new warmth. But I had no heart to participate. I told Kirk of my troubles.

"I'm quitting Jefferson," I said on our ritual walk.

"Then what?" he asked.

"The university," I said.

"Why?"

"Isn't that what you said I should do?"

"Is that what you want?"

"I don't get it, Kirk. You tell me one thing, then . . ."

"So life is shitty right now. That's no reason for going to college. Damnit, Allan."

"I'm not sure of anything anymore. When I went to war, I believed in it. Then after I saw what it was like, I thought it was stupid. I believed in Brodsky and Jan. Who can I trust? It's so damn hard."

Reaching his arm over my shoulder, Kirk grinned. "Congratulations."

"For what?"

"You've just made a momentous discovery."

"Big deal."

"Be in my classroom next Thursday at nine."

"Why?"

"You're taking the late college entrance exam with some of my Lab School seniors."

Once I made the decision to go to the university, I was depressed working at Jefferson Industries. The place seemed dirty. Forcing myself to be respectful to JB and cordial to Jan, I felt hypocritical. I had to quit immediately even if it meant taking a temporary job pumping gas or washing windows until school began in the fall.

JB was sitting back in his chair lost in reverie as I entered his office. The production report of the previous day lay on his desk.

"Hi, Allan. Sit down, son. I'm goddamn proud of you. Your department just broke another record. Bessie did us both a big favor, eh, kid?"

There was no drink on his desk, for a change. His eyes were bright and clear. He was in good humor. He was at his very best: confident and inspiring.

"The new layout's working," I said.

"You betcha. And the deadhead's gone."

"What deadhead?"

"The one I fired."

"She was one of my best workers."

Jerking himself forward to the edge of his chair, he said, "Look, I'm not going to argue with you."

"I know why you fired her. You were getting even with Jan. Isn't that right?"

He walked to the door and closed it. "What are you getting at?"

"You and Jan have a thing going."

"That's a lot of crap."

"No, you are, JB."

"What's your trouble?"

"I'm quitting."

He stood motionless. Immaculate in his crisp white shirt, red silk tie, gold engraved cuff links, he seemed suddenly pitiful.

"I see," he said, sliding slowly into his chair. "Everything I planned for you is out. Is that what you're saying?"

I nodded.

"What in hell's wrong with you, Allan? You're giving up the opportunity of a lifetime. Anyone would give his right arm to be where you are. What in hell's wrong?"

"I'm going to college."

He pondered for a moment, then said, "Wonderful, excellent. I'll pay for it."

"The GI Bill . . ."

"You'd owe me nothing. It would be an investment. In four years you could take over. I'd be ready to step aside then. It would be perfect for both of us. I wish someone had given me a chance like this when I was your age. Instead, I keep paying—well, that's another subject."

"I don't need your money, JB. The GI Bill will pay for everything."

"You came here with nothing. Now all of a sudden you've got it made, and you tell me to take a hike, after all I've done for you."

"I don't owe you a thing, JB. I gave you my best."

He pondered a moment. "Yes, I've got to admit, you did. I suppose we're even. Right?"

He stood up. I took his hand as he extended it across his desk. "You can always use my name as a reference. But I think you're an unappreciative sonofabitch."

I strode from his office, ending my career in lampshades.

While I was emptying my desk, Jan approached and asked what I was doing.

"I've quit," I said. "I suppose you know it's over with us, too."

"What? Why?"

"I know about you and JB."

She stood by silently as I collected my personal items. When I was about to leave, she began sobbing.

"I'm sorry, Allan. I'm sorry."

"No more than I am," I said and darted out the door.

I wrote Bessie that I had quit. In her return letter she said: "I'm thrilled that you've decided to go to college, dear boy. But in your last letter you seemed so happy at Jefferson. After Julian had offered you such a wonderful opportunity, what changed your mind? And you needn't be polite. I want the unvarnished truth."

"As you say, Bessie," I began in reply, "it's all chaos."

Lenny

The two happiest days in most men's lives are the day of their wedding and the day they drive off in their first new car. In neither case can it be said that the typically rapturous character of these events applied to my friend Lenny Gladfeld. From the first day he got his driver's license at age sixteen, he had a new long gray Cadillac at his constant disposal, meticulously maintained and methodically filled with gas. As for his wedding, although he married a remarkably beautiful, sweet-tempered and intelligent girl, qualities I can verify personally, he was miserable the entire time.

Lenny and I met during my first month at the University of Chicago. Before we introduced ourselves, we had studied several afternoons a week amid the prim echoes of the high vaulted university library. We were drawn by its simulated ancient serenity, a refreshing contrast to the raw atmosphere of commercial Chicago only a few blocks away.

After a couple of weeks we smiled at each other in recognition of our mutual dedication to this academic environment. He was slight and had a pixie smile—an appealing smile—a smile that seemed to say life was a lark. Since I thought life was quite the opposite, I made no effort to introduce myself. Besides he had a streamlined look, too fast for me.

One afternoon we happened to sit across the table from each other. When I raised my eyes from a book by Aristotle to contemplate his statement on the soul, our gazes met.

"I'm not sure he's worth it," he said.

"You mean . . ."

"Who you're reading—Aristotle."

"But it's required," I said, intrigued by his audacity.

"Anyway, I don't agree. Take his definition of the soul; he says it's the source of movement, the end, the essence of the whole living body. Not bad stuff, I'd say."

Lenny laughed. "Hell, that 'stuff' held science back a thousand years. No offense. I'm sure you'll get an A. Well, at least a B." He reached over and shook my hand. "Lenny Gladfeld at your service. Of course, you and I know that Freud discovered the soul," he added.

"Of course," I said, impressed. "Name's Pete Albert."

From that conversation on, I can't say that I was ever bored in Lenny's presence. Although he was barely twenty and I was twenty-four—a recently returned World War II veteran considerably matured by my overseas experience—his exuberance, his sophistication, and his obvious brilliance compensated for what I took to be his naivete and excessive insouciance. From that beginning our friendship thrived.

I was best man at Lenny and Lisa's wedding. Standing only a few feet away from the shining couple and staring at their strangely solemn, beautiful faces, I heard the clergyman incredibly declare, "I now pronounce you man and wife." I've heard those words, that announcement with its illusory finality, hundreds of times—in the movies, at scores of weddings of relatives and friends, at my own daughter's and my own three weddings. Why, I always wondered, was it "man" and wife? Why not "husband" and wife? Isn't that what Lenny had become, a husband, qualified or not? No, there was no sense to it, to the marriage, none at all.

In my first year at the university I rented a room off campus on 57th Street with a small, welcoming family. Lenny lived in an elegant high-rise with his parents in the East Seventies near Lake Michigan. On most Saturday nights he picked me up in his brand new 1948 long green Cadillac and we drove dreamily along the eight or so miles of the Outer Drive bordering the lake to the Near North Side. There we dined in splendor at the renowned Imperial House. Having come from a lower-middle class family and a poor small New England industrial city, I was dazzled by all the unfamiliar luxury. At the beginning he paid the entire tab, but soon I insisted on paying my own way, painful though it was.

"It's nothing to me, Pete. My father's paying for it."

"Well, I can't keep taking. Anyway, I can afford it," I lied.

"On your measly government stipend?"

"No, I've got a few part-time gardening jobs."

"You mean you actually work?" he said, clicking his tongue. "You poor guy. I feel sorry for you."

After awhile our dining-out binges inclined more toward drinking than eating—with Lenny that is. He often got out of hand by the end of the meal and would erupt into a boisterous tirade against his father.

"I hate the bastard," he would seethe.

"But why? He gives you everything," I'd argue, thinking that I could penetrate the alcohol.

"Exactly why I hate him. He makes sure I owe him."

"You're mixed up, Lenny. He loves you."

"Too bad for him. I still hate the bastard."

He would then commence blubbering, which would embarrass me. I would call the waiter, pay the bill, and hasten our departure whether or not we had finished the meal. Lenny's capacity for liquor was considerable: He never got so drunk that he lost his reason. And he always let me take the wheel on the drive home.

"Why are you slowly destroying yourself?" I once asked as our glorious Caddy carried us down the highway.

"Am I? Hey, I have an excellent idea. Let's go to a hospital. I'll walk into emergency and say, 'Here I am, you lucky people. My friend says I'm addicted to alcohol. Cure me. I dare you.' "

So I drove him to a hospital, but when we got there he reneged, saying, "I will someday, though. I really will."

In a few months I got to know Lenny's parents. They frequently invited me to dinner at their sumptuous apartment. Afterward Lenny and I would spend hours in his room listening to his enormous classical record collection.

Lenny's father, a power in the Chicago scrap metal business, was a small man like his son. Both men projected an overweening self-confidence. The father lacked the son's wit and cultivation, and the son lacked the father's intensity and sense of clear purpose. When they discussed matters in my presence, which was rarely, Lenny was always curt; his father would react with pained silence.

On one dinner occasion the father advised Lenny that the Cadillac wouldn't be available for his use on a particular Saturday night. Lenny retorted bitingly, "Hell, why tell me? It's yours. Are you asking my permission?"

"I figured you'd like to know so you can make other plans," the father explained.

"Oh, sure," Lenny went on, his tone unaltered. "You always have my interest at heart, don't you?"

His father shrugged. "There's no pleasing this kid," he muttered, lifting a spoonful of soup to his lips.

"Please, both of you, don't, don't," Lenny's mother pleaded, fixing an apologetic gaze on me. "Out of respect for our guest."

The mother assumed the role of protector and constant arbitrator, although she wasn't well and the task appeared to exhaust her. She had angina, and recently it had been discovered that she had diabetes.

The loving center in a hostile circle, she attempted to draw me in with her. "I am so happy that Lenny has you as a friend," she confided. "You are such a good influence—like an older brother. I wish I understood what he's got against his father. It hurts me to see him so bitter."

I too failed to comprehend Lenny's hostility toward his father. "I think he should get some help," I suggested.

"Help? What kind of help?"

"Psychological help, Mrs. Gladfeld."

Lenny

"He's not crazy, Peter. Are you saying he's got something wrong with his . . .? "

"No, no. I'm only saying he should talk to someone professional who can help him discover what's at the bottom of his unhappiness. Then he can deal with it."

She sighed. "I think Lenny needs someone, a role model, to show him how to be happy. A good friend like you. Or maybe a nice girl."

I nodded, realizing that she hadn't understood. She expected more of me than I could deliver.

Of all the weddings I ever attended, I would say Lenny's was the loveliest, most moving, and most doomed from the start. It took place on a clear, gentle September afternoon in the lush green Eden behind the bride's home. Who could possibly have known that Lenny was anything but happy and in love with Lisa as he kissed her passionately after the vows? Perhaps too passionately. And afterwards at the reception everyone could only assume his eyes sparkled from genuine joy, although I knew it was due to his steady consumption of champagne. Who could have doubted the convincing mask of a smile on his good-looking broad bony face? Among the entire well-wishing swarm of relatives and friends who embraced and fussed over the couple all afternoon, only he and I could have known his dread.

Only I knew he had supremely deluded himself. I fed his delusion, I suppose, inadvertently. I had begun doing it as we were driving in the Cadillac from the funeral of a mutual friend whose suicide stunned us both. Justine couldn't bear living without her companion and former teacher, Doctor Banner, with whom she had shared a life for many years.

"I had no idea how desperate she'd be if the doctor died," I said full of remorse over our friend's death. I blamed myself for not having been more aware of Justine's plight and attentive to her needs.

"We are all blind to each other, Pete. It's the way things are. I think what she did was absolutely wonderful. What courage! What a woman!"

Then impetuously Lenny pulled the car off the highway into a small rest area and sat crying behind the wheel. "I wish I could do it. God, how I wish I could do it," he sobbed.

After composing himself he spoke of his enormous shame and relentless self-hate. "I don't know how much — how much to tell you — about — about myself," he stammered.

"For God's sake, Lenny," I said awkwardly. "Someone would think you had committed murder or something."

"Maybe I've done worse," he said, turning his head away.

"Worse? What could be worse than murder? Rape? Maybe torture," I said playfully as I waited for him to gather courage.

"Will you still be my friend, Pete?" he said pitifully, peering straight through the windshield across the pale suburban prairie, "when you realize I'm homosexual? "

I was stunned. This was 1948, long before homosexuality was out of the closet and accepted as a sexual option for better or worse. Nothing I could recall in our past had provided a clue. We sat silently for a few moments.

Finally he said, "You can't despise me any more than I despise myself, Pete."

"Hell, I don't despise you."

"But I've lost you."

"You are what you are, Lenny."

"I know I've lost you."

"You're still the same guy you were when we first met in the library," I said reassuringly. "So what's changed?"

"Noth — nothing, I suppose," he said haltingly. "But now you know."

"No big deal," I said.

"Look, our friendship isn't based on — I mean, I know you're damned heterosexual."

"You never gave me cause to suspect anything but friendship between us, Lenny."

"I want to be like you. God, I want to be normal."

At last I had some insight into Lenny's mysterious suffering. The least I could do was to stand by him. As a friend I asked no questions, made no judgments. As a friend I simply accepted. He was an unhappy soul, a good soul, and that was all.

At the wedding reception I sat beside him at the bride and groom's table.

"Sorry fella," he said grinning and grasping my hand in both of his as if he meant it.

I said what every decent fellow says when he loses in love. "What the hell. The best man won."

And when later I kissed Lisa ever so gentlemanly, tears surged into those soft green eyes that still bewitched me.

"I wish you every happiness," I said, never more sincere in my life. I knew she hadn't loved me but worshipped him. And I knew he wished for nothing more than to be in love with her and make her happy. And I knew that neither was possible.

I had set my heart on Lisa, Lenny's future wife, when she was an incoming freshman. I spotted her about the campus on the first day of my third year at the university. (My relationship with my former girl, Vicki, had ended six months earlier. Music was my unfair competitor. Her parents had removed her from the university and sent her east to study piano with a famous teacher to prepare her for a concert career.)

Lisa's effect on me was instantaneous. I hadn't the faintest idea what she was like. With infatuations, such specifics don't matter anyway. The victim merely sees what he or she imagines. Quite simply she was everything I wanted, my dream girl, with smooth blond hair that cascaded like a waterfall, a delicate marble brow, and an erotic gaze. I imagined that her slender, small-breasted figure when naked resembled the statue of a Greek goddess. In a few days I located her dorm, discovered the paths she followed routinely, introduced myself, and took up walking her to classes. By the time I introduced her to Lenny, she and I had become firmly linked.

In my desire not to neglect Lenny, my dates with Lisa usually included him as well. We were a constant triad, dining elegantly at the Imperial House, picnicking at the dunes, sailing on Lake Geneva, strolling through the arboretum west of the city, and on Sunday afternoons viewing exhibits of masterpieces at the Art Institute.

Lisa was flippant and fun loving, and lived for the moment, certainly never for longer than the day. It was all for laughs; nothing mattered — but it did. This was no scatterbrained beauty; she missed nothing. Though Lenny was all fun in her presence, and he was good at it, she knew better.

"Don't you think Lenny is really hurting inside?" she asked several times when we were alone.

Being more inhibited, I shared in the fun but at a distance. Lisa was often impatient with me. "Why are you so serious? I mean, if you can't have fun, what's the use? Don't be a lump; you know what I mean, a lump?" But Lenny understood, saying with a laugh, "Be easy on him, Lisa. Don't you realize he believes in tomorrow?"

I suppose Lenny's presence helped to conceal the true incompatibility between Lisa and me. She was aware of it long before I knew or would admit it. The concerts I enjoyed bored her. She had no interest in the novels I read and raved about. The art films we saw together were "too slow moving" she said. It seemed nothing we did together was right.

I invited her to see the flower garden that I had been maintaining for the previous three months. Located in the university neighborhood, it belonged to Doctor Kocna and his wife. The garden was a glorious riot of late spring bloom. It had to delight her, I thought. She walked quickly through it, unimpressed, politely said it was "nice", and spent the next two hours in the living room rapt in conversation with Doctor Kocna.

Kocna, a chunky, round-faced man in his mid-fifties, was a world renowned psychiatrist from Romania. With gentle, searching eyes, he riveted his attention on every syllable Lisa spoke. His words, although plain and measured, seemed rich and meaningful. His aura was inspirational. What was not right he could make right; what was not well he could make well. No need to be unhappy; he could eradicate all misery of the mind. He transported Lisa across rainbows.

"Lovely, lovely," he said, supporting Lisa's chin with his outstretched hand to study her profile. "Estonian forebears you say? Yes, yes, I have seen others from Estonia who are also quite beautiful." He spoke with a slight trace of an accent.

His appreciation, however, exceeded the clinical. I had the impression Lisa had affected him on a subliminal level as much as she had me.

"Can you help my . . . our friend, Doctor Kocna?" Lisa asked, unmoved by the doctor's admiring attention.

"Of course. Without doubt. But then, can you persuade him — this Lenny — to see me? My treatment is quite unorthodox, you understand."

"Frankly, I think all he needs is to get away for a while and dry out and he'll be okay," I said, embarrassed that Lisa was imposing on the doctor's professional capacity.

"Perhaps, Peter, but we must learn why he drinks. We would eliminate the drinking preliminary to treatment by simply depriving him. And he will accept that constraint once he is in our secure environment. You see, this is not psychotherapy. After only a few sessions of my new gas inhalation treatment, he will already change for the better."

"It sounds miraculous," Lisa said, instantly a devoted believer.

"Have him see me. You may be sure I can make him well," said the doctor as we said good-bye. If God were on Earth, he would sound like Kocna.

During the weeks I worked in Kocna's garden, Mrs. Kocna often brought me a cool drink. A heavy woman with a puffy face that hinted of once great beauty, she spoke with a soft, thick accent of her husband's former achievements. It was he who had invented chemical shock treatment. It was he who had pioneered the neurological approach to psychiatry. And now there was his newest innovative technique which promised to revolutionize the treatment of both neurosis and psychosis.

Upon looking up the literature on his original work in the medical school library, however, I learned that his method had produced uneven results and indeed had been considered dangerous by some experts. In a more recent journal was a reference that praised Kocna's technique as being advanced for its time, but found that the conclusions he reached were arrived at for the wrong reasons. In other words, his discovery was serendipitous, not the product of genius.

Nothing that I told Lisa about Kocna persuaded her that he was other than a great healer. Indeed, she said my skepticism toward the doctor was symptomatic of my generally negative attitude toward life.

Our relationship ended on a warm May afternoon in Jackson Park. We were lying on the lawn behind a hedge. Trying to kiss her in the brief intervals between passers by, I was failing desperately.

She was annoyed with me. I had brought up Kocna's credentials again. "You're always so damned careful about everything," she complained.

"Only when it's necessary, Lisa—and Lenny means a hell of a lot to me."

"No more than to me—more than you know. Oh, for God's sake, Pete. Haven't you seen?"

Had I heard her correctly? Wasn't there a song, *More Than You Know*, that said everything the words implied?

"You mean you like him?" I said, partly questioning, partly stating a fact.

"Yes, a lot."

"And what does that mean?" I asked, already knowing the truth.

"It means I . . . I love him," she said, nervously pulling at a tuft of grass. "I'm sorry, Pete."

"You can't love him," I said, as if giving her an order.

"Don't be silly," she said with contempt.

"What I mean, Lisa, you mustn't love him."

Seeing the pain in my increasingly misty eyes, she said hesitantly, "Why, why do you say such a thing?"

"Because he . . ."

I stalled in mid-sentence. Should I have said, because I loved her? Or imagined I did. I hadn't ever given thought to marrying. We hadn't reached that stage. Of course, in hindsight I see we never would have anyway, with or without Lenny.

Or should I have said, because she could never be happy with Lenny because Lenny could never be happy with her because she was a woman? Yet how could I be sure of this? What did I really know of Lenny's complexity?

"Because—well, how does Lenny feel?" I asked.

"I haven't asked him. For your sake. He's so fond of you." She looked away. "He and I just have more fun being together than you and I. Haven't you noticed?"

"Having fun isn't the same as loving someone or spending a life together," I said, wishing I hadn't.

"That's just what I mean," she said, bolting from her reclining position. "You're so damned serious. Who cares what happens next! Why do you worry so much? You're a gloom, Pete."

We walked along the Midway to her dorm in wretched silence. It was all over—no doubt before it had ever begun.

"Let's be friends," she said as we reached her door.

"Sure thing," I said. "That's all we ever were, anyway."

"We can still have fun together, the three of us."

I shook my head. "I don't think so, Lisa."

Then she kissed me. It was full of sadness. How desirable and beautiful she was. Would Lenny see her so? How could he? I worried for her. As she said, that was my trouble.

That week I avoided the library to make sure I wouldn't run into Lenny. That weekend Lenny didn't call, that is not until Monday evening when normally he never would call. He said it was very important; that he had to see me right away. In less than ten minutes he was sitting on the bed in my room sober but distraught. At that moment I'd have rather seen him drunk.

"Lisa," he began, "Lisa said—I don't know how to say it."

"My friend Lenny lacking for words! Unbelievable!" I exclaimed, mimicking his usual sarcasm. "I suppose she told you it's all over between us."

"Then it's true?"

"Why should you doubt her?"

"Well, you know how she is," he said, seeming more at ease.

"Yeah, I know how she is."

"You won't mind if I see her?" he went on warily.

I assumed he meant on a casual basis, for going out on the town. "She's not mine, never was. How can I mind?" I said, trying to disguise my hurt.

"Pete, I don't want this to come between us. If I had the slightest suspicion that this would jeopardize our friendship, I'd drop her."

"It's Lisa's decision. How can I blame you? she's all yours, Lenny."

Lenny

"It can't be serious, of course, but we do have a great time together."

"I fully understand, Lenny. You don't have to explain."

He never did explain, even when barely a month later the wedding invitation appeared in the mail. Until her wedding day almost three months later, I hadn't seen Lisa—except to wave to from a distance—since the afternoon we kissed and parted at her door. Only once more, the Saturday after his visit, would I spend a customary evening with Lenny at Imperial House. Much had already changed. He didn't mention Lisa, nor, for that matter, did he get drunk.

They spent their honeymoon in Hawaii, paid for by Lisa's parents. They returned to a luxurious, amply furnished apartment in the East Seventies, paid for by Lenny's father. After a few weeks of settling in, they invited me to dinner.

It was a most unhappy evening, beginning with drinks that never stopped. Lisa had prepared a delectable Italian meal, her specialty, but Lenny said it couldn't compare with Luigi's in the Loop.

"It was delicious, Lisa," I said. "See, clean plate. You have a hidden talent. And I thought I knew all about you."

"Well, I could tell you a thing or two more about her," Lenny said cuttingly with a booze- thickened tongue.

"And you dare to talk. My God," Lisa screamed.

Tears welled up in her eyes. She suppressed sobs as I pitched in to clear the dishes from the table while Lenny helped himself to more liquor.

Married barely two months, their trouble had begun. Perhaps it began sooner, perhaps in Hawaii. Had Lisa thought she would be the solution to his deep unhappiness? Had Lenny thought she could make him like most men? How he yearned to be normal.

There were no more dinner invitations. Not wishing to witness their misery, I made no attempt to contact them either. After a winter passed, during which I worked the night shift in a gas station on 51st Street, Lenny's mother phoned.

"Could we see you, Peter?" she asked in a trembling voice. It was about seven in the evening.

"Certainly. When would—"

"May we visit you?"

"Well . . . yes. I suppose the landlady will allow us to use her living room."

"Tonight, Peter?"

"Tonight? You mean—hold on." I checked with the landlady and returned to the phone. "It's okay," I said. After Lenny's mother hung up, the alarm in her voice still haunting me, I continued holding the receiver.

Less than a half hour later Lenny's mother and father entered the living room. His mother hugged me tightly to her and hung on.

"Oh, it's so good to see you, to see you looking so well," she said. How gaunt she had become since I last saw her. A sallow pallor showed through the layers of her makeup. It was obvious she was dying.

Lenny's father took my hand in both of his. "Thanks for seeing us like this. On such short notice," he said, his eyes pleading.

"Tell us, Peter, tell us, please, about this Doctor Kocna," Lenny's mother began. "Lisa says that you know him too."

"Sit down, won't you?" I said, startled by her mention of Kocna. "Well, I only take care of his garden. Hasn't Lisa told you . . .? "

"What do you think of him? Is he any good?" Lenny's father asked, remaining standing. "We understand he's using some new method, some kind of gas, at the Chicago Psychiatric Hospital."

"But why are you—"

"He's treating Lenny," Lenny's mother interrupted.

"Making a guinea pig out of him is more like it," said Lenny's father. "I don't think he knows what in hell he's doing."

"Doctor Kocna's quite famous in his field, you know," I said, hoping to ease their concern, and my own.

"So what? That's all Lisa says. I don't care how famous he is," said Lenny's father.

"Lenny doesn't know us any more, Peter. Can you believe he no longer knows his own parents?" said Lenny's mother, wringing her hands.

"He's out of it, completely out of it," said the father. "He was fine when he went in. Drinking a little too much maybe, but basically fine. I'd like to know what in hell this man has done to our son."

"Maybe a person has to get worse before getting better in a case like this," Lenny's mother said, putting on a smile. "Would you see him, Peter? Maybe he'll know you. Then you can gab together the way you used to and it might bring him back. He always admired you so much, Peter."

"Mrs. Gladfeld, I'll go to the hospital tomorrow," I promised. "And Lisa, does she spend much time with him?"

"It's as if she doesn't exist," said Lenny's father.

"She always ends up crying when she's with him," said Lenny's mother.

"As if she's invisible when he sees her," said Lenny's father.

"It's so sad, so very sad," said Lenny's mother, tears filling her eyes. "He was so brilliant, so wonderful. And he married such a beautiful, sweet girl. Oh, oh, what have they done to our son?"

When I arrived at the hospital during afternoon visiting hours, the receptionist informed me that only immediate family, whose names were listed, could see Lenny. I then asked to see Doctor Kocna. I was told that if I was willing to wait he would see me in a half hour.

I sat in the lobby watching visitors come and go, patients wander through in bathrobes, and doctors in wrinkled white coats race by. No one exchanged pleasantries; no one smiled.

It was a deadly, joyless place. I could imagine how Lenny must be suffering in this antiseptic atmosphere.

Promptly after a half hour an orderly approached and led me through a jungle of corridors to Kocna's office. Surprisingly, the doctor's office was no larger than a cell. Wearing a starched white coat, looking immaculately professional, he rose from his desk to shake my hand. His manner held a hint of impatience.

"This is a surprise, Pete. I'm sorry you had to wait."

"I hope I'm not imposing."

"Certainly not." Motioning me to a chair beside his desk, he sat down and leaned towards me. "How can I help you?"

"I tried to see Lenny Gladfeld, and they wouldn't—"

"Lenny is your friend?"

"Well, yes, of course. He's Lisa's husband."

"Oh, yes, yes. I see the connection. Striking girl, Lisa. Bright, charming. You brought her over to the house, didn't you?" His eyes became momentarily distant as he recalled the day. A fateful day, I thought.

"I'd like to see him, Doctor."

"I'm afraid Lenny is one of our less fortunate cases." He leaned back and murmured, "One of the few who hasn't responded to my treatment."

"I'd still like to talk to him," I said, restraining my rising frustration.

"There's no point, Pete. I'd rather you didn't."

"But, what's the harm?"

He shook his head, making his heavy jowls wobble. "No, no harm, but no point to it." Looking at his watch, he moved toward the door. "I have a lecture to give in exactly three minutes. Sorry to leave like this. Now be assured you needn't be concerned about your friend. We are constantly developing new approaches." He led me into the corridor. Holding my arm, and with a look of piercing sincerity, he said, "One must never give up. See you in the garden, eh?"

I called Lenny's parents and informed them that I was unable to see Lenny but that I did see the doctor. Parroting his words, I said, "They are constantly developing new approaches. One must never give up."

"We don't know what to do," Lenny's mother replied. She paused. "We think he should leave that place and try another doctor. Don't you agree? But Lisa won't hear of it. She swears by this Doctor Kocna. Maybe—maybe you could talk to Lisa. Would you, Peter? Would you be so kind?"

I hadn't spoken to Lisa since the evening of the unhappy dinner at their apartment months before.

"May I see you?" I asked Lisa over the phone.

"About what, Pete?" Her voice was thin and lusterless.

"About Lenny. I tried to visit him but—"

"There's nothing to talk about."

"I'd like to see him, anyway. I'd like to help in some way."

"Thanks Pete, but I think it's better—actually, there's nothing you can do. I'd rather you left me alone."

"I'm sorry, Lisa. I didn't mean to—"

"So am I, Pete. Maybe some day."

I quit the garden. Lenny's mother died two weeks after our phone conversation. Lisa, appearing drained and ghostly, hardly acknowledged my presence at the funeral. Although Lenny loved his mother—she was easy to love—he was not there. I never saw him again. As far as I know, he remained in the hospital forever, one of Doctor Kocna's mistakes.

Staying Young
For my daughter Suzanne

"At least you could have unpacked first," my wife said as I sat on the bed and listened to the phone ring at the other end. She lugged a bag to the bed and heaved it up onto it, making me bounce.

"I've waited more than five years to make this call," I said as the ring continued. "Looks like nobody's home." But I let the phone ring, reluctant to cut it off.

My wife removed her belongings from the suitcase and placed them neatly in the bottom drawer of the dresser. She always gave me the high drawers, the most convenient ones.

"What a beautiful motel room," she said, spotting a vase of freshly cut flowers on a writing table in front of the window wall. She looked out at rows of palm trees that lined the shade-dappled lawn of a park below.

The ringing stopped.

Hearing an indistinct, throaty voice, I shouted, "Hello, hello, is this Maxie?"

As my wife listened, she gazed across the park past a cliff which dropped sharply to the bleached Santa Monica beach fringed with white surf. "Beats New England," she said partly to herself. We were on a winter vacation, our first in twenty years, having left a cold, snowy January behind six hours earlier.

"This is Hal, Maxie. You know, cousin Lena's son."

Sounding like a hoot owl, the voice repeated, "Who? Who? Who?"

"You mean he doesn't remember you?" my wife interjected.

Motioning for her to be quiet, I pleaded, "Lena's son. Chicago. Remember?" I was going back twenty-five years.

"After all, he should remember," said my wife. "It isn't that long since you last wrote him."

But she was wrong. All of eight years had passed since I sent my last unanswered letters to Maxie. Since I saw him he had become an aged man. Memory is like an old photograph album that imprisons the past in obsolete images. I could not allow Maxie to grow old in my imagination. Perhaps being fifty, I wanted no reminders that the past actually held more of my life than the future.

I pictured Maxie's large, stocky frame, rounded in the middle, moving like a steamship across a room, his enormous, beaked nose and thick gunmetal hair sculptured into waves that swept back in a pompadour. I remembered his great cheeks bulging and rippling as he spoke.

I begged: "Maxie, for God's sake, this is Hal."

Over a period of twelve years we had faithfully corresponded, confiding our most sacred thoughts, informing each other about our daily lives. Writing of his two beautiful daughters born a year apart soon after his marriage, he had revealed that he was worried he might be too old to help them enjoy a normal childhood. But he confessed they revitalized him, causing his heart to swell at the sight of their freshness, their agile loveliness. Yes, his life revolved around theirs; nothing else was more important.

I had written of similar joys, though less emotionally. Our letters described the idyllic years of two happy families. Thus, despite the three thousand miles separating us, our friendship flourished — until, for no reason that I could fathom, Maxie stopped writing. My last three letters remained unanswered.

"Yeah, this is Maxie," he replied finally, in a monotone. "What do you want?"

"It's been a long time, Maxie. How are you?" I paused, waiting for his next response. "How are you, Maxie? This is Hal. Don't you remember me?"

His coldness confounded me. I expected him to be warm and welcoming. It made no sense. Had I insulted him somehow in an old letter, making him angry?

How different this was from our first phone conversation back in 1950. A student at the University of Chicago under the GI Bill, living in a ramshackle, bedbug-infested apartment near the school, I was twenty-two then and Maxie was fifty-six.

Maxie had picked up the phone on the first ring back then.

"Is this Maxie Smithfield," I had asked timidly.

"Well, it all depends on who's inquiring," he shot back gruffly.

"This is Hal Arnold. My mother's your . . ."

"You're Lena's son?"

"Yes, and . . ."

"Sonofa . . . this is a surprise. How's cousin Lena these days? Say, whatta piana player she is. Whatta . . . she's only gotta hear it once, and she'll play it like she always knew it. Did you know . . ."

"I know," I interjected. "My mother asked me to look you up to say hello."

That was a polite distortion of the facts. Not having seen Maxie in thirty-five years, not since he was a young man passing through Boston, my mother had heard that he had settled down in Chicago and had become a rich man. Three years earlier, just as I was leaving Newton, Massachusetts for the Midwest, she said, as if Chicago was extraterrestrial, "He's living out there, and I'd like you to give him my regards. But don't be influenced by him. He has a reputation." She pressed her lips into my cheek. "Just call him up but you don't have to see him."

Truly independent for the first time during those early years in Chicago, I was dazzled by the novelty of my freedom and the vitality of the place. Or was it due to the times—the late forties, early fifties—or was it the time of my life when I had no cares, when I was innocent and uninhibited? My friends were young and old, affluent and almost destitute, brilliant and ordinary, artistic and political, of varying sexual preferences. We shared concerts, plays, art shows, parties, poker games, jazz in the deep of the night, ethnic restaurants, afternoons in the sun by Lake Michigan, walks through the arboretum. Three years passed before I found an interlude of boredom sufficient to stir my dormant curiosity about Maxie and lead me to make that first call.

"I like Lena," Maxie had gone on. "I'm sure glad you called, kid."

"Well, I'll give her your best," I said, although Maxie suggested nothing of the sort.

"Sure, sure, you do that, and tell her . . . say, how'd you like to come over?"

"You mean . . ."

"I mean, now. It'd be great meeting Lena's kid. Hell, we've got some of the same blood in us, y'know."

"Well, I was in the middle of studying."

A part of me insisted on heeding my mother's warning.

"You at school? I'll bet you're brilliant. Any kid of Lena's has to be."

Maxie's flattery when added to my increasing curiosity was compelling. And wasn't my mother needlessly overprotective anyway?

"I can't tell you how long it's been since I've seen someone from the family, kid."

"My name's Hal."

"Sure, sure, Hal." There was a pause before he added the cryptic words. "Y'know, kid, it'd be nice to be with someone I can trust for a change."

"Tell me how to find your place," I said, bracing myself for the worst corrupting influence imaginable: the wholesale pursuit of money, high living, and God knows what else.

Maxie's apartment building was situated in a high-rise strip known as the Gold Coast on the north side of the city near the lake. I knew the spot, having passed it often in my used '48 Chevy sedan on trips along the Outer Drive, the ribbon of highway that borders Lake Michigan. It was a section I had never expected to visit, a part of Chicago that like a glamorous woman, might well have bewitched me were I not sure that beneath it all, the city's personality was ugly.

And I was convinced in advance upon entering his building that Maxie was Chicago's corrupt soul creature.

After I introduced myself the doorman admitted me, as Maxie said he would. Maxie's apartment was a garish display of opulence—in a word: voluptuous. It would have suited Arabian royalty. As I stood in his doorway, he took my hand, then embraced me.

"Lena's boy," he murmured.

Awkwardly trying to return his embrace as his gold brocade robe slid in my grasp, I was embarrassed by his emotion.

"Welcome, kid, welcome, welcome." Bedazzled, I nodded. "Ah, I see Lena in you, in the nose, especially the nose." He held his head high to show off his profile. "It's the Smithfield nose. Here, sit down, kid, sit down."

I fell into a massive overstuffed chair, enveloping me. Immediately Maxie began pacing back and forth across a vast Oriental carpet.

"Christ, kid, my nerves are shot. Just excuse me. Okay?"

"Sure thing," I said, startled.

"Listen, kid, take my advice: Never get married. Women ain't fit for men." He marched back and forth, flailing his arms. "She cleaned me out. She cleaned out my bank account, took my car, even my, my daughter—everything. Goddamn her, goddamn women."

"Gee, I'm sorry, Maxie, really sorry."

"Thanks for your sympathy kid. Damned nice of you. I guess I need an ear pretty bad." After softening for a moment, he erupted again. "Can you beat it? It's the second damned time."

"Honest, Maxie? She did it to you before?"

His pacing stopped.

"Hell, no, she's my second wife."

"Oh."

"The first one did the same damned thing."

"You mean both wives cleaned you out?"

A broad smile rippled across his face. "Yeah, kid. I'm a sucker for a woman."

I understood Maxie's problem. I let him know that women had power over me, too, so we were brethren in spirit as well as blood. His steam subsided and he talked for hours about relatives I never knew back in the "old country," and, after they arrived at the turn of the century, back in Boston. No doubt we had descended from an immoral lot. How, I wondered, could my parents have turned out so decent and hardworking.

"Didn't you know your mother was an artist?"

"An artist?"

"I mean an 'artiste', kid. She was an accomplished pianist."

"I know, I know, Maxie."

"Did you know I fought in Palestine for the Jews before there was an Israel?" I shook my head. "I bummed around the world on a tramp three times. Did you know I speak four languages, each one without an accent? I can tell you, nothing in this world surprises me. I've seen it all: From bad comes good and from good comes bad. Irony, eh? Nothing surprises me anymore."

"Well, you've sure done well," I said.

"You call this 'well'. Hey, I make a few hundred thou a year, plus, and what's it got me?"

Struggling up from my chair, I said: "I've got to go, Maxie."

"Sure, sure, kid. I guess I bent your ear quite a lot."

"It's been a real pleasure."

He hugged me as we walked to the door. "Let's get together again. After all, we got the same blood, eh?" I reached out for his hand. "I'll show you how to live, kid." He winked.

On another Sunday afternoon, I lay on the cot in my small room contemplating my meager existence on a subsistence budget: $80 a month from the government, $50 more doing odd jobs such as window washing and gardening. I didn't mind my "poverty" except from time to time I yearned for a more elegant meal or a night on the town.

The phone rang. The angel Maxie came to my rescue and the routine began.

"How about dinner out, kid?"

"Gee, Maxie, I can't. Exams tomorrow. I've gotta pile of studying to do."

"Hey, you'll think better on a full stomach, kid."

"I appreciate the invitation, Maxie, but . . ."

"When did you last have a decent meal? Probably not since you've been in Chicago."

"That's true."

"Well, c'mon."

"Gee . . ."

"At seven. In the lobby. Pick me up in the Chevy."

When did I tell him I had a Chevy? God bless Maxie. I simply knew he would give me a wondrous evening.

Body gleaming, engine humming without a hint of tappet noise, my dark green Chevy constituted my major material wealth and my pride. No museum piece received better care. Maxie would ride in style; he would be impressed.

Maxie's wife "stole" his car. Convinced that one day he would get it back, he refused to buy another, so he used cabs.

According to Maxie, dining at Royalty House, basking in its luxury and communing with its guests, is to experience the best Chicago has to offer. As we approached its canopied entrance, a uniformed doorman, the tails of his coat whipped about in the wind like writhing snakes, opened the shining brass portal with grandiloquence.

"Evening, Mr. Smithfield."

Maxie patted him gently on the arm. We entered a purple-carpeted foyer in the center of which hung an enormous silver chandelier from a high, rococo ceiling. I felt dismally ill-dressed in my simple brown tweed sport jacket—my only jacket. In tuxedo attire, the maitre d' approached.

"Ah, Mr. Smithfield, so good to have you this evening."

He snapped his fingers and a beautiful middle-aged woman wearing a silky evening gown slithered behind Maxie and gently reached her arms around his chest, hugging him briefly as she slipped off his coat.

"So good to see you again, Mr. Smithfield," she cooed.

"This is my cousin Hal," said Maxie.

"So good to meet you," said the woman. The maitre d' bowed and led us to a secluded corner. A colony of tables stood on a one-step rise above the rest of the room.

"Your usual table, Mr. Smithfield," said the maitre d', his fingers exploding again, activating a platoon of waiters standing nearby.

Scanning the spacious room like a hunter, Maxie nodded here and there to a familiar face. The room was almost entirely purple—the walls, ceiling, draperies, even the tablecloths—but the napkins were white and the marble floor a transparent milk.

Three waiters, whom Maxie knew by name, hovered over us so that the level of our wineglasses never fell below the half point.

"See that fellow over there?" Maxie said, indicating a distinguished white-haired man seated nearby. "He's chief honcho over at Consolidated Motors. One of my best customers."

"He looks important," I said.

"Powerful man—tells the mayor what to do." Maxie sighed in admiration.

A bald, mousey old man ambled by with a svelte young woman hanging on his arm.

"That's Benny Hingman."

"Oh," I shrugged.

"You never heard of Benny?"

"Never. Should I have?"

"Hi, Benny," Maxie called. Turning to Maxie, Benny nodded and smiled wanly. "He wrote 'My Darling, I Love You With All I Got.' Great song, y'know. Benny's the best lyricist alive."

Watching Benny wend his way among the tables, I wondered at the seeming incompatibility of package and contents. Maybe the attractive young woman sees something beyond Benny's outward appearance. Maybe she's not his mistress, only his daughter.

"Benny's a damned lucky guy," a wistful Maxie said. "He's never lonely."

The next few hours were full of happy banter and shameful gluttony. No doubt Maxie charmed me partly through my stomach, but he gave much more. I found him intrinsically irresistible: He was good-natured, warm, generous.

The waiter delivered a silver dish on which lay the check. Maxie signed it, then placed three ten-dollar bills under it. I envied the waiter; thirty dollars was a fourth of my monthly budget.

I had trouble dealing with Royalty House, finding it fascinating on the one hand and repellent to my Spartan nature on the other. I felt like a misfit who didn't belong in such surroundings. I turned down Maxie's Sunday night invitations more often than not. Still I chose not to be totally deprived and even bought a good topcoat, which qualified me for the ritual of the subtle embrace executed by the lovely coat lady.

After an early dinner at Royalty House one Sunday evening, Maxie proposed we drop by the Hot Stuff, an infamous bistro on the near north side.

"It's not what you think," he advised. "The entertainment's first class."

The Hot Stuff was a dimly lit, fogged-in cocoon jammed with couples seated around small cocktail tables. At one end of a long bar that stretched the length of a wall were a piano, drums, bass fiddle, and an accordion on a chair. At the other end of the bar was a steep portable staircase leading to the bar top.

"Hi, Maxie," a voice from the crowd shouted.

"Where you been, Maxie?" yelled another.

Waving to the blurred crowd, Maxie worked his way through the gloom to a suddenly appearing empty table nearest the bar. And as suddenly a dark-haired young woman with a hard mouth and determined eyes sat down between us.

"Who's your friend, Maxie?" she demanded.

"My cousin," Maxie replied, grinning.

"Aw, c'mon."

"No kiddin. This is Freda, kid, the bestest with the mostest."

"How do you do," I said.

Ignoring me she turned toward Maxie, who, pulling her to him, whispered into her ear and kissed it.

"No, Maxie, no," she protested. Removing his wallet from inside his suit jacket, he withdrew several bills, which he folded into a small packet and inserted into her cleavage. "I don't want it. Please, Maxie."

As she tried to foist the packet back on him, Maxie threw his hands in the air. "Take it. You deserve it a hell of a lot more than a lot of people I know. You've brought me much joy, Freda." Turning to me, he said, "She's putting a daughter through college."

Freda kissed Maxie fervently on the lips while he patted her behind.

"Wait'll you see her perform."

"I gotta get ready," she said, rising.

I wondered how old she was then to have had a college-age daughter. Maxie must be pulling my leg. Freda had to have been thirteen or fourteen, maybe younger, when her daughter was born. I remembered Maxie's words: nothing's a surprise.

Soon after taking their places, the musicians opened with a lively jazz piece, catching the attention of the crowd. Everyone clapped their hands and pounded their feet to the rhythm. An eagerness was in the air.

Then Freda appeared and mounted the staircase, followed by a lithe shining blonde and a sunset redhead. Wearing tantalizing gauze gowns fringed with silver tinsel, which barely hid their naked bodies, they waved and blew kisses to the maddened crowd. Maxie clapped uncontrollably as they swirled along the bar in a sexy ballet. To the slowing beat of the music, the three women unfurled their filaments item by item in a precision rite.

"Atta girl, Freda," Maxie shouted. "Wow 'em. Show 'em all ya got."

Blowing him a kiss, tassels hanging from her nipples, she twirled and twisted as she lay bare her unshaven crotch.

When I used to tell my wife stories about Maxie, I made sure never to mention the Hot Stuff. And in Santa Monica that Sunday night I knew I wasn't on the line with the same Maxie who had taken me to the infamous bistro.

"He seems strange," my wife said. "Are you sure he remembers you?"

"Of course he remembers me. He just said so."

"Maybe he's senile," she speculated.

The possibility had occurred to me. But he was simply hostile, hardly irrational, and incoherent.

I tested his memory. "Do you hear from Freda, Maxie?"

"Go to hell," he said.

I shared an apartment in a deteriorating South Side walk-up with a med student and a law student. We lived in excellent harmony, respecting each other's independence and giving moral support when ill or disappointed in love. Being former GIs, our lot in common was comparative poverty, the pressure of a heavy study load and a yearning to break out from time to time and rejoin the life of the city. To relieve the monotony we were happy simply to have dinner every Sunday afternoon in a Chinese restaurant on 63rd Street where the El clattered overhead.

After meeting Maxie, my boredom assuaged, I rarely joined my apartment mates on our weekend flings and instead returned home late Sunday nights babbling stories of Chicago's fabulous night life. Intrigued by my tales of Maxie and confident that they could make a meal that would meet Maxie's high standards, the boys insisted I invite him for dinner. Although skeptical, I consented, and to my surprise, Maxie accepted.

That momentous evening I was like an apprehensive housewife giving our usually disordered apartment a final check when I heard Maxie's knock on the door. Wearing a homburg hat at a rakish angle wreathed by his silver mane, Maxie stood in the doorway. He was impeccable, dashing, dressed in a dark blue suit, a figure of elegance.

"My god, this isn't Royalty House," I exclaimed.

"Hey, I'll bet it's a hell of a lot better."

"It'll only be a simple dinner, Maxie."

"Well, these'll give it class," he said, handing me a bag containing two chilled, moist bottles of champagne.

The boys shook Maxie's hand and excused themselves to return to their chefs' duties.

"Quite a dedicated team," Maxie observed.

"We're honored to have you," I said. Struggling to make conversation as he sat in a decrepit overstuffed chair whose arms wobbled, I went on: "Milt, the tall one, is planning to be an internist."

"Is that so? Great field. There's a real need for internists these days."

"And Lou is pretty busy right now preparing a moot court case."

"I always said we need good lawyers. I mean as against bad lawyers, of which we've got too many already."

After the boys brought out the dinner from our small kitchen and we settled around the table in the living room, an awkward silence began.

"You going to specialize in litigation law, Lou?" Maxie said, rescuing the moment.

"Well, to tell the truth, I don't know."

"I'll tell you that's where the big money is. Y'know I was a personal friend of Darrow's."

"Clarence Darrow?" Lou piped.

"'Course. Y'know the case where he defended the guy accused of poisoning his wife for the insurance?"

"Was that Darrow's case?"

"Didn't they teach you that one? Darrow downed the poison so-called—exhibit number one—like it was a draught of beer right in front of the judge and jury. 'Course the defendant, just as guilty as sin, knew it was real strychnine."

"Strychnine?" Milt and I blurted.

"Hell, the defendant nearly died of shock. It was real alright, but Darrow showed how the stuff couldn't kill an ant."

"Are you sure Darrow was the defense lawyer?" Lou persisted.

After wafting down champagne, Maxie rolled on: "'Course as soon as the jury left the room to deliberate, what d'you suppose Darrow did?" Giving us no time to reply, he said: "Hell, he rushed over to Cook County Hospital, had his stomach pumped out, and returned to the courtroom in time to hear the innocent verdict."

"Unbelievable," I said.

"I'd say that's a lawyer with guts—guts he's willing to risk literally," Maxie cackled. "They just don't make 'em like that anymore."

Lou shook his head.

"Don't believe me, huh, Lou? Well, I'll tell ya I set the whole thing up. That's right. I was in on the deal, knew Darrow's strategy right from the start. Hey, it was me who drove him over to Cook County zipping around the Loop like

I was a World War I aviator in a Spad." After filling his glass again with champagne and gulping it down, he broke a new silence. "An internist, eh Milt?"

"Maybe. I'm not sure," Milt said, looking away.

"I s'pose you've heard of Anton Carlson—he's the Nobel prize winner who . . ."

"Yeah, I know who he is."

"'Course you do." Addressing Lou and me he went on. "This guy had his stomach sliced open in an accident, Okay. Well, they had trouble sewing him up, so good old Carlson, seeing an opportunity, studied his insides—you know the digestive tract, that kind of stuff—and learned how it all worked. Now they call Carlson the father of gastroenterology, right Milt?"

"How do you know so much about Carlson?" Milt asked.

"How do I know . . . ? Hell, who do you think gave him the idea?"

"You, Maxie. It was you," we sang.

"You betcha. I suggested the whole thing. It was a golden opportunity to learn how the tummy works for the benefit of mankind." Maxie belched resoundingly. "He even found out what causes burps."

"Gas," said Milt. "Just plain gas."

"Right, Milt. I see you know your stuff."

What a shameful evening, I thought. Being hostage to Maxie's incredible stories we drank champagne until at midnight Maxie called a cab and departed, reciting the code of Alcoholics Anonymous.

For months afterwards I refused to deal with Maxie, refused to answer his phone messages, refused to forgive him for the shame I felt for being associated with such an out and out liar. Did he think we would swallow his stuff? He had toyed with us and I was insulted. But I was disillusioned too. Why did he always have to be bigger than reality? I had come to love the genuine Maxie and hate the one he pretended to be.

On a bright, cold, windy December afternoon while walking home from class with my head down like a fish against current, I failed to observe a cab parked near the entrance to my building. After I entered the small hallway, Maxie leapt from the cab, catching the hall door before it locked shut.

"Listen, kid . . . ," he said as I turned in surprise.

"The name's Hal."

"Sure kid. Let's talk. I'd like to know what I've done."

I vented my complaint about his actions the night he came to dinner.

"You mean that's all that's eating you?" Laughing, he slapped his thigh, which only intensified my outrage.

"I was ashamed of you," I screamed.

"I'm sorry, truly sorry, Hal," he said, his voice quickly quiet and solemn. "I won't even try to defend myself."

"They're my closest friends, Maxie."

"Sure, sure. Listen, I don't want to lose you, kid." His eyes welled with tears, causing mine to do the same, and we embraced as best we could in our bulky overcoats.

"How about dinner Saturday night, kid?"

"At Royalty House? I find the fuss tiresome, Maxie."

"This time at my place, a real quiet dinner. I want you to meet somebody."

"I don't know," I said, expecting he had a Freda or a Benny in mind.

"It's important, kid. Look, bring a date. By the way, I've moved."

"You're kidding."

"To the classy building made of glass on the lake front."

"You mean the Mies van der Rohe?"

"That's the one. Twenty-fifth floor."

"Gee, Maxie. I'm impressed."

"Yeah, kid. Figured you would be. And there's more yet. So I'll expect you, huh? You and your girl?"

How come Maxie's taste had radically changed? Compared to his former elaborate and ornate apartment, the daring, simple yet pleasing new glass apartment building was the extreme opposite. His manner had also changed: He sounded more serious, more restrained, less bombastic perhaps.

The motel room facing the ocean in Santa Monica evoked a sense of deja vu. It reminded me of Maxie's glass apartment that fronted on the stark expanse of Lake Michigan. I could imagine that Nora was about to enter, appearing as I had seen her at that first meeting.

In desperation, I tried to keep our phone conversation alive. "How's Nora?" I asked.

"She's OK."

"Can I talk to her?"

"No."

"Why not, Maxie? What's wrong?"

"She's gone to work."

"She works?" I remembered how anxious she had been to quit her job back in Chicago.

Maxie drew a deep breath. "She's a nightclub hostess." She *was* very attractive, perfect for the job. She must be doing it to keep busy. Surely they wouldn't need the money.

"How's the PR business, Maxie?"

Silence: I could hear his breathing and a radio or TV in the background. Better drop the questioning.

As the panelled elevator ascended without a tremor to the 25th floor, Joy said, "He must be rich."

"Rich enough to say whatever comes to his mind without worrying about the consequences," I said. "So don't be surprised, okay."

I had been dating Joy, a dark-haired blase beauty, for a few months with middling success. She was so beautiful I had to stand in line along with a lot of other guys. Maybe Maxie's outrageous charm would blow her off her feet and by association help me gain points.

"Wait 'til you meet his friends," I said.

"What do you mean?"

"They're real characters."

The elevator slowed to an imperceptible stop.

"Oh, then this should be fun," she said, coming alive.

A dapper Maxie stood in the doorway of his apartment ready to greet us. Embracing me he bellowed: "Fantastic, kid, fantastic. And this must be the South Side charmer who . . ."

"This is Joy. For God's sake, Maxie."

As he took her hand and kissed it, I looked the other way, but Joy was entranced and giggled.

The apartment's decor was astonishing: Gone were the Oriental rugs, the bulbous overstuffed furniture, the lavish colors. All was subdued, plain, sparse—appropriate to the building but not to Maxie. A decorated Christmas tree standing in a corner of the living room was even more astonishing: Although not religious, Maxie made a point of cultivating his Jewish identity.

Nora entered smoothly from the kitchen, walking as models are trained to walk, or as Filipino country ladies walked with baskets on their heads. Nora was prim, quiet, in a stylish black dress that made the most of her fine figure. Her features were clean and delicate and she smiled often and easily. In every way, it seemed, she was Maxie's opposite.

Holding her by the waist, Maxie said, "Meet Nora."

"Maxie simply raves about you," she said, taking my hand. "It can't all be true."

"You must know how Maxie exaggerates," I said, fearful of what stories he might have made up about me.

Leading Joy by the arm to the dining room table, Nora pursued small talk as a smiling Maxie and I followed. After seating ourselves Nora placed her hand over Maxie's and said: "Hal, you must know too that Maxie only seems to exaggerate." Then she turned to Joy and began chatting.

"Where in the world did you find her, Maxie?" I said.

"Y'know she's younger than my daughter."

"She's younger than me too," I said.

"Actually I'm older than her old man."

Nora was clearly in charge of the evening, directing Maxie in helping to serve dinner, and leading the conversation but revealing little about her own background. Joy, ordinarily unresponsive, had become animated while I, usually talkative, basked quietly in her charm.

"How long have you two known each other?" I blurted at last.

"Three months, wouldn't you say, Nora?"

"Three glorious months," said Nora, rising to retrieve four stem glasses from a nearby cabinet. Obviously she was familiar with every detail of the apartment.

"She's made me young again, kid. I feel like forty, hell, maybe thirty." Sweeping his arm through the room, he added, "Hey, isn't this a terrific spread?"

After Nora filled our glasses, I raised mine in a toast: "To Maxie's exquisite taste." As Maxie and Nora sipped they gazed across their glasses at each other like adoring teenagers.

Standing up, Maxie toasted, "To my beautiful wife," and withdrew from his pocket a diamond ring and wedding band, which he slipped onto Nora's waiting finger. "We got married when nobody was looking."

Obviously he had fully recovered from his second wife's leave-taking. I realized then why he had been trying to reach me all the while I had refused to take his calls. Feeling mortified, I was also filled with joy and embraced him and then Nora who pressed her lips to mine.

"I'm so glad you approve, Hal," she whispered. "He needs your friendship. So many don't understand—our difference in ages you know."

My memory of that evening in the glass apartment seemed more immediate and real than my unconvincing conversation with Maxie from the motel room. What had happened to Maxie and Nora in L.A.? Come to think of it, why did he ever leave Chicago, a city he loved, where he knew important people, where he had made his fortune? Why did he choose to begin all over again while in his late fifties. Had he really thought he was forty again, or thirty?

"How are the girls, Maxie?"

"What girls?"

"Your daughters, Mimi and . . ."

"They don't live here."

I had forgotten they would be grown up and on their own.

"Well, how are you?"

"Me?"

"Yes, how are you feeling?"

"Not so hot."

"You're not feeling well?"

"I'm not feeling so hot."

"Can I see you, Maxie? I'm nearby in Santa Monica." A silence ensued. "My wife is with me. You've never met her, Maxie. We'd like to come over and visit."

"No, don't."

"What was that?"

"Don't come over."

"I don't understand, Maxie."

A click, then the dial tone sounded. Stunned, I said: "He won't see us."

Sitting beside me, my wife drew me to her. "What do you think has happened to him?" she asked.

"I've lost him for good. I guess he's ill. After all, he's in his early eighties now, and Nora's still full of life in her forties. Christ, I remember he thought old Benny Hingman had it all together."

"Benny Hingman?"

"Yeah, the songwriter—always had a young chick hanging on his arm. I think Maxie's real trouble is he's ashamed."

"Ashamed? What do you mean?"

"Of having failed." I kissed her.

"Failed?"

"Yeah. Maybe Nora's working because she has to. I got the feeling he knows he's no longer the person he used to be — the incredible winner I knew. He doesn't want me to see him in decline."

"How sad."

"Sooner or later we all fail, y'know," I said sadly in resignation. "I wish I could tell him that."

MIDDLE AGE

A Sentimental Concerto

"**B**ut, Daddy, do you think she'll remember you after so many years?" my sixteen-year-old daughter, Betsy, asked. We were driving from our suburban home to Worcester center.

"Well, thirty years *is* a long time. Hell, I doubt if she'll even recognize me."

"You don't look so old, Daddy, even if your hair is gray."

I reached over and gently touched her cheek. Gray? I was virtually bald. But I was still Betsy's shining knight.

Our destination was Mechanics Hall, a Greek Revival auditorium, an acoustical marvel, built during the Civil War. We were to hear the famous pianist Victoria Kendall play the D Minor Mozart Concerto with the Boston Symphony.

I had heard her play the piece often (without an orchestra) on the campus of the University of Chicago when we were students there. The daughter of a wealthy family, she was only eighteen and I was twenty-three, a veteran fresh from the war in the South Pacific, living off a meager stipend under the GI Bill.

"It's too bad Ma caught the flu," Betsy said ruefully.

"Yeah, she'll miss a great concert." I responded.

"I think she's jealous."

"Don't be ridiculous."

"Didn't Victoria Kendall used to be your girlfriend?"

"Sure, but I married your ma. And we had you."

Betsy smiled. "Daddy, what's she like?"

"Who?"

"Your old girlfriend."

"I wish you wouldn't refer to her that way."

"What's she like?"

"It's been thirty years. I haven't the faintest idea."

"Daddy, I mean when you knew her."

"Like you. She was like you—quiet and serious and very determined."

Betsy squinted under the glare of the mercury vapor lamps as we turned onto Main Street.

"I'm not like that at all," she protested.

Back in 1946 I had asked my friend Kirk, an instructor at the university's Laboratory School, the same question: "What's she like?"

"For one thing, she's beautiful."

"Aw, c'mon, Kirk. When you say that, I know she must be a dog."

Kirk, forty-five years old, was pleading with me to take Victoria, one of his students, out on a date. Infatuated with him, she sent him love notes, camped at his office door, and called him at home in the evening. A decent, civilized man, not wanting to inflict hurt, he didn't know how to get rid of her.

"I mean it. She's a Roman goddess."

"Then she's got plenty of guys."

"No. No one's interested. You see, there's a problem."

"I knew it. A real oddball."

He drummed his fingers on his desk as he searched for words. "You see," he said finally, "the most important thing in her life is the piano."

"That's a problem?"

"It's her hands. This poor, beautiful girl's thumbs are ugly, bony spindles. She was born that way."

I was interested. I was interested in anyone who was an underdog, no matter how. Kirk arranged to have me meet her in his office one afternoon.

Her surname then was Ricardi. She was certainly a dark beauty. Her eyes were a soft liquid umber. Sheafs of brown hair fell to her shoulders, framing her face like an Egyptian queen's. Lithe and slender, she walked smoothly, as if balancing a basket on her head. She wore a conservative but very expensive skirt. Her clothes, Kirk said, always had pockets so she could bury her hands in them. During wintertime she wore special gloves to hide her defect.

After we were introduced and the three of us chatted for a while, I asked, "Vicki, how'd you like to accompany me to a piano recital at Orchestra Hall next Thursday evening?"

She glanced at Kirk.

"He won't bite you," Kirk said and laughed.

"I don't know," she said, staring at the floor.

"Dame Myra Hess is soloist," I added.

She raised her eyes, excited. "Are you sure? She's my favorite pianist."

"Of course, I'm sure. You'll go?"

"I wouldn't want to miss her for anything."

After she left to attend a class, I commented to Kirk, "Well, obviously, I don't count. I have to bribe her."

"Give it time. She'll come around."

"I do like her."

"I thought you would," Kirk said, grinning. "If I were your age . . ."

Vicki lived in the posh East Seventies district in a French-style country house with large windows framed by ruby velvet drapes. There were Oriental rugs everywhere and a grand piano in the living room. Raised in a lower middle class family, I had never witnessed such opulence before. Indeed, I could hardly afford the price of our tickets.

"I don't have a car, Vicki. I'm sorry I can't take you out in finer style," I said.

"I don't mind," she replied. "I'd be willing to walk the whole ten miles downtown just to hear Myra Hess play."

"Well, you won't have to do that."

We took the trolley to the Illinois Central commuter train. Its wheels clicked and clacked down the tracks like castanets as it hurtled us toward the Loop.

"Oh, this is fun," she said. "I never travel the IC." We sat side by side jostled by the sway of the train. Streaks of light flashed across the window by our seat. Her eyes darted. She seemed exhilarated by the sounds of the train and the people around us. She read every advertisement within view. The ride was clearly an event in itself for her.

Orchestra Hall is higher than it is wide. From the uppermost balcony the stage looks like a miniature model, but the music is surprisingly strong and clear. To this day, I've saved that evening's program. Myra Hess played an early Beethoven sonata, several Chopin pieces, then the incomparable Mozart A Major sonata, the Number 11, with its excruciatingly sad and delicate andante.

Entranced, Vicki lost herself in the music while I visually caressed her every feature. It was too soon to become involved with her, I thought. But as I watched her, I found myself falling in love. I had a strange premonition of her destiny. I felt like a diver ready to plunge into a dark pool of unknown depth. Still, I chose to dive. I didn't care if I drowned. It would be worth it.

"If only I could play like that," Vicki exclaimed as she applauded. Myra Hess bowed to the cheering audience. "Oh if only I could. I'd give anything, anything." Caught up in the excitement, she momentarily seemed to forget she had spindly thumbs. But after Dame Hess left the stage, Vicki buried her hands within the folds of her skirt.

Soon we became inseparable. We met every school day at Ida Noyes, the student lounge. There she practiced her limited repertoire on a fine concert grand that stood in the main room. I sat in the corner of the room reading *The Brothers Karamazov* or Thorstein Veblen or the classics.

Kirk was enchanted with our love affair.

"I didn't ask you to fall in love with her, you know," he said. "Be gentle with her. She's very sensitive." I took his advice.

Vicki's parents were not as pleased. Her mother, a small gray-haired prematurely aging woman in her late fifties, had given birth to Vicki in her early climacteric. She blamed herself for her daughter's defect. She seemed subdued, perhaps by the burden of her guilt. Or was it because of her powerful, macho husband, a large, rotund man in his mid-sixties? He ruled the family like a severe shah. They spoke to each other and to Vicki only in Italian.

The father was clumsy in his dealings with Vicki. Although her freshness and liveliness dazzled him, he had no understanding of how a teenage female felt and acted. He treasured her as he would an ornamental jewel. She reciprocated with respect and affection but not love.

He resented me. Unknown to Vicki and me, he had ordered his henchmen to keep us under surveillance. They followed us on our walks through Jackson Park on warm spring afternoons. They watched us kiss in the evening shadows. They attended the concerts we went to. Soon the father's patience cracked and he warned Vicki to stop seeing me.

"You'll have to meet me at the corner of my street from now on," she said as we walked across the Quadrangle. "My parents forbid me to see you. I made an awful scene and said some terrible things."

"They hardly know me. I don't understand your father. What's he got against me? It doesn't make sense."

"I know, dearest," she said, grasping my hand. "They make up excuses."

"Like what?"

"You're too old for me."

"Too old? I'm only twenty-three."

"But you've been through the war."

"You mean they're holding that against me? What do they think I am, a hardened old wardog who's caught a dozen doses of the clap?"

We sat on a bench holding hands.

"I told them how much I love you, that there's no way in the world they can break us up. I got so angry, I threw my books at them. It's so unfair. They hate you because you're not one of them."

"Christ," I muttered, "I should have guessed they were anti-Semitic."

As we entered Mechanics Hall Betsy asked, "Daddy, were you in love with her?"

"I'm in love with your mother," I replied.

"I know. But that's now. Were you in love with her then?"

"Yes. She was a wonderful girl. Now let's find our seats."

"Did she love you?"

"Do you have to know everything? We go this way. We're up in the balcony."

"But, Daddy, I want to know everything."

The moon was full and bright. A fresh breeze from the western prairie rustled the dry brown leaves that bordered the sidewalk. Vicki and I had walked the two miles from the Illinois Central train station to her street rather than wait for the trolley.

"They'll be asleep," she said. "I think it will be all right. Walk me to the house."

As we embraced and kissed at the foot of her driveway, a spotlight was suddenly turned on, catching us in its glare. We heard an angry, raucous voice shout, "Stay away from my daughter, you sonofabitch."

Two men appeared at the edge of the light. One of them, wearing a bathrobe, was Vicki's father. He held a gun pointed at me. "I'll kill you," he shouted, "if you ever come here again, you godamned—"

Vicki lunged at him, swinging her handbag and beating him on the head with it. "Run, Pete," she screamed, "run. Please run."

Terrifed, I couldn't decide whether to help her or take her advice.

"How can you do this, Vittoria? How can you strike your

father? I'm only thinking of you," her father said, shocked and hurt.

The other man, also in a bathrobe but much younger, drew closer to me.

"Call him off, Daddy, or I'll leave your house forever," Vicki threatened. The father signaled the younger man to quit.

"Please go, Pete," Vicki pleaded. "I'll see you tomorrow." Then she dashed to the open front door of the house where her mother had stood ringing her hands watching.

As Vicki cried herself to sleep that night, her father stood outside her door begging forgiveness. He had created a chasm between his daughter and himself that would never be bridged. Indeed, instead of keeping Vicki and me apart, he had only driven us closer together.

The musicians had drifted onto the stage until every seat was finally occupied. A cacophony commenced as they tested their instruments, drowning out the buzz of the audience. The hall lights were dimmed and the audience became silent. The conductor entered the back of the stage, bounded to the podium, and bowed to the applause. He turned, raised his baton, and with a flick activated the soft strains of a Mozart serenade. I drifted into a sort of sentimental reverie and reminisced over those days long ago with Vicki.

"Just tell him I'm Vicki's cousin," the man standing at the door said to my landlady. "Tell him I've come in peace."

Leaving him waiting in the entry hall, the landlady knocked on my bedroom door and informed me of the stranger's presence. "What does he mean 'come in peace,' Peter," she asked. "You may use the living room, if you wish."

When he entered I immediately recognized him as the younger man who had stood ready to attack me the night of the confrontation months earlier.

"Victoria's father sent me," he said.

"For what?" I asked.

"What do you want?"

"I don't understand," I said.

"What are you after? If it's money, we're prepared to—"

"Get the hell out of here," I said.

"Just wait a minute. Just wait," he said, pushing his hand against my chest, then withdrawing it. "Here's ten thousand." He pulled several bundles of one-hundred-dollar bills from his pockets and flipped through them like a deck of cards to show me they were the same throughout. "Take 'em, and stay away from her. You understand?"

"Tell Mr. Ricardi to shove it," I said.

His eyes narrowed, becoming slits. "You'll get nothing, nothing. He'll cut her out if she keeps seeing you."

"Get out," I said.

He turned to the door, flung it open, and slammed it behind him. From the window I watched him enter a large black car. As it pulled away I caught a glimpse of Vicki's father in the passenger seat.

At the end of the Serenade, as the audience applauded, the conductor bowed and motioned the orchestra to rise, then he left the podium. Returning quickly, he was preceded by Victoria threading her way through the violin section. The audience burst into applause again as she stood by the piano and bowed. I stared at her and didn't recognize her. There on the stage stood an absolute stranger. Still, her mannerisms were familiar: the way she slid onto the piano bench, and held her hands over the keyboard waiting for the entry cue. Her eyes were as bright as ever. She still clasped her fingers together to hide her thumbs. Her figure was lithe no longer; rather it was almost buxom. Her face was rounder and lined. This was far from the image of her I had held so sweetly for so many years.

The conductor raised his baton, and Vicki, becoming

alert, waited as the first orchestral notes filled the hall. After her fingers struck the keys, I knew it was my Vicki. It was her unmistakable magic touch.

"Daddy," Betsy whispered, "what's wrong with her thumbs?"

"Wrong? There's nothing wrong. Listen to her playing. Would you call that wrong?" I said, annoyed. Suddenly mention of her handicap made me as defensive as when Vicki and I were young.

"But Daddy, I mean—look at them."

"I know, I know. It's nothing. She was born that way. Now listen, will you?"

"Oh. You didn't tell me."

"I'm sorry," I said regretting my harshness. "I'd forgotten." In fact, I had forgotten her thumbs an hour after I had met her in Kirk's office so long ago.

That first summer after we had met, I served as a waterfront counselor at a boys' camp in Maine. My first task was to herd a hundred rich kids from Central Park West in New York City aboard Pullman sleepers in Grand Central Station and nurse them all the way to Portland. It was a torrid summer night and some of the kids were impossibly unruly. I was hot and depressed and longing for Vicki. Perhaps I should have stayed in Chicago, I thought.

I wrote daily to tell her how much I missed her, and she wrote daily of her similar anguish. Then one day in early August she was on the phone.

"I'm here," she said.

"Here? What do you mean?"

"In Maine."

"What! I don't believe it. Where?"

"In Harrison. At the motel. Isn't it wonderful?"

"Oh Vicki, it's marvelous, marvelous!"

"I miss you so. You can't imagine how much."

"Oh, yes I can, my love. But your parents. Do they know where you are?"

"They think I'm in Bennington having an interview. They want me to transfer there. When can I see you, Pete?"

"I'm sure I can talk the director into giving me the night off."

"Good, my darling. I'll be here."

We went out to dinner, then spent the night together in the motel. It was a difficult night. Vicki was plagued with a hernia that was causing her severe pain. All night she lay curled up in my arms. She should never have come. The next morning we found a local doctor who recommended that she immediately return to Chicago and have surgery performed. When I returned to camp I was almost dismissed for overstaying my leave. The director kept me on only because he couldn't have found a replacement so deep into the summer.

Vicki's parents never ceased trying to keep us apart. They threatened to stop paying for her piano lessons and college tuition unless she transferred to a school far away from Chicago. She felt she had no choice; the piano was her life. So she chose Bennington College partly because of its liberal reputation but mostly because of Silkanov, the renowned piano teacher in residence.

Silkanov, a short, thin, balding man, still in his thirties, had taught several young up-and-coming pianists then on the concert circuit. During Vicki's first interview, he was impressed by her determination, but more important, after hearing her play, he was amazed at how well she had overcome her handicap. Indeed, it intrigued him. What a challenge Vicki would be. What a feather in his cap were she to make the concert stage.

That fall Vicki enrolled at Bennington. Immediately Silkanov took her under his wing and strove to dominate her. To meet his demands that she perform ever more difficult pieces, she practiced endless hours into the night. His insistence on technical perfection was implacable. Both teacher and student had merged their private compulsions toward a single goal: Vicki's consummate mastery of the piano. After several months, Silkanov's demands finally drove Vicki to the brink of physical and mental exhaustion.

In the little spare time she had, she managed to write me every day. She wrote about the small hints of Silkanov's approval as if they were the most momentous rewards. "I played the Chopin Twelfth Etude for him last night," she wrote. "And when I was finished he didn't say a word. Isn't that marvelous? You should meet Silky, my love. He's so incredibly inspiring. I must tell you what he said the other day: If I should keep on as I have been, I'll be good enough for the concert stage by the time I graduate. Isn't that wonderful? I can't believe it. Oh, my love, I'm so confused. What should I do? I want you and I want the piano too. Can't I have both? Can't I? Help me!"

Her letter tore at me. I resented Silkanov. Because of him I was bound to lose her, I thought. My reply to Vicki offered her little solace. "How can I help? You know I want you, only you, but if you decide on a concert career, how can we be together? How could we raise a family? No, darling, you really can't have both me and the piano. This Silkanov worries me. Are you sure his interest in you is strictly professional? After all, you are beautiful, irresistible. You are my life and I feel it ebbing away."

Yes, I was consumed with jealousy. Silkanov was my nemesis. Just as Vicki's parents had tried to tear Vicki and me apart, I now tried to do the same to Vicki and her teacher. Soon, during the Christmas break, I would meet Silkanov. I vowed that somehow I'd reveal him to Vicki as he really was: a man ambitious for his own advancement even at the cost of Vicki's health.

That night at Mechanics Hall, if I hadn't forgiven him before, I did then. There on the stage was living proof of his remarkable dedication to Vicki's cause. Only because of him could her hands with their spindly thumbs have produced the incomparable torrent of melody as they tripped across the keys.

The last sounds of the D Minor's first movement faded into a hush. Vicki had awed us with her perfection, with the delicate nuances she gave to the music, with her incredible control over the keyboard. Still under the spell of the first movement, we heard the soft, slow second movement begin. Each note was distinct and clear and increasing in emotional intensity. The piano sang with pure feeling. My eyes had become bleary with tears. I was caught up in the thrall of her virtuosity. For a brief moment I loved her again as I had once loved her.

Betsy stared at me, puzzled by my sudden burst of emotion.

"Daddy, you're crying."

"I can't help it, Betsy. It's just so terribly beautiful," I whispered.

Her own eyes filled with tears. "I know, Daddy."

Before the concert, as we were driving toward the city, I had felt anxious about meeting Vicki. Although I was afraid of what I would find, I was most afraid of what she would find. Ever since my college days I clung to an image of how I should turn out by the time I reached forty. I thought that by then my life would be interesting, challenging and important to the world and, of course, that I'd be financially well off. Only the last item came to pass. My life was simply ordinary. I lived in a middle-class suburban house, served on the board of selectmen in town, owned a thriving realty business, and drove a Mercedes. So what? Vicki had arrived. I had yet to arrive, or maybe I already had and was on my way out.

A Sentimental Concerto

"Come to Bennington during Christmas vacation and stay with me," Vicki had written. "I'll tell my parents that I have to remain on campus for my piano studies. I don't want to see them anyway. Please come, my darling. I want you to hear how much I've progressed so you'll understand that it's been worth it."

I understood—she wanted me and the piano too. And I understood that it was impossible.

We registered at the small hotel in Bennington as Mr. & Mrs. Amadeus Mozart. In those days, only married couples could sleep together with a clear conscience in hotels. I remember the hotel as if it were yesterday. It was an old three-story structure on a street corner. The room on the second floor facing the street was clean and cheerful and freshly painted. I was exhausted, having driven my '48 Chevy for twenty-two straight hours from Chicago via Route 20 through every city, town and hamlet. There were no superhighways then. I slept through Friday night into Saturday afternoon while Vicki sat by the window reading a book.

On Saturday evening I met Silkanov in the student lounge. He bounced up from his chair to greet us when we arrived, kissed Vicki on the cheek, and shook my hand firmly.

"You may not realize it," he said, "but I've known you for some time." His eyes were dark brown and they danced as he spoke. "Vicki has told me all about you."

"And I know all about you," I said in a challenging tone.

Silkanov was not what I expected. From Vicki's description, I envisioned an overpowering, physical titan. Instead he was a small, dark, balding, ordinary looking man. Only his eyes gave a hint of his dynamism.

"Vicki talks of you constantly," he went on. His voice was unexpectedly smooth, strong and booming, belying his small stature. "Except when she's playing her music, of course," he laughed. It was a surprisingly deep laugh, as if from a man far larger than he. "Thank God she has you, something besides music." He fastened his eyes on Vicki's. "There's a time for music, and there's a time for living. Both are important. Live life fully—love, enjoy and suffer—otherwise the playing will be empty. I can make anyone with talent a virtuoso of technique. Ah, that's easy. But I can't teach one how to feel. That, life has to do. Only from life can one learn how to interpret a Beethoven sonata so that it moves the listener. Only from life. Forgive me. I'm going on like a raving fool."

"Not at all. You make sense," I said, struck by his intensity.

"Has Vicki played for you yet?"

"No, I'm looking forward to it."

"Well, you're due for a pleasant surprise. She's made enormous strides. You know, Peter, we have a common interest: Vicki's welfare. I hope you and I will become fast friends."

If Silkanov had seemed to be a threat to my relationship with Vicki, he easily dispelled it during those first moments of our meeting. As he said, we both had her welfare at heart. And it was obvious that his interest in her was strictly professional.

But as he spoke, I observed from the corner of my eye that Vicki was watching him with adoring eyes. Silkanov reminded me of another older man and teacher, Kirk, with whom Vicki had had an infatuation.

We sat around a coffee table in the lounge and had the room to ourselves. Vicki spoke of her future. After graduating she planned to study in Europe with another teacher, a friend of Silkanov's. He explained that by then she would have learned all he could teach. It would be time for her to experience the world.

"I'm happy for you, Vicki," I said unconvincingly.

"Please, darling, try to understand."

"Play the Schumann sonata for Peter," said Silkanov. "When he sees how much you've progressed, I'm sure he'll understand."

"Would you like to hear it, darling?"

"Of course. I haven't heard you play since Ida Noyes."

"Yes, that was before Silky," she said as she rose to go to the piano. She sat on the piano bench, gazed into space momentarily, and began playing. In no time she became totally absorbed in the music. For all she knew, Silkanov and I had disappeared.

"Her power of concentration is superhuman," said Silkanov. "The world must not be deprived of such an extraordinary talent, Peter. Don't you agree?" I nodded. "She has even more. She has what's needed to succeed: the desire, the compulsion, the dedication. It's a rare combination."

"Well, it's obvious she's compensating for her handicap. She's trying to prove that her hands are as good as any normal person's."

"She has no handicap, Peter. How can you say that? Listen to her play."

"But she thinks she has."

"Do you realize that Cortot has heard her and has agreed to take her after graduation?"

"Alfred Cortot?" I had his records and knew him to be one of the greatest pianists of our age.

"None other."

"Where?"

"Lausanne. He no longer performs but he still teaches a handful of exceptional pupils."

"I see. Well, that's certainly a wonderful opportunity."

"I know it must not be easy for you, Peter. But we must not deny her or the world her future."

"Are you saying I'll have to give her up?"

"Not at all. She loves you. But you'll have to share her. Music will be the center of her life. The question you must ask is can you live with it."

I stared off into space, listening to the Schumann. It had come to sound more like a sad wail.

That night in the hotel room Vicki and I made love for the second time—and last time. She clasped me to her in a kind of desperation as if sensing that it would be our last time together. "Hold me," she begged. "Don't let go. Don't ever let go." We clung to each other, praying that time would stand still. But we both knew these would be our final hours. I kissed her brow, her eyelids, her cheeks, her neck and tasted the salt of her warm tears as our lips met.

"Don't cry," I pleaded.

"I know I won't see you again. Will I? Tell me the truth."

I began sobbing over the loss that had already begun.

The orchestra and piano completed the last chords of the concerto's spirited finale. Instantly applause swept through the hall like a cresting wave. Shouts of "bravo" pierced the roar. Vicki bowed gracefully, perhaps demurely. What sweet irony. Little did I know thirty years before in Orchestra Hall that she would realize her wish—and that I would bear witness to it. Now, right before my eyes she had attained the stature of her idol, Myra Hess. The audience stood in unison as Vicki had five curtain calls.

During intermission Betsy and I rushed from our seats through the crowd down the red-carpeted stairs to the room behind the stage. There the musicians stood in small conversational groups smoking and drinking coffee. Off to the side, I spied Vicki surrounded by autograph seekers, mostly young people. Betsy joined them as I stood by a wall waiting patiently for them to disperse. Vicki was animated and witty. Her admirers constantly burst into laughter at her remarks. As she happened to glance in my direction her eyes momentarily met mine. She stared for a moment, transfixed, then returned to the program she was signing. It was Betsy's.

Had she forgotten, or had I so changed that she didn't recognize me?

An old man in white tie and tails suddenly emerged from the throng of musicians and strode toward Vicki. He was a small, bent man, bald except for a white fringe of hair above his ears. He held a woman's fur coat in his arms, which he gently draped over Vicki's shoulders like a cape.

"As usual, you were fantastic, my dear," I heard him say hoarsely.

Vicki turned slightly and kissed his cheek. "I play only for you, Silky. They no longer matter."

He smiled wanly as they walked toward the door, she holding his arm, supporting him. I stood rooted in place, feeling like an outsider. I was thunderstruck that my old pain still lingered.

"Daddy, aren't you going to speak to her?" Betsy asked.

I shook my head.

"But why? I don't understand."

"She doesn't remember me."

"How do you know?"

"She saw me."

"Oh," Betsy said. "Look, I've got her autograph. I told her I play the piano too and how much I enjoy it. See what she wrote."

On the program that Betsy handed me Vicki had written, "For Betsy, May music fill your life with as much joy as it has mine. Vicki Kendall."

The lights flashed, signaling the end of intermission.

"You'll love the next piece, Betsy."

Betsy read the program. "It's Berlioz' Fantastic Symphony," she said. "I don't think I know it."

"Just wait. You'll see." I hugged her. "It's like you, simply fantastic."

Search for Euphoria

Emily is nuts about me. I can't imagine why. I'm ordinary looking, actually shorter than most, balding, and I wear thick glasses. But, in her eyes, everything I do is perfect. There are plenty of guys around who are more talented and better looking. And they're on the make. Emily won't see them for dust.

"You know what I like about you?" she says.

"Haven't the vaguest," I say.

"You're deep. I mean, you're not like the others. You're always thinking. You've got ideas on every subject. Religion, meaning of life, sex, taxes — that kind of stuff."

I smile and shrug. Why argue? It's nice being appreciated even when you don't think you deserve it.

Emily's one of the Kenmore Square gang. (That's the square near Fenway Park where the Sox play. They're my team. What a year we're having, eh? Excuse me, I go off track sometimes.) The Kenmore Square gang consists of about ten guys and gals who meet randomly for breakfast at Sampson's — a kind of hole-in-the-wall — between 7:30 and 8:30 every weekday morning. It's been our ritual for years. We're from all walks of life, but despite that, we have something in common — perhaps our humanity — and we're always happy to see each other. When one of us has a birthday or is laid up, the gang always sends a card signed by all.

But this is about Emily and me, mostly her. She always takes the counter stool next to me. In fact, if she arrives late and that stool is occupied, she graciously asks my neighbor to move.

Emily is fifty-five years old, a widow whose deceased husband left her plenty, I think. She isn't a bad looker, for her age. She has a nice figure, and a smooth face with bright, youthful green eyes.

We talk a lot about her investments. I give her good advice, it seems, because the investments I recommend do well. Too bad I don't follow my own recommendations. She believes in me more than I do.

Of course, we discuss other subjects too, deep stuff like religion, the meaning of life, sex, and taxes, not the usual small talk that goes on over a morning cup of coffee.

Little by little I learn about her past. Though right now she's a successful real estate agent — judging by her duds she's doing damn well — she reveals that she used to be a nun.

"I went twenty-five years without a guy," she says, sighing. "It took me all that time to realize I was sacrificing my womanhood. Life's short. I don't want to miss anything."

"Hell, no," I say.

Then she says: "I'm seeing this man, an executive with a big company. He's always drifting from one outfit to another. Oh, they're good jobs but he's going nowhere."

A few months later she's seeing someone else.

"He flies his own plane," she says. "We have good times skipping down to New York or Nantucket. But something's missing. He knows how to make love, but he doesn't know how to love — know what I mean? He bought the plane with a portion of some fire insurance money and when the rest of that's gone I don't know what he'll do. The pity is, neither does he.

"Why do I attract such losers? At first they seem so wonderful, until I get to know them. But with you, it would be different. You and I hit it off pretty good, don't we?" she says, leaning over and rubbing her shoulder on mine.

"I guess we do," I say, asking myself what next.

"How would you like to do some socializing? I mean, come over to my place and have a drink after work."

I'm honored. Never had a woman proposition me before.

"That's very nice of you, thanks, but I'm married, and I don't think my wife — "

"Do you tell your wife everything?" she asks.

Of course I don't tell my wife everything. When I want variety, you can bet I don't go where I'm known. One-night stands, no involvement — that's my policy.

"I love my wife, Emily. Anyway, I've got enough troubles already."

"Troubles? I'm no trouble," she says. "Sweetheart, I could make your troubles go away."

What does she know? I'm facing an IRS audit, business is bad, and one of my kids is on drugs. "I like you, Emily," I say, "but let's just stay friends."

"Sure," she says, "that's nice too."

Still, I feel good knowing that someone nifty like Emily wants me, an ordinary guy.

For Christmas I give her a book of warm poetic insights about life.

"You're very thoughtful," she says. "I keep the book on my bedside table to read before I fall asleep. It helps me feel better about myself."

Emily is a fountain of information about all the people who frequent Sampson's for breakfast. She knows their business and drinking problems, whose kids are going wild, and whose marriage is in trouble. And she keeps me informed of her love life with the latest boyfriend. Like all the others before, each has his deficiencies. After hearing about her losers, I must admit I'm not so bad.

From the other guys in the breakfast gang, I learn that some of them visit her after work and unload their troubles, among other things. If she's such a listener, who does she have to talk to? Me. Who else? I can sympathize because I understand her frustration searching for a dream man. I can sense her desperation.

When she left the convent, she was about forty-five years old. In less than a month she married a guy thirty years older than herself.

"He was a beautiful man," she says. "They don't make them like him anymore."

"Maybe that's the trouble. The men you're seeing now are too young. What did he do for a living?"

"Oh, he was independently well-off. Retired contractor. I remember him from when I was a kid, never dreaming that someday . . ." She becomes teary. "We had five gorgeous years together."

"Good memories, huh?"

"The best," she says, as if "the best" would never happen again. Not having faith in the future is depressing. She is touching my heart.

"He died of cancer. I nursed him for more than a year while he was dying. It was the longest year of my life. The medical bills took most of his money. After he was gone I had to do something to support myself. I never thought I'd become a savvy business woman. I take after my father. They broke the mold after he died."

"I think I remember him. Wasn't he in insurance?"

"The biggest agency in town," she says proudly. "When I have to make a business decision I always ask myself: What would my father have done? It works. For an ex-nun, I think I'm doing okay."

"You sure are," I say with a touch of envy. She is doing a lot better than I am. "Maybe—it's just a thought—I'm no psychologist, of course—but since you've had two extraordinary men in your life, maybe no one else can measure up."

She thinks for a few minutes before replying.

"I don't think so, at least as far as my husband was concerned. He was a bastard."

"I thought you said—"

"Our early love died." Her voice grows husky with emotion.

"You mean while he was sick?"

"No, before that. He thought I expected more from him than he could—well, give."

"You mean—"

"Sexually. I accepted his limitations. I didn't need him; I wasn't always faithful."

"I'm confused, Emily. What was he: beautiful or mean?"

"It depends. Our first couple of years were happy, then he changed."

Or did Emily give him cause? Was she still looking for her dream man?

In June she invited my wife and me to an afternoon party at her place on the Cape. Located in an open meadow on the bay, it used to be her family's summer house. She uses it half the summer and her married sister uses it the other half.

"My sister," she said, "doesn't enjoy life. She thinks I'm too loose. Well, at least half the summer you can have a good time at the place. Now, don't forget to bring your swim trunks and tennis racquet."

My wife begged off, saying she'd rather spend the afternoon at the flea market. More to the truth, she seemed to resent Emily. I suppose I raved about her a bit too often.

Emily's spread at the Cape was quite something: a free-form swimming pool, two tennis courts, and a nine-room Victorian mansion.

Tables brimming with platters of catered food and a portable bar stocked with liquor were set out on the sunny lawn which rolled down to the blue bay. A cooling breeze came off the water. Yes, it was quite something.

Everybody from the Kenmore Square crowd was there. I played tennis most of the afternoon.

After the game, Emily suggested, "You're all sweaty. Why don't you take a shower?"

"I don't want to impose," I said.

"Not at all. Use the shower off my bedroom. Follow me. I'll get you a towel."

She left the room and I undressed in the bathroom. I stood under the warm water with my eyes closed, feeling completely relaxed. Then the shower door opened and in walked Emily without a stitch on.

"I need a shower too," she said, "and two can do this better than one. How about washing my back?"

Well, she's right there like an engraved invitation. What does a guy do? "What about your guests?" I said.

"They're all feeling too good to miss me. I want to do it with a winner for a change." So she grabbed me by the kazoo and I was done for.

In the late afternoon the air had cooled off and I was feeling refreshed and loose after the shower. Taking a beer, I helped myself to some food and mingled. Emily, looking chipper, took my hand and said she wanted me to meet someone.

"This is Jeff," she said, introducing me to a shriveled sort of man. He looked as though he might be recovering from an operation. He pumped my hand and conversed as if he'd known me all his life.

Emily hugged us to her in each arm and says, "My two favorite men," then walked away.

In none of the conversations I've had with Emily did I ever hear of Jeff. Where, I wonder, did he come from? It's strange: I felt a little jealous even though I have no claim on her.

"What a terrific gal," said Jeff.

"You bet," I said.

His eyes caressed her while he talked. I had the feeling she was the center of his universe.

"When did you two meet?" I asked.

"Six months ago. She sold me a town house on the Hill. Lots of fun, that gal. Never figured I'd fall in love at this time of my life, but I ain't arguing."

I felt sympathy for him because I don't think he stood a chance. Didn't Emily have a painful experience with an old guy already? And this one looked as though he's ready to go cold. She was too smart to make the same mistake twice. Still, he was very personable. He talked calmly, he was sure of himself, and he seemed full of kindness. I couldn't help liking him.

"How about a beer?" I said.

"No thanks," he said. "Haven't had a drink for over a year. I'm an alky, you know. Quit cigarettes too. That gal's given me a reason to keep living."

"Emily's something," I said. "She can keep a man on his toes."

"Next weekend I'm taking her to Quebec City," he said. "She's working too hard; I told her she ought to get away. But you know Emily—she's got her own mind and says no. I bought the plane tickets anyway. 'It's up to you,' I said. 'Either you go with me or I throw the tickets away.' So we're going."

I found myself rooting for him.

I see Emily at Sampson's for breakfast on Monday. "What in the hell's going on?" I say. "Why did you keep Jeff a secret?"

She shrugs. "I didn't really," she says. "I see him occasionally. Sure, we went to Bermuda one weekend last winter and Paradise Island another weekend, but he's just a casual friend. There's nothing serious between us."

"Are you sure?" I say.

"Certainly. He just likes my company and I like his. That's all there is to it."

"Hell, he's spending a fortune on you, Emily. It looks to me like he more than just likes your company."

Emily smiles and says, "He's lonely. All he's looking for is a traveling companion. Anyway, he's too old for me. You know how I am. I need a horny guy."

"Well, you may not be serious about him, but I think he's serious about you," I say, reluctantly poking my nose in.

"Yeah," she says, wincing. "Is that what he told you?"

"No. That's what I see."

"I told him to forget it. Don't even think about getting serious."

"You're a tough gal."

"He's in his seventies, diabetic, a reformed alcoholic. He knows what I went through the first time. And worst of all he can't get it up. We don't sleep in the same bed."

"Oh, that's rough," I say, feeling pity. My god, he's got a gal who's great in bed and he can't enjoy her. He may as well be dead.

Business being bad, I try my hand at writing sexy stories to supplement my income. And what do you know, a girlie magazine buys them. I tell Emily about it, and she goes right out and buys the magazine. After reading my stories she can't contain her admiration.

"We've got to celebrate your literary success," she says. "Visit me after work. Just a drink and you can leave."

Since I'm feeling pretty good about myself, I go along. But I don't leave—right away, that is. What happens in the apartment is great material for my next story. I'm a married man. The next time Emily invites me over after work, I tell her no dice. It could become an addiction.

Just before Christmas she breaks the news.

"I'm getting married," she says.

"That's wonderful," I say. "Who's the luckiest guy in the world?"

"Jeff," she says.

"But I thought—"

She nods. "I know what you're thinking. It'll be okay. He says I can do whatever I want so long as I don't tell him about it. He realizes I have my needs."

"What a terrific guy," I say, astonished. "He's crazier about you than I thought."

"Yes," she says. "I think I can make him happy. Y'know I love him—not the way I love you—but there's no chance with us, is there?"

"C'mon, Emily."

"You'll see me once in a while, won't you?"

"I told you I can't. I wouldn't be able to stop."

"You can put me in one of your stories," she says.
I already have, in a dozen versions.

The wedding took place in a gigantic cathedral. Only a small gathering of family and close friends attended. Emily's sister appeared relieved that her sister was going legitimate but some of the guys from the Kenmore Square gang were sad. They were probably her lovers and didn't realize that the wedding wouldn't change a thing. Jeff, of course, was on cloud nine.

"I told you I'd marry her," he said to me.

"You're perfect for her, Jeff," I said. "I wish you all the happiness."

"I'm not perfect," he said, "but I've got a ticker full of love."

I wondered whether he thought I was one of her lovers too. But I don't think being with her a few times qualified me as her lover. And seeing how Jeff adored her, I was sure I'd never be with her again.

After six months Emily told me that the marriage was working out. Jeff was getting the steady companionship he wanted and Emily was finding elsewhere what she couldn't get from him.

One morning over a second cup of Java, she asks me to write her life story. "Maybe it'll help some poor, confused kid like I was."

"I don't know whether I can handle someone's life story, Emily."

"Sure you can. It's not much different from some of the stories you've already written."

"What do you mean?"

"Things have happened to me."

"Like what?"

"I can't tell you," she says.

"Christ, Emily, how can I tell your story if you don't tell me. You don't make sense."

"I mean I can't tell you face to face, not yet, but I can put it in writing—a kind of synopsis."

"Sure, that would be okay, for a start," I say, anticipating, eventually, a sizzling description of her sexual encounters with some of Boston's rich and famous—maybe an expose. She reaches in her bag and hands me an envelope.

"This will tell you what happened to me," she says as she slides off the stool to leave. "If you think you can make a story from it, I'll fill in the details later."

Ordering a third cup of coffee, I open the envelope on the spot and began reading. I am in absolute shock. The poor, poor kid. Suddenly I understand why she is the way she is. Here is most of what she wrote:

"We were so close. It was perfect happiness. Euphoria. I was completely satiated, wanting nothing more. I was his first born.

"He was always there when I needed him. When I was sick he sponged my body with cooling alcohol. When I panicked in a house fire, he took me in his arms and placed his hands between my legs. When I broke my arm, I retreated to a corner of the kitchen, letting no one help me. Only to him would I surrender my horribly fractured limb.

"When I was bigger I slept by myself on the studio couch in the parlor. Often he came to me and after an abundance of pleasure, a super abundance, which was more than I could bear, it became wrong.

"I still can't accept what happened, but I remember it too well. I remember I had to escape. And I had to punish myself and maybe him too.

"So at seventeen I entered a semi-cloistered order where I would never be allowed to go home or to see him unescorted. But even after pronouncing my vows of poverty, chastity, and obedience, even after years had gone by, my longing did not leave me, the longing for that time of bliss and perfect peace.

"One day on a family visit, he stayed behind as we said good-bye. In a dark hallway he kissed me hotly—an open-mouthed kiss with his tongue reaching for mine. I pushed him away in disgust. What he had done was so bad, so revolting to me.

"A chronic depression settled over me like a dark menacing cloud. None of my duties for the order, neither my studies nor my prayers, relieved me of the constant growing pain deep within my innermost being. I waited for something to happen; I longed for someone to rescue me. I lived in a fantasy. I reached for God, trying to sublimate this cruel desire for pleasure and happiness. I wanted to be reborn, be a child again and have my father.

"My white-haired confessor said I must grow up. He said I was a woman, a woman with a lovely body capable of leaving the convent and finding joy if I wished. He would prove it to me. I was in my early twenties then and he was in his late sixties. Several times, at his request, I removed my habit and stood before him naked while he gazed at me, proving, he said, that I need not be ashamed of my form. No, we never had sex. In fact I refused to believe that I had a 'hole,' a normal vagina; often I tried to pry it open with my fingers to prove that I had one. Then one day my confessor slipped his hand under my habit and inserted his index finger beneath the flap of my vagina without damaging or hurting it and stimulated me so that I would know, he said, that I was intact as a woman. Later on he did it often, making me flow and know I was a woman. He was my father, to whom I could confide anything, and I was his child begging for help.

"I left the convent after twenty-five years. When my father came to get me, all he said was: 'Why didn't you talk to me and tell me of your unhappiness?'

"I could not live in the same house with him. I found my own place and in less than a year I met and married a man thirty years older than myself. He thought I was a virgin, so we had sex before our honeymoon 'so that it would be more pleasant afterward,' he said. He was my father again.

"I became pregnant but lost the baby, a boy, after two months. I just knew it had to be a boy.

"Having sex with my husband did not satisfy me. I wanted real sex with someone young and vital. Then suddenly at our very own pool I found the right one—a big, beautiful Tom Selleck type with smiling eyes. He had come to see my husband on business and stayed the afternoon. He came again when my husband was away. I was in the pool and I invited him in to hold me, just hold me, nothing more. He took off his clothes and walked down the pool steps into the water and reached for me as I came to him. Our joining was spontaneous. I knew I had found what I was hungering for so long—his wet body against mine. It was ecstasy.

"After that, we met often. But once the first irresistible pangs of passion were satisfied, we tried to stay apart for both our spouses' sakes. He was only the first of a long list of men with whom I experimented. To me, all of them were losers. Only the inaccessible men, those who were married, appealed to me. What was I looking for? Who? My father?

"Now, my lover, the one I most enjoy, comes to me from time to time. We love each other very much. But he is married and so, now, am I, and I know I can't really have the man I love because the first man in my life loved me too much. So I live in a fantasy world of unfulfilled bliss searching endlessly for that state of euphoria I knew in my childhood. And sadly I know when I find it, it will not be mine to keep. Not until we are together, my father and I, for the rest of time."

Emily's story is better than anything I could write. When I see her the next morning at Sampson's, I say: "Read your story." She avoided my eyes and waited. "It's great."

"Then you'll do it?"

"Are you sure you want to tell everything? I mean it's very personal."

"Absolutely everything. It would be dishonest to hold back. If my story could do some good, keep some poor girl from turning out like me, it would be worth it."

"I'll use fake names, disguise a few things."

"No. I think real names will have more impact."

"I'm really sorry for all your suffering, Emily. You've got courage."

"Courage, huh?" she says, winking. "Let's talk business. How much money do you think we'll make?"

"I haven't the vaguest—but probably a lot if I find the right publisher."

"Okay. How do we split it?"

"You're way ahead of me," I say.

"How about 60/40? Ladies before gentlemen."

As I say, Emily's a sharp cookie.

El Presidente, El Morro

The he motel in Albuquerque left much to be desired.

"But it's rated three-star," Norman insisted. "Why do you blame me? I went by the book."

"I don't care," Janet said petulantly. "I don't want to stay here." With a sweep of her hand she pulled down the bedspread. "They didn't even change the sheets from the people last night. See how wrinkled they are."

"Christ, it's ten at night. We'd never find anything this late." Norman sat on the bed and bent his head into his hands.

"Always the pessimist. How do you know unless you try?"

"All I know is I drove five hundred miles today and I'm exhausted."

"Well, I'd have been happy to help you drive. But no, you've got to do it all."

"With you driving I'd be more tired."

"You've got to run the show. El Presidente."

"For crissake, shut up, Janet."

They stayed in the undesirable motel and fell asleep back to back, clinging to their own edges of the mattress.

Janet had wanted to visit the Southwest for a long time. She had never been there in Georgia O'Keeffe country. O'Keeffe was one of her favorite painters. She had hoped the journey would bring her and Norman closer, bring them back to the way they were during the early years when the kids were small and he was struggling to build his business. It would be a second honeymoon, something every couple needs after twenty years.

They had made plans three times previously, once even securing plane tickets, which Norman had canceled because of pressing business. He had an exaggerated sense of his importance, as if the business wouldn't survive without him. El Presidente Norman.

The next morning, they awoke early. From the motel window they could see hundreds of colorful hot-air balloons drifting lazily in the sky against the purple-hued mountains. It was the first day of a week-long annual balloon festival.

"Look at that one," Norman exclaimed. "It's gorgeous."

"And that one," said Janet. "I've never seen anything like it. The air's full of them."

What a way to begin the day, Norman thought. The entire sky was a celebration. He envied the balloon people. They just soared, free with the wind.

"Now, aren't you glad you came?" Janet asked sanctimoniously.

"Sure, I'm glad," he said. "Who said I wasn't?"

Damn her, spoiling his pleasure in such an awe inspiring sight.

Driving west on the interstate, they stopped at Acoma, an ancient Indian village perched on a lonely mesa jutting high above the flat desert. A decrepit school bus took them up a steep, dusty grade to a cluster of low, thick-walled adobe structures.

"They're so poor," Janet said, observing the primitive dwellings.

As their guide led them through the windswept dirt streets, she recited the town's history. Native women displayed hand-wrought silver jewelry on tables set before their hut entrances. On one table, Janet saw a silver necklace she liked.

"It's quite beautiful," she said.

"Thank you," replied the Indian woman.

"Did you make it?"

"Yes, I make."

"Where did the design come from?"

The woman shrugged. "From here." She pointed to her forehead.

"Remarkable."

Janet had a sharp eye for quality in craftsmanship and art. Norman admired her appreciation. He wanted to learn from her, but he never told her so.

"Do you live here?" Janet asked, pointing to the simple hut.

"Yes, and here I work."

"Remarkable."

Janet bought the necklace, and the woman gave her a small set of earrings as a gift. An unspoken rapport, it seemed, had developed between the artist and the connoisseur.

"Let me pay you for the earrings," Janet insisted.

"No, no. For you."

"Thank you. They're lovely."

Smiling, the woman nodded.

As the school bus descended into the desert, Janet commented to Norman, "It's so sad being stuck in this awful place."

"I wouldn't say it's sad," Norman replied. "The woman seems happy."

"I know," Janet marveled. "I suppose she's got all she wants."

They returned to their car and continued westward on the interstate across the dry, barren countryside. During the next couple of hours a wind gradually arose. Soon mesquite was tumbling across the highway. Severe wind gusts buffeted the car, swerving it from its lane.

"Damnit, we need gas," Norman observed. "I should have filled up in Albuquerque." He spread the map across the steering wheel to locate the next town.

"For God's sake, either pull off the road or let me have the map," Janet said impatiently.

"No, I can do it," Norman said, accelerating to seventy-five.

Janet stared ahead in silence. Why does he always have to run the show? Why . . . why?

Though the wind continued to increase as they headed west, Norman maintained their speed, which made Janet more anxious. She would have been at ease were she driving. But she knew he would give her no peace. Do this or do that, he'd say, or go faster, or pass the car ahead. She felt trapped.

They turned off the highway onto a secondary road, which after fifty miles took them to El Morro National Monument. An imposing mesa rising a thousand feet above the desert, El Morro is the site of ancient Zuni ruins. Over the centuries passersby had stopped to drink from the cool spring-fed pool located in a rocky cavity at the foot of the mesa.

In late afternoon, with the massif looming in the distance, Norman broke the silence. "You'll be impressed with this place, Janet. I've read a lot about it."

"Well, I hope we don't stay too long. It's been a long ride and I'm tired."

"You can stay in the car," responded Norman. "I'll climb the mesa by myself."

"Do you expect me to just sit here alone? No, I'll go with you," she said grudgingly.

At the visitor center a park ranger directed them to a path that would take them up the escarpment to the heights.

Starting at the spring-fed pool, they walked beside the vertical face, gazing in awe at pictographs, names, vignettes, and rhymes carved into the stone, some bearing dates going back a few hundred years. They were so enthralled that they held hands and smiled, their accumulated resentments forgotten.

"Look at this one, Norman," Janet said.

"Yes, it's wonderful. I've never seen anything so interesting," replied Norman. They were enraptured, sharing the experience of discovery. It was longer than they could remember since they'd been this way together.

Because their side of the escarpment shielded them from the wind, they had no notion that it had been increasing steadily and that now a gale force was blowing on top of the mesa. The day was brilliantly clear, with high cirrus clouds splashed here and there.

As the engravings petered out, the path began winding upward among low shrubs and eventually into tall trees indigenous to a more temperate zone. As the grade grew sharper and the path entered a series of steep switchbacks, Norman, who had neglected to keep himself fit, had to rest.

At last, they stepped onto the top edge of the mesa. The wind was gusty and strong, and Norman pressed his white admiral's cap farther onto his head. The wind seemed harmless enough. Gazing across El Morro's summit, they were surprised at its vastness and the extent of the trek that lay ahead. The path seemed more like an obstacle course of ledge upthrusting in a variety of shapes and sizes. In the distance they could barely make out the ghostly adobe ruins of an ancient village.

Arrow symbols etched in the rock beckoned them on. After following them toward the center of the summit, they found themselves crawling on hands and knees, clawing any small cranny and pressing themselves as tightly as possible to the rock as the full force of the howling winds hit them.

Finally, they lay prostrate afraid to move.

"I can't go on," Janet said.

"We have to, Jan. We can't stay here. We have to. Try girl, try. Hold on to me."

Bracing himself between two large rocks, he reached for her hand. Inch by inch, crawling like lizards, they worked their way forward along the path to the very rim of a steep, enclosed, horseshoe-shaped canyon.

"I'm afraid, Norman. I'm really afraid."

"Look, let me go first and I'll lead you along the edge," Norman said.

Frightened himself, he realized that one misplaced step would topple them into the canyon. But he was more afraid for Janet. Never in their twenty years of marriage had they faced such an ordeal—literally a matter of life and death.

"No, I want to be with you," he heard Janet say. "I want to die with you. You mean more to me than . . ."

The poncho she was wearing ballooned up around her, muffling her words. Slowly he pulled her with him. How he loved her, cared about her. He hadn't felt this way in years. Janet tried to complete her sentence. "You mean more to me than" . . . Than what? He couldn't hear her above the howl of the wind. Finally the words came, "than my own life."

It was as if someone else had spoken, she thought, as if the words had issued from God. What did they mean? Why did she speak them? Of course she could go on without him. She knew that their marriage had so deteriorated that if things didn't change she would have to leave him. So where did those words come from?

Eventually they were in the lee of the wind and they stopped to rest before completing the perilous course.

"We'll make it okay now," Norman said.

"You've been wonderful, Norm, thank you."

They crawled on past the ruins, too exhausted to view them.

"We'll come back another time and take a look," Norman said, "when it's dead calm. Right, Janet?"

"You'll come back," she laughed.

At last they reached the sheltered face and the easy path down to the visitor center.

"We could have been killed," Norman said on the way down.

"Why didn't they warn us?" Janet said.

"I'll give that ranger hell."

At the headquarters a different ranger than the one who greeted them was on duty.

"The winds are ferocious on top. We could have been killed. Why in hell don't you warn people?"

"Didn't you see the sign?"

"What sign?"

"On the path before the incline."

"We never saw a sign."

"It's there. The top's closed off."

"We must have been too engrossed to notice it," mused Janet.

"I must be blind," Norman said.

Lost in thought, they drove in silence for several hours to their next destination, Chinle. They were in awe of each other. They had found feelings they didn't know they had, feelings that had been submerged under layers of petty hurts. In the crisis their lost love for each other had resurfaced and overwhelmed the bitterness that had insinuated itself into their marriage. On the mesa they had abandoned their protective defenses and felt suddenly open and free. It was truly remarkable.

When they reached Chinle Janet remained in the car while Norman went into the motel to register. The clerk had no record of their reservation.

"My travel agent made it weeks ago," Norman said.

"Do you have a confirmation slip?"

"I never received one."

"I'm sorry, sir. We're booked solid."

Norman, fuming, returned to the car. "No wonder the Japanese are taking over the world," he shouted. "The way businesses in this country operate, we're handing it to them on a silver platter."

He was on a roll. "I thought you took care of everything," he ranted at Janet. "Wait'll I see that goddamned travel agent. You can't depend on anybody these days. When you make motel reservations you've got to insist on getting confirmation slips. Do you understand?"

Janet had been listening to his bombast for years. Turning him off offered her no reprieve. He seemed to be blaming her for what went wrong at the motel; he always blamed her. And she was ready to accept the blame. Yes, she made a mistake. She should have asked for a confirmation slip.

They found a room in another motel several miles away. It was just as bad as the room they had stayed in the previous night. But Janet was too weary to complain. She knew it would be useless anyway, considering Norman's foul mood.

While Norman was in the bathroom getting ready for bed, Janet stood before the dresser mirror trying on her new necklace and the earrings that went with it so well. She stroked them, relishing their smooth metallic feel. She stepped back to see the entire picture. How beautiful they were, even more so than she remembered while they lay on the open-air table.

Tears welled up in her eyes as she thought of the Acoma lady, a true artisan; no, she was much more—a creative artist. How happy she seemed on that dusty, windswept mesa. How satisfied. If only she herself could find such reward. Janet let herself weep gently. In the mirror she watched her unhappiness flow into the room.

"Your turn," Norman said, emerging from the bathroom and turning on the TV as he sat on the bed to watch.

The nightly news featured the balloon festival. Several balloonists were being interviewed against a background of balloons floating gently upward, filling the sky just as he had seen them that morning in Albuquerque. How he had envied the balloonists their abandon. They went wherever the wind took them, on the edge of risk, of possibly losing control. If only he could live on the edge and be released from his need for order and security. But hadn't he found such a freedom on El Morro? Hadn't he discovered a depth of feeling that he had forgotten he possessed?

He could almost cry. He hadn't cried since he was a boy. He had forgotten how. Anyway, he certainly wasn't going to start now. And not in front of Janet. El Presidente Norman.

Janet came from the bathroom and without a word crawled into bed and pulled the blanket up around her. Norman turned off the TV and the bedside lamp. Assuming fetal positions with their backs to each other, they clung to the outermost edges of the bed and soon fell into a lonely sleep.

The Elaborate Crapshoot

I've come to the conclusion that business is nothing but an elaborate crapshoot. Take Chris, one of my clients. I was at his office preparing his company's P & L, when he had an anxiety attack. I had just presented him with a negative bottom line for the latest quarter. He took a few tranquilizer pills and laid down on a couch across from his desk.

After he stopped hyperventilating, I said, "Let's have a relaxing lunch and talk. It would do you good to get away from this place."

"Okay," he said, "I could use a drink."

I was surprised; he never drank. In fact, he was quite fit. A lap swimmer. Swimming kept him sane, he said. He was a trim man. He moved quick and easy like an athlete.

We drove downtown and had lunch in the dining room at the Manger hotel. It's a quiet spot where the waiters are old and the guests and staff take their time. After ordering highballs we clinked glasses.

"To no more anxiety attacks," I toasted. "Y'know, Chris, this was no accident. There was a reason." He nervously fingered his knife. "I think you're worried about what could happen."

"Worried? Hell no." He held his arm out. "See, steady. I've got everything under control. It won't happen again."

I put down my glass and looked seriously into his lean face. "I know red ink isn't easy to take time after time."

"Look, I'm no Pollyanna, Fred. I realize I've got problems. The goddamn recession isn't helping. The competition's brutal, but I can handle it. I've been down this road before."

"You've left something out. The agreement with Stan. Isn't the first principal payment due next month?"

Chris had bought out Stan, his ex-partner, four years earlier. Their agreement called for seven annual installment payments. It further stipulated that in the event Chris defaulted, Stan would take over the company. Were that to happen, Chris stood to lose virtually his entire personal wealth.

As we sliced into our steaks, I continued, "I'm sure you realize there are no miracles."

Chris raised pained eyes to mine and after making several false starts finally said, "I'll deal with the payment when the time comes."

"Then it will be too late, Chris. As your accountant, I urge you to plan ahead. You always have. It's been one of your strengths. Why not now?"

"Because nothing can be done."

"Surely—"

"Let's change the subject. Okay?"

"Do you think that will make it go away?" I realized I was being pushy, but I'd never seen Chris like this. He had always thrived on challenge, on accomplishing the impossible.

We used to play a little game. When I came to the office each quarter to do the books, he'd write down the expected bottom line figure on a piece of paper and seal it in an envelope. At the end of the day we'd open it and compare his figure with my results. Invariably he was so tuned in he'd be off by no more than a percent. And when the bottom line was red, he'd laugh and say, "Oh well, black gets boring after a while."

It wasn't like him to give up. I simply couldn't let him wallow in futility.

"Look, I'm in a corner," Chris admitted. "If I fall into a depression I might never pull out of it. I can't give in. So long as I keep up a front, I'm functional."

"The anxiety attack is telling you that doesn't work. You're only kidding yourself, Chris. Let's talk about it."

He downed the rest of his drink. "I—I can handle it. Honestly, Fred." Then suddenly his bravado cracked. "The truth is I've given my best, but it's just not good enough."

"It's not over, not by a long shot," I said poking my fork into the air for emphasis.

"Somehow I've managed to fail. I rolled dice and lost. That's the way it is."

"You have to do something, anything."

"Like what? I've run out of ideas."

"Let's examine the cards you hold."

"Well, the bank's out."

"One option remains. You could approach Stan. Ask him for relief."

"No way, never," Chris said slamming his fist on the table, making the plates and silverware jump.

"Why not, Chris? What alternative is there?"

A curious leer crossed his face. "Hey, wait a minute. Just you wait a minute. I'm really not powerless, after all."

This remark caught me off guard. "What do you mean?" I said cautiously.

"I could take the whole goddamned thing down with me."

"For God sake, Chris, you wouldn't want to do that."

"If Stan's unreasonable I sure as hell would. I'd lose everything if he takes over. What more could I lose?"

"You're bluffing. This isn't like you."

"I don't know whether I am or not. We'll have to see, won't we?"

He now had the spark he needed to deal with the issue. He asked that I be present at the meeting between Stan and himself. "We'll need a neutral party," he said. As the company's accountant, I had remained on good terms with both partners.

We met in Chris's office late one steamy August afternoon a few weeks after the lunch. Stan, jowly and pot-bellied, trying to appear casual, lounged on the couch across from Chris's desk. I sat on a stiff office chair in a far corner. Both men, their eyes hard, avoided each other's gaze. Chris opened the discussion.

"I take it you've looked over the latest P & L?"

"Yup," Stan replied.

"And you see that we're in the red and have been for the past couple of quarters?"

"I'm not surprised after the way you run the business," Stan quipped.

"For Christ sake, you know goddamn well times are tough," Chris shouted. "We'd be bankrupt by now with you at the helm."

"If you knew what you were doing, you'd be able to stay in the black regardless of the times."

"Let me remind both of you," I cut in, "that the purpose of this meeting is not to fire barbs at one another."

"Actually, I'm not sure why I'm here," said Stan.

"Maybe it's because you know the company doesn't have enough cash to meet the note that's due next month," Chris said sarcastically.

"Well, that's one thing we can agree on," said Stan grinning.

It was obvious Stan held all the cards. Chris paused. I could tell this was hard for him. He had his pride. He didn't want to beg. Finally he said evenly, "The fact is I can't raise the cash. The bank's out of the picture, especially now with the economy getting worse."

"So what are you getting at? What do you want from me?" asked Stan.

"More time."

"More time? You're kidding."

"More time—just on the principal. I can meet the interest payment. What have you got to lose?" said Chris calmly.

"I've got everything to lose—the whole damned company," Stan shrieked, his face flushing scarlet. "This is incredible. You're expecting me to—"

"Why not? You can see the company's in trouble. If you took over, you'd only inherit a bundle of problems," Chris warned. "Do you want that? If you give us some time, I know I can bring the company into the black."

The Elaborate Crapshoot

"Hey, fella, if I take over it will be in the black. It won't owe me a thing."

"Not a chance, Stan. Were you to run the company, it would be sure to go down. You'd lose it all—in less than a year. Admit it, Stan. You're a great salesman but a lousy manager. Give me a chance and we'll both win—the company will survive and you'll get your money."

"There's nothing more to talk about," said Stan rising to leave.

"Well, there sure as hell is and you'd better listen," Chris screamed as he bolted from his chair, his right arm punching the air. "You'll get only a shell, do you understand? I'll strip the company of every damned asset it has. I built this business while you were out there playing and living off its fat. You're not going to get it. Never. Not as long as I have breath in me."

As Stan stormed from the office, I stood with my arms outstretched in a gesture of hopelessness. "Well, we knew it was a longshot," I said.

"He doesn't want the money," Chris whispered hoarsely. "He only wants the business."

When Chris and I said good-bye after the meeting I had no idea it would be his last. On his way home that evening he had a fatal auto accident.

The receptionist was new as were several of the office staff. Chris's former office, now Stan's, had been freshly panelled and newly carpeted. Stan was seated in a large black leather chair behind a new teak desk when I entered. Unlocking his hands from behind his head, he clambered up from his chair to shake my hand.

"Welcome aboard," he said. "Ready to go to work?"

"Ready. What desk should I use?"

"The one you always use in the spare office." He handed me an envelope. "Let's compare figures when you're done, okay? I know I'll be right on."

"Really?" I said, skeptical.

As I was about to leave, he said, "About Chris—I mean his family. How are they doing?"

"They're okay. He had a lot of insurance."

"You know I'd be glad to help out if—"

"You could speak to his wife," I said, stating the obvious.

"I called and she hung up on me."

"I see."

He fidgeted in his chair and asked hesitantly, "What exactly happened? I mean how did it happen?"

"He was alone. There were no witnesses. He ran off the road into a tree."

"That's awful."

"It's quite a puzzle. He was really an excellent driver," I said. Stan sat unresponsive staring into space. "I'd better get to work. Excuse me, Stan."

"Oh sure, Fred, sure."

Late in the afternoon I had completed the P & L. It was crimson—an unprecedented loss. Statement in hand, I went into Stan's office and found him gone—"gone for the day," said the receptionist. Curious, I opened the envelope lying on his desk containing his figure. It was absurd. He had anticipated a ridiculous profit. Chris had him pegged. Stan was a consummate dreamer. In less than a year the company declared bankruptcy.

The Mentor

If I learned nothing else in business, I learned never to hire friends and relatives. But I did anyway—twice. The first time . . . well, no need to go into that. It was the second time that shook me to the marrow.

We had invited my wife's "successful" cousin, his wife, and their son and daughter-in-law to spend a fine summer Sunday with us at our cottage on Pleasant Lake. During the twenty years Jan and I had been married, we'd seen them only at weddings and bar mitzvahs and funerals, where we exchanged small talk and promised to get together but never did until that Sunday.

Starting as an engineer with an expanding plastics materials company, Cousin Russell had moved up the ladder to become second in command and owner of a minority piece of the business. When after a few years the owner died, he purchased the remaining shares at a favorable price from the grieving widow. Though we had business in common, I couldn't relate to Cousin Russell. His success, plus his background as marine captain in World War II, inflated his ego too much for me.

"It's all luck," he'd say about his success, grinning proudly, his chest expanding so that you knew he didn't believe that. "A matter of being in the right place at the right time, that's all."

Before I was on my own in business, I had been moving from one job to another trying to make a living. In fact, when I'd meet people I hadn't seen in a while, the typical greeting was, "What are you doing NOW?" It was embarrassing. Too independent minded to work for anybody for long, I was a "failure." Successful men like Cousin Russell didn't mingle with losers like me.

To make a long story short, eventually I started my own business making toys. After a rough ten-year period and, as

Russell would say, some luck, I became quite successful. Now that I was a winner, Russell was ready to accept my hospitality. By then he had become a bigger deal still. Within a year of acquiring his company's stock, he turned around and sold it to a large conglomerate for an enormous price, securing himself a position near the top.

"Don't say anything to anybody, Joel," he said to me as we sat on the pine-shaded porch overlooking the sparkling lake that afternoon, "but they're grooming me for the presidency."

"You don't say," I commented.

"But don't say anything to anybody."

"Not a chance."

Then he revealed the real reason why I was so fortunate to have the opportunity to sip highballs with him.

"Y'know, I took Nathan into the business after he quit college." A troubled look crossed his paunchy face as he stared off across the lake.

"Yeah, I heard," I said, also having heard that his son was no longer there. Until his father hired him, he had moved around a lot; he had a reputation for being "unstable." Shades of my earlier days.

"He's a bright kid, y'know, and he did a great job for me, but sometimes it's a mistake having your son aboard, especially when you're in a political situation like mine and you could be accused of nepotism. I mean he was earning a big salary, and some people were making remarks. Know what I mean?"

"I sure do," I said. "Why, when I had to let my nephew go—"

"As I say, Nathan's a good boy, bright, hard-working; I did all I could for him. So if you can find a place in your organization where he'd fit in, I'd appreciate it. All the kid needs is an opportunity to show what he can do, a spot where he can find himself. Know what I mean?"

"Sure, sure Russell. It so happens we're looking for a salesman."

To this day I'm not sure why I was so hasty. Maybe I had empathy for the kid whose job experience sounded much like my own in the early days. But Nathan was no kid; he was thirty-two and newly married.

"Look, talk to him. If you don't think he's for you, it's okay. No favors, see."

Before I had a chance to confer with the lad his mother cornered me while I was lighting the charcoal.

"All Nathan needs is a chance to find himself," she said with a distant look. "Y'know, Joel, of the four kids, he's my favorite. I can't explain it; he's the one I love the most."

"I'll talk to him, Rachel."

"You won't be sorry, I promise you. So—"

Then Cynthia, Nathan's wife, popped up beside me while I was treading water during the afternoon swim.

"Thanks for taking Nathan in, Joel."

"Huh?" I said, shocked. When did she hear that?

"You won't be sorry. All he needs is a place to find himself."

"Not so fast, Cyn. He's got to go through the procedure—the interview and tests, that sort of thing."

"Oh, I understand. But isn't that mostly routine?"

"Sure, just routine. I'm sure he'll work out."

Finally, I got to talk to the man himself in the outdoor shower. Nothing like interviewing someone when he's nude; no trappings to hide under then. Though shorter and rounder than his father, he was solid and barrel chested like him. I noticed he had a big scar at his left hip.

"Ski injury," he explained. "It's worth a cool thousand a month for the rest of my life."

"How's that?"

"I sued. Dad's company had an ace lawyer."

"Look, Nathan, we've got this sales job available—"

"Anything, Joel. I'll do anything. I'm not fussy."

"I was going to say, it's not up to me. You'd have to come in like anybody else and have an interview with our sales manager. Of course, I'll put in a word for you, but it's his decision."

"That's okay, Joel. I'm not asking for any favors, just an even chance. I'm looking for a spot where I can make a career—y'know, a spot where I can find myself."

Well, sure enough he called Ken, our sales manager, the very next morning, Monday, and made an appointment for that afternoon. I was impressed with his swift action.

Ken came to see me in my office after Nathan had left.

"We hired him, Joel."

"You did?"

Surprised by the early decision, I didn't know whether to feel relieved or wary.

"I hope you're not letting his connection with me influence you."

"Not in the least. He's certainly bright, highly motivated, very personable. After six month's training, I think he'll make a good man for the New York metropolitan area."

"You told him that?"

"Of course."

"And he went for it? He'll move?"

"Of course."

"That's a tough market. Those New Yorkers will haggle for a half cent. Are you sure he'll be okay?"

"The way I size him up, Joel, underneath he's a real sharpie. He can out-haggle 'em all, mark my words."

"Okay, you're the boss of sales. He's your choice."

So began a mentorship that I had never anticipated.

During the training period in which he served as an ordinary worker in the plant, then as a draftsman in the design department and finally handling phone sales in the front office, he was consistently interested, dedicated, and high-spirited, displaying a humorous side that delighted his co-workers. In each department he quickly became one of the crew and won their favor.

As I strode through the facility every morning, passing by his station, he would greet me with a smile.

"How's it going?" I would ask.

"Great," he'd say.

"I hear good reports," I'd say.

"I love it here," he'd reply.

Yes, the reports were glowing. He caught on fast to every assigned task. He was a natural. I began relaxing about having a relative aboard, feeling that he was an asset after all.

"He's smart, Joel, smarter than any of the others," Ken enthused.

From favorable comments such as these, and from my own observations, emerged my first glimmerings of his greater potential. Being in my late fifties, I wanted to ease off and enjoy the fruits of my success, but to do so necessitated finding someone to take my place, someone trained in my ways, familiar with my style of doing business. When nothing negative developed, I came to see Nathan as a possible successor—that is after a few years of careful grooming.

When his stint inside was completed, he was assigned to train under our other salesmen in nearby territories. To a man, they found him congenial, quick on the uptake, bound to be a "sure winner." Ken, impatient to send him to New York, cut short his sales training period.

"The kid's a natural, Joel. There's nothing more our men can teach him."

"I hope you're right," I said. "You're sending him into a lion's den, y'know."

After only a few months on his own, he racked up sales at an unprecedented rate. In the tough New York market where buyers are known to have no mercy, it was all the more remarkable. Just as he had captivated his co-workers during training, he now captivated the customers.

He had been staying in motels, returning to his home in Boston on weekends. He had agreed to relocate to the New York area within six months, but when the time came he hadn't yet moved, claiming that he and Cynthia could find nothing that pleased them. He asked for more time.

One Monday morning when he should have been in New York calling on the trade, he appeared in my office.

"I'm sorry to bother you, Joel," he said, "but I think it's time we had a heart-to-heart talk."

This was the sort of thing I dreaded. If Nathan had something to say, he should say it to Ken, not me. That's what I would have said if he weren't my wife's cousin's son. Instead I said, "Something troubling you?"

I motioned him to sit beside my desk.

"Actually, yes."

He paused, thinking how to begin. "I'm not earning enough, Joel. I need more money."

Our salesmen's earning arrangements had always been satisfactory to everyone; this was a surprise.

"You should ask your boss, Nathan, not me."

"I did."

"And?"

"He gave me the usual line—you know, I'm working under the same salary and commission as the other salesmen and he can't make an exception."

"Well, he's right; it would cause a problem. I'm sure you can see that."

"I understand. That's why I'm here."

"I don't get you."

"I'd hoped that you'd make an exception in my case. No one else has to know."

"I'd rather not do that," I said stiffly.

"I see."

"Look, Nathan. Under our compensation plan, when you sell more, you earn more. You've been at it only seven months. Give it a year, eighteen months, maybe two years and you'll be right up there. Just be a little patient. It'll come."

"The trouble is, I'm used to earning a hell of a lot more. I was making five times as much with my father."

"Not when we hired you, you weren't."

"Well, that's true."

"As I say, Nathan, be patient. It'll pay off in a bigger way than you realize. Anything worthwhile takes time."

"Actually, to tell the truth, it wasn't my idea to see you. Russell suggested it. He was shocked when he found out how little I was making."

That angered me. What right did Russell have poking his nose into his son's business, into my business?

"Let me ask you this, Nathan: Were you happy working for your father?"

"I hated it. I was bored. I had nothing to do—I just drew a weekly paycheck."

"Do you like what you're doing now?"

"I love it. Absolutely."

"In this job you can hold your head high. You're accomplishing something; you have a goal to work toward. Don't you agree?"

"Yes."

"Then what's money got to do with it? You're earning enough now to get by, right?"

"Well, we can't exactly afford to eat out every night."

"Who can when they're starting out? For the first three years I was in business, we ate only hamburg. Something's worthwhile only when you work for it. I think you found that out at your father's place."

His moon-shaped face broke into an easy smile. He seemed relieved.

"You're right, Joel. I really appreciate your taking the time..."

"Anytime, Nathan, anytime. Now you get out there and show those New Yorkers what real selling is."

I should have told Nathan that his father was the problem and not the job. I realized the father could also be my problem. How could I expect to win over the son's allegiance when the father was so powerful? Because of the father, Nathan's talents had been wasted until he joined us. Now I would see what Nathan was really made of.

IT'S ALL CHAOS

I said nothing to Ken about the episode, in case he'd resent Nathan's going over his head. A few weeks later Nathan asked that I meet him for lunch at his father's club.

"What's on your mind?" I asked. I wanted to beg off, but, after all, he was my wife's cousin's son.

"It's the same old problem."

"You mean—"

"They're pressuring me, Joel. They keep telling me I'm worth a lot more than you're paying me."

The club, an old oak-panelled mansion with a broad veranda running along its brick face, was strictly for men. The only women present were the waitresses. Russell had suggested I join and offered to sponsor me. "You should start rubbing elbows with these kind of men," he said. "Nothing important happens without them."

When I arrived, Nathan, in a dark blue suit, was waiting in the lobby, which was carpeted with an enormous Chinese rug. At the rear of the hall a broad oak staircase rose smack up the middle, then separated both right and left to the floor above. A brass chandelier, hanging all the way from the second floor, hovered above me.

I followed Nathan through a narrow doorway into a brilliant dining room that looked onto the veranda. The maitre d' greeted Nathan by name and led us to a small table covered with a white linen tablecloth. We took our seats before two settings of fancy china and dark blue napkins. Several members seated at the other tables said hello to Nathan. He was quite at home in his father's circle.

"Does Ken know you're not in New York?" I asked.

"Not yet. But I mean to tell him. Cynthia's pregnant, y'know," he said in a grave tone.

"I see. Congratulations."

"She wants me around. It's not going easily for her."

"You mean there are complications?"

"No, no, she's fine. She just needs my support."

"Of course."

"And after we have a child, there'll be additional expenses."

"Not while they're infants. Wait till they get to high school and go to college."

"Joel, I really need more income."

"It'll come. Don't worry. I told you before, our system guarantees it; the more you sell, the more you make. That's the way it operates and no one's ever complained."

Why doesn't he get the message? I wondered.

"But Dad says, even my mother..."

"Look, Nathan, what they think is their business. But all that matters is what you think. You knew about our compensation system when you were hired. You thought it was fair then. It's still fair."

His eyes shifted from mine to the tablecloth and back before he replied.

"Yes, it's fair."

"Then be your own man. Tell them how you run your life is your business. You'll feel much better about yourself working for what you earn. When you worked for your father you were paid well, but you hated it. Do you want another free ride?"

"Hell no, Joel. I'm not looking for favors."

"Good, because you won't get a handout from me. We're a team; everybody gets paid for what he contributes. No more, no less. That's the way it is. Take it or leave it."

I put aside, at least for a while, my mission to groom Nathan as my successor. But I took a fatherly interest in his development. Having been coddled by his parents all his life, he had never learned the value of accomplishing something on his own. Nathan had made Russell his model. No wonder he could never hold down a job: he expected to be paid for who he was and not for what he did.

He had to learn that self-sufficiency and reward for achievement generate self-respect. I believed I could, with patience, transform this intelligent, talented young man into a responsible person, for his sake as well as mine.

A few weeks later Nathan phoned from the road.

"Russell would like to meet with you and me—join him for dinner at the club."

"I'm not sure that would be a good idea," I said.

There was a pause.

"It's not about me," he said. "I took your advice and told him to stay out of my business."

"Atta boy, Nathan. I'm proud of you."

"So how about it?"

"What's on his mind?"

"Let him tell you, Joel—a proposition."

At the club you'd think Russell was some kind of emperor. The waitress hovered over him, keeping his glass filled with wine. A steady flow of fellow members came to our table to confer with him. All of them knew Nathan.

"Meet my cousin Joel," he said to each one. "Owns the biggest toy company in the East."

This falsehood embarrassed me.

After each person left our table, Russell explained who the man was: a judge, a senator, the president of our largest bank, a local newspaper columnist, and so on. Throughout, Russell was experiencing a high.

"That's what counts in this world, Joel—contacts." His eyes swept across the faces in the room. "Do you realize that this country is run by just a few hundred persons? They're the makers and the breakers; the rest don't matter. Know the important people and you can get anything done."

"What's on your mind, Russell?" I asked.

"Joel, I want an honest answer. Have you thought of retirement?"

"Retirement? Someday maybe. But not yet. I'm still going strong."

"How old are you? Fifty-seven, sixty? I don't mean retire now; I mean three years, maybe five years down the line."

"I suppose someday I'd like to take it easy."

"Right, but before you can retire you'll need someone to take your place, someone to run the show as competently as you do."

"That's right."

"Nathan would qualify, don't you think?"

"He could be a possibility," I said, glancing at Nathan who had been intently following his father's words.

"Here's another possibility. How would you like to cash in?"

"Cash in?"

"Yeah, sell the business. Become a free man, spend winters in Florida and summers up here at the lake."

"As I said, Russell, I'm not ready."

"Who's talking about retirement now? I'm suggesting that you sell the business with the stipulation that you'll stay on as CEO. Bring Nathan back into the office, teach him the ropes, and when you're ready to take it easy in a couple, three years, everything will be in place."

"And you're the buyer."

Russell grinned.

"Who else? I'd give you a good deal. You see, Joel, it's worth a lot to see my son's future secure. He tells me he likes the business and he likes you. With young blood at the helm and you and me guiding him, the business is bound to take off like never before. How about an after-dinner drink?"

"No, no thanks," I said, referring also in my mind to his proposal, which struck me as being as ridiculous as anything I could imagine. Although I knew someday I would ease off, and had considered Nathan as a candidate to take over, I figured that I would eventually sell the company, but to the employees.

"No need to give me an answer now. Think it over and get back to me. Okay?"

"Sure, Russell. I'll get back to you."

Weeks passed and I delayed, wishing that his proposal would go away. Moreover, I feared crossing him and causing a rift with my wife's family.

Nathan mentioned casually one day, "Russell's wondering when he might hear from you, Joel."

"How's your father doing these days?"

"Great. His company's board is meeting next week. He's slated to be chosen their next CEO. It's in the bag."

"Fantastic," I said. Maybe that would distract him from trying to negotiate a deal with me.

Russell phoned me at home the evening after the board meeting.

"Where've you been, Joel?" he demanded. "I expected to hear from you."

"Well—"

"It looks like I didn't make CEO."

"Gosh, I'm sorry, Russell."

"It's that goddamned widow."

"What widow?"

"My deceased partner's widow. She screwed me royally—claimed I cheated her when I acquired her husband's stock. She sued me and the corporation."

"That's awful."

"Oh, yeah, it's been tough. Because I was shrewd enough to find a willing buyer and negotiate a favorable deal for the stock, she brands me a crook."

"Well, she's got to prove it, doesn't she?"

"Not with the judge we got. He's an old friend of her husband's, so of course he decided in her favor."

"I suppose you can appeal."

"The corporation doesn't want any more litigation. They're going to pay her off. I've had enough. I turned in my resignation this morning."

Russell must have anticipated the possibility of an unfavorable verdict and the termination of his career at the corporation. Acquiring my company would not only help his son, but it would also provide him with a means to rechannel his own future.

"What are you going to do?" I asked, not that I gave a damn.

"Well, we'll do some business, you and me."

"I've been thinking it over, Russell. I'm not ready to sell."

"What?"

"I don't want..."

"You don't even know what I'm offering."

"Money isn't an issue. It's not what I want, that's all."

"I see. Well, if it's final..."

"It is."

He expended a breath of disgust.

"Which brings me to another matter: Why won't you do better for Nathan?"

"I don't think that's your concern."

"Hell it isn't. He's my son."

"But he's our employee. It's not our policy to deal with parents of our employees."

"You're a sonofabitch, Joel."

"Russell, I'm hanging up."

"You goddamned sonofabitch."

Click. He beat me to it.

A family rift was now in place. I wondered whether Nathan was finished too. I didn't have to wait long to find out. The very next morning Ken tossed a stack of phone bills on my desk.

"Take a look at these, Joel—Nathan's credit card calls for the past four months."

The bills listed scores of phone calls made from Nathan's home throughout the day. Other calls originated in cities far from his assigned territory. Most were made to Florida and Hawaii, some to England. None of them destinations where we did business.

"It must be a mistake," I said. "Did you check with the phone company?"

"I did. They're real."

"Why would he do this? I can't believe he was faking his itinerary," I said.

"You'd better believe it. Just compare the times and locations of the phone calls with what he wrote down in his daily sales call reports. They don't jibe. I phoned a few customers indicated on his reports. They haven't seen him in months. The bastard hasn't been working, Joel. I know it's touchy, he being your relative, but I want him out." I winced. "But damnit, he had so much promise. Everything about him seemed right. I never dreamed he was like this."

"I thought he had seen the light."

"What do you mean?"

"When you didn't give him more money, he came to me. I've been mentoring him — trying to teach him some values. I thought he understood. Look, Ken, I'll handle him."

"It's my responsibility, Joel. I hired him."

"No, the family will blame me no matter who does it. I'm responsible: I let you hire him."

When Nathan phoned in that day, I asked him, "Where are you?"

"New York," he said.

"Are you sure?" I questioned.

"What?"

"Never mind. I want you to drop everything. See me in the morning."

"Maybe you didn't hear me. I said I was in New York."

"I heard you. Did you hear me?"

"What's up, Joel?"

"We've got to talk."

"About what?"

"Look, Nathan, do as I ask. Be here."

"I'll be driving all night."

"I suppose so," I said icily.

At 11:30 the next morning he walked into my office.

"Good morning, Joel," he said. Taking a seat beside my desk, he noticed the monthly phone bills stacked on my blotter.

"It's a lousy morning," I said.

He laughed nervously. "Why do you say that?"

"When did you first become disenchanted, Nathan?" I said, meeting his eyes directly.

Without a second's hesitation, he replied, "A year ago maybe."

"That long ago? You mean you've been putting on an act all that time?"

"You don't know how to run a business, Joel. Russell could make something of this company. You know what's wrong with you? You're a small-time thinker."

"You may be right on all counts. But how I run this business is no business of yours, or Russell's."

"Sure it is. My future depends on it."

"Not for a long time. By your own admission, you haven't worked in our interest for a year. Apparently you never got my message. You could have been something with us. You've been leading me on. Well, now you're done."

"You can't fire me, Joel. I resign."

All this happened five years ago, but even now as I write about it I tremble with anger and sink into despondency. To believe in someone, to look out for their interest, and then to realize that it wasn't mutual—that in fact I was despised, is the ultimate betrayal.

What happened next that day with Nathan revealed the extent of my outrage.

He headed for the door.

"Just a minute. The car keys."

"How do I get home?"

"I'll have someone drive you."

"I need the car."

"The car's not yours. I want the keys."

He shook his head. I felt a surge of anger unlike any I had ever known. I struck his chest with my full fist, taking his breath away. I was terrified at what I had done.

"Now give me the goddamn keys."

"You're gonna have to deal with my lawyer for this."

"Give me the keys and get the hell out of here," I screamed.

He refused and ran into the outer office.

"If you take that car," I yelled after him, "I'll call the police and have you hauled in for theft."

He threw the keys on the receptionist's desk on his way out. I never saw Nathan again, nor his father, nor, for that matter, anyone else on that side of my wife's family.

The Liebestod

S. H. Bronstein pressed the intercom button on his desk. "Come into my office, Loretta."

For the past week he had rehearsed what he would say. Leaning forward in his executive chair, he rearranged his pens, his blotter, the stacks of reports, and the paperweights on his already meticulous desk.

Loretta appeared with pad and pencil in hand. In her mid-twenties, she was as fresh and attractive as a fashion model.

"Close the door," Bronstein ordered, glancing at her casually. He looked askance at her snug slacks which accentuated the curves of her firm buttocks. He observed the revealed outline of her breasts beneath her blouse.

"Certainly, Mr. Bronstein," she said, shutting the door behind her. She sat in an upholstered wing chair facing his desk.

The desk was an elegant piece of furniture, a Queen Anne mahogany table. During one of her rare visits to his office, Bronstein's wife had commented, "You could play ping-pong on it when you've got nothing else to do." "Don't bother me," Bronstein responded.

Loretta admired her boss's office. She liked that its traditional air contrasted with his business — manufacturing video games.

"I'm ready, Mr. Bronstein," she said, perched on the edge of the seat.

"You've been here, let's see — how long has it been, Loretta?"

"Just over a month."

"Well, I think it's about time to start calling me Sam."

She squirmed, casting her eyes toward the thick, beige carpet at her feet. The other girls in the office addressed the boss as Mr. Bronstein. Even the executives referred to him as SH.

"Do you find that difficult?" he asked.

"Yes, Mr. Bronstein," she replied.

"Am I really so frightening?" he continued.

"Well—," she laughed nervously, "yes— sometimes."

He frowned. "When you get to know me, you'll find there's nothing to be afraid of. I'm quite harmless. You've been listening to the others, haven't you?" She nodded. "Well, call me Mr. Bronstein in front of them. But when we're alone, it's Sam. Okay?" Loretta nodded again, with little conviction. "I'm really very pleased with your work, y'know. You're the best I ever had. Don't let it go to your head though."

Her eyes brightened. "Thank you Mr. Bron—, Sam."

He grinned. "Now that wasn't so painful, was it?"

She remained wary. He was given to violent outbursts. She had witnessed them.

"I'd like to get to know you better, on a professional level, of course," he said. He watched her face but her expression was inscrutable. "After all, we spend more time with each other than we do with anyone else."

The incoming call light on Bronstein's phone blinked. Loretta rose and headed for the door and her office.

"Take it here," he ordered. She picked up the instrument.

"Consolidated Games," she announced. After listening briefly she covered the mouthpiece with her hand. "It's for me."

"That's okay. Go ahead. I'll keep busy." Taking some documents from a pile, Bronstein pretended to be involved.

"Well, I can't talk now," Loretta said to the caller. "I'm sorry. I can't help it. I'll see you tonight. Not now—please—we'll talk about it later." She raised her eyes to the ceiling. "Yes, I'll be there around six." Agitated, she hung up.

She calmed herself while Bronstein loosened his tie. "Sit down and take it easy," he said, motioning her back to the chair. "What you need is a drink."

She stared into space. He snapped his fingers.

"Hey, snap out of it. Are you okay?"

"I'm fine, thank you."

"It's none of my business, but as your employer I'm concerned. Who was that?"

"That was my husband."

"Your husband? But I thought you were unmarried. Your application said . . ."

"I mean my former husband — really my husband who will soon be my former husband. Or whatever," she laughed.

"Now that's better. I take it you're getting a divorce."

"Yes, I've filed. We're separated."

"I see. Separations, divorces, that sort of thing — they can be very painful."

"Are you . . ."

"No, no," he chuckled, "but I broke up with a business partner once and they say that's like a divorce."

Her voice quavered. "It's hard getting used to."

"I can imagine." He paused. "How long did you say it's been?"

"What? Oh, we've been married two years."

"No, I mean how long have you been separated?"

"Not very long," she said wearily, lapsing into silence.

Rising from his chair, he suggested, "Let's have that drink now."

"I suppose I still love him but . . ." Her voice trailed off.

"It must hurt," said Bronstein.

"But his abuse was just too much." Her eyes welled with tears, which she dabbed with a small lace handkerchief retrieved from her sleeve.

"Life is very hard," he said. He resisted the impulse to embrace her and gently stroke her hair. "But you'll have no trouble finding someone else, a beautiful girl like you."

She smiled at him through tears.

"If there's any way I can help."

"I know you mean well, but I can handle this myself."

"Of course, of course."

How different he seemed now from the hard-hitting man she was used to. Salt and pepper hair flowed along the sides of his head. His face, though creased with signs of late middle age, had character. Tiny crows-feet flared back to his sideburns. But his eyes looked tired. He'd be an interesting portrait subject, she thought. Having dabbled in acrylic, she had a painter's eye. During lunch hour she would often forgo eating just to browse through the art museum nearby.

He walked across the room to a large hutch. Opening its cabinet door, he asked, "Is there anyone else? I mean are you seeing . . ."

"I'm not ready, really. I'm still quite mixed up."

"I understand."

Her eye caught a print on the wall to the right of his desk. It was a reproduction of Degas' *Prima Ballerina*.

"I've had it with men, for a while anyway."

He poured wine from a decanter into two stem glasses. "This will make you feel better."

Loretta looked at her watch.

"It's not 5 o'clock yet," he said smiling. "The boss won't mind if you take a little wine." He handed her a full glass, then he sat on the edge of his desk, one leg dangling. "But you've tried."

"I'm sorry. Tried?"

"You've tried others. You've gone out with some of the men in this office."

She flushed. "Well, they asked me out. I thought it would help, but it only made things worse."

He lifted his glass and held it high. "To the right man," he toasted.

The telephone light blinked again. Placing her glass on the edge of the desk, she picked up the receiver.

"Consolidated Games. Yes, Mr. Parker, he's here. I'll see if he's free."

Bronstein signaled that he would take the call. He snatched the receiver from her hand.

"Bronstein," he said gruffly. "Now you listen to me, Parker. Either you get that production line going, or I'll get a new manager. Do you read me?" He slammed down the receiver in its cradle, muttering, "Goddamn ninny."

Ignoring Loretta, he stared out the window at the orange sun sinking in the murk between two skyscrapers. Dusk had the color of a dirty shroud. Observing Loretta's reflection in the window, he turned. "I'm sorry," he said, "sometimes you gotta be rough." Lifting his glass, he swigged down the wine. "Now where were we?"

Loretta wondered what his personal life was like. There were no family pictures in his office. He wore no wedding ring. Besides the Degas, a replica of Chagall's *The Violinist* hung on one wall and Manet's *The Fifer* on another. How could he be so coarse and an art lover at the same time?

"What were we talking about?" he asked.

"It's getting rather late," she said.

"Say, I just had a thought. How would you like—now, you don't have to if you don't want to—how would you like to join me for dinner tonight?"

"Oh, I'm sorry, Mr. Bron—I mean Sam—, but I couldn't tonight. You know—my husband."

"Oh, yes. I forgot. Some other time then."

"I'm really not ready. It will take me awhile."

"Of course, of course. I do understand."

"Thank you. I appreciate your thoughtfulness."

"But you've gone out with other men."

"Yes, once or twice."

"So what's wrong with me?" he demanded.

"Oh, it's not you. Believe me, it's not you." She cast about for words. "May I ask a personal question?"

He smiled. "Of course."

"Did you select the prints for this office, or—"

He broke into a laugh. "I sure did."

"Really, they're quite beautiful."

"And did you notice? They have something in common."

She studied each one closely. "Music?" she said.

"Right. Music. How about some more wine?" He refilled her half-empty glass. "Do you like music?"

"Oh, yes."

"Then you shall have some." He rushed across the office to a stereo cabinet. She glanced at her watch.

"Isn't it terrific that we both love music?" he said, handing her an album. "Do you know this one?"

She shook her head. "No, I'm afraid—"

"You don't? I'm surprised."

"Well, it's not my sort of music really. I—I, do you know the Beatles?"

"Who?"

"Bruce Springsteen?"

"I've heard of him."

"Tina Turner?"

"No."

"Dire Straits?"

He inserted the disc into the player. "Listen to this," he said. "Listen to real music." The early strains of Wagner's *Liebestod* flooded the room.

She glanced at her watch again. It was time to leave. Were she late she knew her husband might accuse her of trysting with some imagined paramour and strike her.

Swept up in the music, Bronstein glided to her chair. He reached for her hands, pulled her up, and clasped her to him. The music gathered momentum. His mouth suddenly met hers in a devouring kiss. He cupped his hands on her buttocks. She struggled to wrench his hands away. The music reached a crescendo. She tore herself from him, whimpering, "No, no, please, no." The music died. The hum of the amplifier filled the room. The phone on his desk blinked. She picked it up but was unable to speak.

He took it. "Yes? Okay, I'm late tonight. So what? I have some problems. Of course, everything's all right. I'll be awhile yet. Look, go ahead and eat alone. I'll grab a bite out before I get home. No, don't wait for me. I don't know when I'll be done here. For Chrissakes, you heard me."

The Liebestod

Loretta headed for the door. "Good night, Mr. Bronstein," she said.

He covered the phone with his hand. "Wait a minute, please, wait." He lifted his hand from the instrument. "It's nothing. Nothing's wrong. I'll be home when I get there." He hung up.

"I'm late already," she said. "I have to meet my husband."

"I'm afraid my emotions got the better of me," he said.

"He'll be terribly angry," she murmured, opening the door.

"So let him," he shouted. "You're getting a divorce. What do you care? Tell him to screw himself."

She paused and turned. Bronstein was right. She suddenly realized she did hold some cards after all.

"Why don't you like me?" Bronstein pursued, taking advantage of her hesitation.

"It isn't that I don't like you."

"Then what?" he asked plaintively. "Am I too old?"

She shook her head. "It's not that. It's just—I mean—aren't you a married man?"

"Is that all?" he said. "Please sit down. I'd like to explain something." She remained by the door; he sat on the edge of his desk. "I have my business, my passion, and my family. And I keep them separate. Understand? One has nothing to do with the other. Am I a married man? That's a meaningless question."

"I don't think it's a good idea to get involved with a married man, Mr. Bron—Sam."

"I'd be good to you," he said. "We'd have wonderful times."

"I—I'm sorry, Mr. Bronstein. I really need my own space. I'm tired of being treated like a toy. I want someone who'll respect me. Do you know what I mean?"

"You don't get it, Loretta. There are no strings attached. I'd treat you like a queen. You could have anything you wanted—a car, a fur coat, an apartment. You'd have the best."

"Thank you, but I can't. I'm sorry, Mr. Bronstein."

"For Chrissake, call me Sam."

"Please excuse me. I'm terribly late," she said, moving toward the door.

"We can't go on this way, y'know Loretta," he warned. She felt her heart quicken. "Don't come back, unless . . ." His voice faded as he watched her eyes fill with tears. "So, you see it's your decision. I couldn't bear having you here every day without . . ."

She fled through his office door and the main office into the corridor, forgetting her coat. She stepped into the elevator and sobbed while it dropped to the lobby. Rushing into the city street, she flung up her arms and embraced the air. At last, space, space, and freedom.

Bronstein realized he had given Loretta no way out. It was a mistake. He turned on the stereo and played the *Liebestod* again. The smooth, sweeping tones of the violins made him melancholy.

After replenishing his wine glass, he leaned forward in his desk chair and thought of how worthless his power was. He was too old to be attractive to a young woman. Burying his head in his arms he wept. How hard it was, this lesson in mortality. The *Liebestod* reached a climax, then died. The office was still.

Through the dark window he watched the lights of the skyscrapers go out at random. He reached for the phone.

"Parker? This is Bronstein. How's it going? You say you're back in production? You're a good man, Parker, a good man. I knew you'd straighten things out. We'll talk again tomorrow."

Ah, the business. At least he had that. That needed him. He went to the stereo and turned on the *Liebestod* for the third time.

The Accident

As Dave Bentley was talking to his wife on the phone that evening, the operator cut in. "There's an emergency call for Mr. Bentley," she said. "Would you please hang up?"

"Who is it, operator?" Bentley asked.

"The police, sir. Would you please hang up?"

"Right away, operator, right away," Bentley said nervously. "I'll call you back as soon as I know what this is all about," he said to his wife.

"I'll be waiting by the phone. I'm frightened, Dave."

"Don't jump to conclusions," Bentley said and hung up.

He knew they were thinking the same thought; the call would concern their son, Arthur. Call it intuition. Dave refused to speculate on specifics. Only a half hour earlier he and Arthur had met and dined together at a Chinese restaurant in town. What could have happened, what terrible thing could have happened in so short a time? When they parted, Arthur, who lived in his own apartment and had a job—he was postponing his sophomore year at college—said that he was going for a bike ride before dusk.

As soon as Dave had arrived home after dining with Arthur, he called his wife, who was summering at their house by the shore. He told her how well Arthur looked and, much to his satisfaction, how well they got along at dinner, especially since this time he avoided bringing up Arthur's pot smoking. Then the emergency call interrupted the conversation with his wife.

The phone rang as soon as he put down the receiver.

"Mr. Bentley."

"Yes." Dave's heartbeat began to quicken.

"This is the police. I must tell you your son has been in an accident."

"Is he—how badly is he hurt?"

"He's alive, that's all I can say, Mr. Bentley."

Alive! What does that mean? Is he barely alive, bordering on death, breathing, unconscious? Or is he just hurt?

"Alive? You mean . . ."

"I'm calling you from the station. The report came in. That's all I know about his condition, Mr. Bentley."

"What happened?"

"Sir, you'll find him in emergency at City Hospital."

"Please, what happened?"

"He was on his bike and was hit by a car."

Dave hung onto the receiver in silence trying to sort his feelings, but all he could summon was a strange numbness. The message seemed unreal, a distorted dream.

"Go right to emergency, Mr. Bentley. They're expecting you."

The phone clicked and the dial tone sounded. He placed the receiver in its cradle, then picked it up and dialed his wife.

"Arthur's been hurt."

There was a gasp at the other end. "Oh my God."

"He's at City Hospital. But it may be nothing, or something very minor." He dared not worry her with the portentous message as it was given to him. "I don't have the facts."

"Where is he?"

"I just told you—City Hospital. I'm going there right now and I'll call you as soon as I know how he is."

"Should I come home? I'd better come home."

"No." Bentley said firmly. "Wait until you hear from me. It may be nothing. So don't worry, okay? It may be nothing."

"Call me as soon as you know."

"Yes, I'll call as soon as I know. I'm going to hang up, okay?"

"Okay."

As he drove across the city to the hospital, he felt remote from the world. The streets, the traffic lights, the other cars rushing by him, all seemed unreal. He knew only the severe pounding of his heart, his terrible fear that Arthur may be maimed or close to death. Strangely he felt that somehow he was responsible; suddenly he regretted that he hadn't given his son enough of himself and that now it might be too late. These feelings were new to him, odd and terrifying.

"I'm Dave Bentley," he announced to the nurse at the emergency desk.

"Yes, sir, follow me," she said instantly as she led him to a room nearby. Afraid of what he would find, he walked like an automaton, falling back, then running to keep up with her. He entered a white room. Lying on an operating table he saw his son, naked to his bloody underwear, a doctor and a nurse bending over him suturing a wound on his forehead.

"No broken bones, Mr. Bentley," the doctor said while tying a stitch. "This is a mighty tough lad you've got here. Are you up to watching, Mr. Bentley? You don't have to stay while I'm doing this, but you're welcome."

"I'll stay," Bentley said, though he had no stomach for it.

The doctor motioned him to the table. Dave stood beside his prone son and gazed into his face, which was bruised and swollen beyond recognition. Glancing quickly at the rest of him, he noticed that Arthur's thigh was raw and his left shoulder was caked with blood.

Arthur spoke, barely moving his lips. "You're not mad at me, are you, Dad?"

"Mad at you?" Bentley replied. "How can I be mad at you? I thank God you're alive." Arthur forced a satisfied smile, but smiling hurt him and Bentley saw that it hurt. "How are you, son?"

"Great, just great, Dad. Never felt better," Arthur said through the pain. His voice was joyous.

He's happy to be alive, Dave thought. He's discovered his mortality—and so young. After telling Arthur that he was going to call his mother to stop her from worrying, he went to the lobby and dialed from the public phone.

"He's banged up, but nothing appears broken," he told her.

"Are you sure? Have they checked him over thoroughly?"

"Of course they have. The doctor seems competent. But I'll make sure they do anyway."

"Good. I think I'll come home."

"There's no need. I can take care of him."

"You? You wouldn't know how."

"What's there to know? I can cook for him, wash him."

"But you have to go to work."

"I own the company. Remember? No one's forcing me to go to work."

"Then bring him here. It's cooler by the ocean. He'll recuperate faster here."

"Let's find out what HE wants, for God's sake," Dave said. "Listen, I've got to get back to him. I'll call you later—from home."

"We've X-rayed him and he's okay on that score," said the doctor after the stitching was completed and the surface wounds were bandaged. "But he's had a concussion. Now, he can stay here the night and we'll watch him, or you can take him home. Only it's important that you wake him every hour, very important, due to the concussion. Understand?"

"What do you want to do, Arthur?" Dave asked.

"It's up to you, Dad. I know how you like to get your sleep."

"I'll take him home," Dave said. Arthur reached for his hand and held it. It struck Dave how rarely he had touched his son. Their joining hands was a new sensation.

Arthur got down from the table very gingerly. As he placed his weight on his feet he immediately began to wobble and he fell into Dave's supporting arms.

"Are you sure you can walk?" Dave asked.

"I can walk, Dad. I know I can. Don't help me."

"Sure, sure," Dave said skeptically.

Regaining his balance, Arthur shook the doctor's hand. "You're a first-class stitcheroo, Doc." Then he limped painfully alongside his father through the lobby and into the car. Suddenly his son was like an old man, thought Dave, old physically and humbled.

The Accident

"What happened, Arthur?" Dave asked as they drove across the city which now seemed real enough.

"This car made a left turn right in front of me. I couldn't stop the bike in time so I tried to veer away, but it was too late. I hit the car on its side near the rear and went flying over it and landed thirty feet away across the street. The gash on my head happened when I fell on the curb. The ambulance guys said I was lucky my neck wasn't broken. I could have died."

"No helmet?"

"I left it at the apartment."

"At the apartment," Dave said, slamming the steering wheel with the palm of his hand.

"That's right."

"You must have been going pretty fast."

"Well, maybe I was. I was going downhill and in a hurry to get home because it was getting dark. But I had a clear road ahead of me when I started down the hill."

"Don't you have lights or reflectors on your bike?"

"I don't usually bike at night, Dad."

"In other words you don't have a light or reflectors."

"That's right."

"Then it's possible the driver of the car couldn't see you." Arthur didn't reply. "Isn't that so?"

"I s'pose so."

"What were you doing riding your bike after dark anyway? Don't you think that's foolish?"

"I was visiting a friend and didn't realize how late . . ."

"I think it was very foolish. You ought to know better."

"Yeah, I ought to know better. I'm sorry if I've hurt you, Dad."

"Hurt me? You've hurt yourself."

"Now I'll know better."

"What a way to find out. But at least you're alive and whole and I thank God."

"So do I."

"I won't ask you whether there was any pot."

"I swear, Dad, nothing."

"Okay, okay. What about the person who was driving the car?"

"He was an old man, by himself."

"Pretty shook up, I gather."

"The neighborhood people who covered me with a blanket said he was crying."

"The poor guy."

"He was coming back from the hospital where his wife is dying of cancer."

"Oh, the poor guy. He didn't need this, did he?"

"I'm sorry, Dad, I'm sorry."

"Well, you didn't know, Arthur."

"I knew, I knew, I knew everything," Arthur moaned, cupping his hands to his eyes.

Dave reached his right arm across Arthur's shoulder and pulled him to him. "No, you didn't, son. You didn't know. Don't blame yourself."

When they got home Arthur called his mother.

"I want you to come here, recuperate at the shore for the next two weeks, Arthur," she said. "You need the care only a mother can give."

"Okay, Ma," said Arthur without hesitation.

Dave sat up through the night to make certain that he didn't fail to wake Arthur every hour. Each time he shook him to verify his consciousness, then let him fall back to sleep. But by early morning it was Arthur who shook his father awake. Dave had fallen asleep despite his intention.

"Time to go to work, Dad."

"Oh, I fell asleep. Are you okay? Are you really okay?" Dave responded, staring shocked at Arthur's unrecognizable face.

"Sure, Dad, terrific."

"No work today," Dave said. "I'm staying here with you."

"Dad, I'm fine. I'd rather be by myself. I can get around." With some irritation he added, "Let me do what I want."

Dave shrugged. "Well, I'll call you through the day. If you don't answer, I'm coming home."

"I'll answer. Don't worry."

Dave shaved and showered and went to work. That evening when he returned home, Arthur had dinner ready for him.

"My gosh," Dave said, "you shouldn't have done all this. You should have rested."

"I wanted to do it, Dad."

After dinner Dave read the *Wall Street Journal* and they watched TV together.

The next morning, a Saturday, they took off in Dave's Mercedes to join Arthur's mother at their seaside cottage.

Arthur gradually improved over the next three weeks by sleeping late into the morning, relaxing through the day reading or watching TV, eating his mother's hot meals and simply submitting to her fussy nurturing. Only a limp remained, due to a badly weakened thigh muscle that had been reduced to a fraction of its original size by the impact of the collision.

Arthur's mother literally dedicated every waking moment attending to her son. Dave took long weekends at the cottage to spend more time with Arthur who he noticed had visibly changed since the accident. Arthur's old daredevil confidence was measurably muted. He now acknowledged that he had limitations. He now seemed to understand that death need not be distant despite youth and good health.

Still, there was something about the accident that continued to haunt Dave. He could never dismiss the idea that had crossed his mind while driving to the hospital—that somehow he had contributed to the cause. Arthur's repeated words, "I knew, I knew," burned in his mind. Furthermore, Arthur was a disciplined person, not on drugs at the time, and certainly not prone to accidents.

"I can't help wondering about the accident," Dave confided to his wife.

"What do you mean?"

"I mean why did it happen?"

"An accident is an accident."

"He was riding his bike without a helmet on, too fast and at dusk. He knows better."

"What are you saying?"

"I mean have I—have we—failed him somehow?"

"You're being ridiculous, Dave. I know our son's happy."

"Then why does he need pot and who knows what else?"

"He picked that up at school from the others. Arthur's well adjusted. Why, he's nothing like you. Haven't you noticed he never gets angry?"

"C'mon the boy's overcontrolled," Dave said with insistence. "He takes after you. Nobody can get into him, even near him."

"You're the one you can't get near," she countered. "Arthur is a typical contented American boy. Why do you insist on always putting him down? He needs you, Dave. He needs your support, not your accusations. Give him a break."

During Arthur's three weeks of recuperation, he formulated a plan to tour Europe alone with the money he would receive from the accident claim. This struck Dave as odd, because his son seemed to bask in all the attention he was getting at home. Why was he suddenly taking steps to go as far away and be as unreachable as possible?

One peaceful evening the three of them went for a walk on the beach and talked.

"I don't understand what you're trying to do," Dave said to Arthur. "You seem to have no goal. All you want is to drift. Why Europe?"

"I have to go away, Dad. I don't know why, but I have to leave."

"But so far away," his mother said.

"The farther away, the better. That's how I feel."

"What have we done, Arthur?" she pleaded.

"Nothing. Absolutely nothing."

"I know your mother fusses over you," Dave said. "She'd like nothing better than to keep taking care of you."

"It's from the heart," Arthur's mother put in. "And I don't fuss over him."

"Yeah," Arthur said. "It's safe and comfortable here. The truth is I'm scared about leaving, real scared."

"I remember the first time I left home for good," Dave said. "Took off for a strange place—Chicago—on my own. I was scared too. It was a long way away—before plane travel was affordable."

"Then you know what I mean," Arthur said.

Arthur picked up some pebbles from the beach and flung them into the waves. Dave watched as they bounced once or twice before sinking. He recalled that when his son was only thigh high he had taught him how to bounce stones off the water.

"For my sake, Arthur, don't leave us. I mean, go back to school and lead a responsible, decent life," his mother said.

"No, Arthur, you should leave," exclaimed Dave. "You do what you have to do."

"Why don't you back me?" his mother demanded. "Why are you contradicting me? He's my son, too. He should go back to college and graduate and get a job and get married and have children like a normal young man. Instead you encourage him to be a bum."

"For God's sake, let him grow up," Dave said stridently. "Let him be a man."

"Be a man? He is a man. He should be like other men and do what they do."

"Don't," Arthur shouted. "Stop it. Let me alone."

"That's right. Leave him alone," Dave said.

"Damnit, you too, Dad. I'm not asking for your opinion."

After a few moments of silence, Dave said, "I want you to do what you want to do, that's all."

"Do you really care what I do?" Arthur asked bitterly.

"Of course, I do. How can you possibly doubt . . ."

"Sometimes, Dad, I think I'm a cipher to you. You don't really care about me. All you care about is your business."

"That's not true. I—I love you," Dave said.

"We both do," Arthur's mother added.

"I'm never sure. I had to find out. Do you know how I found out?"

"Found out what?" Dave asked.

"Whether you cared about me. I found out in the accident."

"In the accident?" both parents blurted in unison.

"I deliberately ran into that car. Do you understand?"

"You deliberately . . ." Dave shouted.

"Oh, my God," his mother exclaimed.

"Yes, I had to find out, and for a few seconds I didn't care whether I died or not. For a few seconds I felt free, hurtling down the hill and into the car, flying through the air across the street, caring about nothing. I was willing to risk death to find out whether you loved me. And I knew whatever happened to me would hurt you both."

"Hurt me? Hurt your mother who fed you at her breast? Who loves you more than her own life. Arthur, I don't understand."

"Don't love me so much, Ma."

"A mother can't just stop loving."

"I wanted you to take care of me. I deliberately crashed so you'd be there. But I feel ashamed of myself when I let you. I—I sort of lose my self-respect."

They turned and retraced their steps in the sand and walked in awkward silence back to the house.

After seeing Arthur off at the international air terminal, Dave and his wife drove back to the beach house. "This is a courageous thing Arthur is doing, y'know," Dave said.

"I simply don't understand him," she said.

"He's finding it hard to break away from us."

"How can you say that? I've always taught him independence."

"So that's why he deliberately smashed himself into the side of a car?" Dave said sarcastically.

The Accident

"I've been a dedicated, loving mother. He comes even before myself. I want nothing more than to see him happy. And he was happy these past few weeks. He was singing."

"Oh, sure, he was your baby again while you waited on him hand and foot."

"But that's what he needed."

"Y'know what he said when I walked into the operating room and asked him how he was doing? He smiled through his bruised and swollen face—it was painful for him—and the first thing he said was, was I mad at him. And when I said no, he said he felt great, never better."

"What can we do, Dave?"

"Nothing. Just let him be, pray and hope he finds himself."

"I hope he calls after he lands so we'll know he's safe," she sighed.

"I hope he doesn't. Then I know he'll be okay."

A Paradise Lost
or
The Great Catboat Murder
of Halcyon Bay

The first call came in at the station late Sunday afternoon, August 20. The day was cool and clear with a mild breeze, perfect for a leisurely sail.

"I saw it with my own eyes," the woman said. "He just tossed her overboard from his boat in the middle of the bay and let her drown."

"Hold on, ma'am," I said. "Go over that again."

I couldn't believe my ears. I figured she must be wacky or something.

"I was watching them through my binoculars from the front porch," she went on. "It was the same blonde woman he's taken out with him before."

"Who was the man, ma'am?"

"She was seated in the cockpit, her hair flying in the breeze, happy as you please and I watched him serve her a drink. Then he sat down beside her. She must have been only half his age. Imagine."

"The man, ma'am. Do you know who the man was?"

"Well, I saw it with my own eyes."

"Yes, ma'am." She was trying my patience. Why do some folks have to drag things out?

"All of a sudden he struck her on the face, then he picked her up and just threw her into the bay. Can you imagine? Threw her as if she were some worthless thing. Well, I was aghast. I couldn't believe what I was seeing. Then he raised the sail and took off down the bay, leaving her to drown."

"Who was the man, please, ma'am?"

"It was Mr. Hixon."

"That's hard to believe. Are you sure?"

"I don't see very good, Chief, but when I look through my binoculars I've got perfect vision. That's exactly who it was."

After that call there were others, all saying more or less the same thing. My common sense rebelled at the story I was hearing. I just couldn't accept the idea that my good friend Doug Hixon, whom I had known all these years, was capable of doing such a deed. Why, Doug was one of the easiest going, gentlest guys a person could ever know. He was the kind of guy who made you feel good when you talked to him.

Yes, siree, when you've been chief in a town for forty years, you see a lot of cases come and go. But I s'pose this is one I'll never forget. I remember clear as the water in our bay when Doug first came out here with his young wife, Ellen, maybe thirty-five years ago, on their honeymoon. They rented a place for the next half dozen summers or so, then they bought a super spot right there on the shore of Halcyon Bay when land was one hundred dollars an acre. They had a small cottage built smack on the sandy beach where you could look across the water to the barrier spit and hear the faint rumbling of the ocean combers.

Ellen and their three kids—good kids they were—would spend the summer there while Doug commuted weekends from New York City, where by the time he was forty he was some kind of important honcho with a big stock brokerage house.

He used to say, "Chief, one of these days I'm going to come here for good. This is my paradise."

I never really understood his saying that then, he being so young and successful—right there in the swim of things. He had everything going for him. I think he had some romantic notion of living a simple life. 'Course, life's never simple no matter how simple it is.

A lot of people who summer out here feel the way he did, but it takes a long time for most to pull up stakes and come here for good. If and when the time comes, they're generally so old, they get in only a few years of living in paradise before they die. Yup, it's true we've got the highest death rate in the state—mostly natural deaths or accidental. We don't have murders. Must be all of fifty years since the last one—long before I was chief.

So I wasn't inclined to rush to conclusions about Doug. Eyewitnesses were one thing; I needed surefire proof, like a body. Lickety-split I drove over to Doug's house looking for him. I found the place wide open, but no Doug. It was as if he just went away for an afternoon sail and he'd be back.

Doug was an expert sailor. He had begun with a small day sailer and worked his way up to a forty-four footer, which he kept in the town harbor because its draft was too much for the shallow bay. He and Ellen and the kids went to Bermuda in her a couple of times; then he sold her, as if all he wanted was to prove he could do it.

After their last kid grew up, Doug chucked it all, although he was only in his late forties.

"Mighty young to be throwing in the towel," I said to him, kidding.

"I've won a few bouts, Chief. No need to be champ," he responded.

He and Ellen moved from the city for good, "away from the wars," as he put it, to their place here on the bay.

It was then he began building his catboat. Took him four years to finish it—the most rewarding years of his life, he said. And I could tell. Working on the catboat gave him a great sense of accomplishment. Besides, he led a warm family life. Ellen was always a peach. She and Doug had a fine love going between them and terrific mutual respect. He was lean looking and quiet. She was small and lively. The kids were something to be proud of—hardworking in the summer at local jobs, serious students and mighty respectful of adults, which you don't see much of these days.

I'd visit him at least once a week to watch his progress on the boat. He'd show me the plans and explain what he was doing every step of the way. No man was ever more dedicated to a project. He built a temporary shelter of polyethylene around the job so he could work in all weather, even in winter.

"It's what I've wanted to do ever since I was a kid," he said.

I was there with all the neighbors that momentous June day when the riggers winched the catboat into the bay. Ellen smashed a bottle of champagne against her prow and christened her *Second Love.* Ellen, of course, was Doug's first love. There was a big party; it was a gala celebration.

Those were the days when everybody knew everybody else and nobody locked their doors. When I think back, I'm struck by how much things have changed. Who could have imagined that Doug, once a veritable paragon in our town—yup, in our society—would turn out to be regarded the way he was right after the incident. They called him a murderer. Hardly a witness I talked to had any doubt that he threw a woman overboard and let her drown even though they knew that such an act was out of character. That's how much we've become strangers to each other. From long experience, I knew what a man does has to be consistent with the kind of man he is. My mind was open until I had solid evidence.

Doug moored "The Love," as everyone soon called her, right in front of their place, 'bout a hundred yards offshore in ten feet of water at low tide on a tremendous white rocket-shaped buoy that was more fit for a battleship. Doug's boat, fashioned after the sturdy fishing vessels of olden days, was broad beamed and had a roomy cabin that slept two and a small galley. To anyone who asked about a head, Doug would laugh and point to the lee rail.

But soon he stopped laughing about anything. Ellen became gravely ill with a brain tumor. She only had a chance to go for a sail in "The Love" once or twice, and in less than three months Doug was alone.

At the funeral he said to me, "Everything was going along so perfect, Chief, just as we planned. I don't understand."

Now, I'm not much of a philosopher, but in my position I see enough happen to give any man pause for thinking. So I said, "Doug, justice is man-made and we matter only to each other. Nothing else in the whole universe gives a damn."

He heard me but I can't be sure whether it helped him any.

Anyway, after that, he just withdrew from the world. Letting his beard grow, which turned out to be almost white, and his hair too—salt and pepper it was, thick and long—he looked old all of a sudden. Still, for a man in his early fifties, he kept himself slim and pretty fit. His eyes gave him away. Sad they were, but alert.

He took to raising his own vegetables and catching fish in the bay and stocking up on canned goods, so he hardly ever had to come into town except to visit the post office once a week.

Oh, he was never unpleasant or anything like that. "How do," he'd say. "It is a fine day, isn't it?"

That's all he'd say and hop into his Jeep to avoid being drawn into more conversation. Antisocial, I s'pose you'd call him.

"Y'ought to mingle more," I'd suggest, "rejoin society, get your mind off the past."

"Thanks for your concern, Chief. I'm doing okay," he'd say, and that's all.

Well, the world wouldn't ignore him as much as he wished. In the next two years houses began to sprout here and there around the bay shore like—well, it seemed to him like Miami Beach. On weekends that pearly blue stretch of clean ocean—it wasn't called Halcyon Bay for nothing—was crisscrossed every which way with the wakes of crazy, roaring powerboats. You could hardly hear the surf moaning off the barrier spit anymore. And the fumes of diesel exhaust fouled the fresh salty smell in the air.

Doug's house was broken into, and all his and Ellen's wedding silverware was stolen. I'm sorry to say it was never recovered. I suspected who did it but had no proof. Ornery kids, twenty, twenty-five-year-old adult kids. Know what I mean? Lived right nearby, always drinking too much, shooting drugs, having wild parties. Why, Doug even had an outboard taken right off "The Love" in broad daylight while she was sitting there in front of his house.

You could see his paradise collapsing right before his eyes. He didn't say much, but I could see he was holding back his anger. It was sad, sad.

Sailing the catboat became the center of Doug's life. It was a way of not only getting away from the past, but also from the encroaching city people who were making the place more and more like a suburb. Regardless of the weather, he went out in her mostly every day—always alone. Having only one sail to be tended to, catboats are easy to singlehand. Doug and the boat would often disappear for a week, maybe two. Someone might spot "The Love" north near Monhegan, and once a fisherman saw her up near Nova Scotia.

When the gale struck in '78, Doug was out there in its clutches. Everyone figured he went down in the storm, but after a couple of weeks he came sailin' up to his mooring as if he'd just taken off for the afternoon.

"Where in hell you been?" I had asked him.

"Wherever the wind took me," he'd said, grinning and with a fresh sparkle in his eye.

Whatever had happened out there, I could see it had caused him to come out of himself. About time, I thought.

Well now, wasn't it likely he was off on another voyage after doing in the blonde, and he'd be back in a few weeks just like before? Sure enough, after I gave the word to apprehend "The Love," the Coast Guard reported having seen a catboat under sail heading east some hours earlier. Of course, it may not have been Doug, except that sailors in boats his size usually hug the shore; they don't head boldly into the open Atlantic. The CG continued their search in earnest, and I issued an order to drag the bay for the "body" although I didn't believe we'd come up with anything. I had to do something to satisfy everybody in town who had already tried Doug in their minds and found him guilty.

What bothered me most was lack of motive. Sure Doug was angry about the cards that life was dealing him. He resented what was happening on the bay and he never got over the emptiness after Ellen's passing. But he had no cause for violence. I knew him well enough after a time to also know his head was screwed on right. His old self had returned part of the way; of course, he never warmed up to be the man I used to know. They say when you lose a limb, it often feels as though it's still there, but you know it isn't. That's how it was with Doug about Ellen and the past.

After his long voyage he began keeping company with women, another good sign. Nothing in the way of a permanent connection developed, although one of our single ladies, of which we have a surplus in all ages, sizes, and dispositions these days, took a real shine to him. Being alone and with her own kids grown up, she kept him warm at night and his place clean, and watched over it whenever he went away on a sea trip. I guess he didn't know how to tell her he wasn't really interested. Well, she got the message when she learned there was another woman. Not exactly another woman, but one of sorts. The one he "drowned."

It didn't take long for the word to spread. You've got to understand Halcyon Bay is probably the least private spot on the coast. All kinds of nosey people watch from the shore with binoculars and spyglasses, keeping an eye on what's going on out there. For some it's an everyday occupation, with only a break for meals. Not that watching is such a bad idea from the point of view of safety. But I can tell you nobody gets away with hanky-panky out on that bay—from drug runners to someone stealing a lobster trap to couples making love on some boat deck.

When Doug went out the first time with a blonde in a bikini sitting in the cockpit, every house on the bay knew as fast as if it were announced over the radio. He repeated this routine for a few weeks, and each time the blonde woman was dressed in a different color bikini. "Maybe she's his granddaughter," the gossipers speculated. When he lowered sail in mid-bay and anchored "The Love," and served the young lady a drink in what looked like a champagne glass, many said, "That awful old man, why, he's robbing the cradle."

Not being in the habit of snooping into other people's business unless my job calls for it, I didn't have cause to investigate the rumor about the new blonde in town, although I admit I was mighty curious. Nor did Doug ever mention such a person when I'd see him. As I think back, though, he said one thing that strikes me as meaning something. We were talking about how fast things were changing hereabouts, how we're losing our quiet and our privacy and our regard for each other, and he said, "Christ Himself couldn't straighten out this mess."

We dragged the bay bottom for two days without finding anything but quahog shells and beer cans and boat ladders. Trouble was we weren't sure where the so-called drowning happened. Some said it was in the middle of the bay; others said it happened nearer the south shore. Then on the third day came the shocker; we found the body. She had on the red bikini everybody said they saw her wearing; she was blonde okay and she was pretty nifty looking. Except she wasn't the genuine article. Now hold onto your hat.

Doug's blonde was a mannikin. That's right. The kind you see in store windows. A real woman-sized display mannikin.

Well, when the local paper got hold of that bit of news, they blew it out of all proportion, taking up the whole first page with pictures of the dummy and the headline: "Body of Murdered Manikin Found in Bay—County Coroner Refuses to Perform Autopsy," which made everybody feel like the damn fools they knew they were without having to be told so.

It's been five years now and Doug hasn't returned. The last I heard of him was when, as I said, he was seen sailing off to the east by the Coast Guard. But I've thought a lot ever since about why he did it. I figured it was symbolic somehow. You know, the young woman, representing paradise, not being real. The drowning being the final destruction of what was once beautiful and virgin. And then the whole act a deception, making fun of everybody and giving us a lesson too. Maybe Doug was telling us not to believe what we want to see and to look at what's really happening to our little corner here.

In a couple of days, as you know, I'm retiring. What are my plans? 'Course, I'm sixty-five, a lot older than Doug was when he retired, and still fiddle-fit. Being a bachelor, I've got no ties. Bought a forty-foot sloop last year with my life's savings. Ten years ago I would have stuck around here. But I think I'll take a cue from Doug and do some sailing around the world. Maybe I'll find my paradise, who knows. Maybe I'll run into Doug in his — if there is such a place left in the world.

Turned Tables

The two men left Bill alone in the room. It was plain and about ten feet square, and the walls were painted gray. A single fluorescent light was mounted close to the low ceiling. The furniture consisted of three folding chairs, including the one Bill occupied.

Nothing about the scene seemed real to Bill. Nothing that was happening seemed real. Only when the interrogators re-entered the room, locking the door behind them, did the reality of the situation sink in.

"Are you ready to cooperate, my friend?" asked the tall, skinny interrogator.

"I don't know what you want."

"I want the right answers, just the right answers. Now, that's not asking too much, is it?"

The squat, fat interrogator never spoke. But his eyes and body movements revealed what he was thinking. Bill could always tell whether he approved or disapproved of his answers.

"What do you mean the 'right' answers. What in hell are the right answers?" Bill stood up.

"Sit down, please," said the tall, skinny interrogator. "Of course, you know the right answers. You've known them all your life, my friend."

"Let's get one thing straight," Bill said. "I'm not your friend."

The squat, fat man turned sad and appeared hurt.

"Look into yourself, my friend. The answers are inside. Everyone knows the right answers if they look hard enough." The fat, squat man nodded vigorously. "I'm merely asking for your cooperation."

"Go to hell," Bill muttered. "You're nuts."

This is unbelievable, thought Bill. He had flown by jet all night, landing that morning in Buenos Aires to close a large computer sale. He had intended to remain there only for the day and return home that evening. As he entered the air terminal, the tall, skinny man and the fat, squat man approached him and requested that he follow them to their car. He assumed they were his customer's emissaries. But after a convoluted drive through the city, they ended up in the bare gray room with the three folding chairs.

"Now, now, my friend," said the tall, skinny man gently. "Surely you will know that telling me to go to hell and calling me nuts would never qualify for the right answers."

At first Bill was terrified. What could these strange men want with him? After all, he was only a businessman trying to close a simple transaction, far from political, and hardly a threat to anyone. Now he was not only confused but angry.

"I'd like to know what I've done. I mean have I done something wrong?" Bill demanded. "Are you the police? Have I broken your law?"

The tall, skinny man and the squat, fat man laughed, the squat, fat man uncontrollably. "Broken our law?" said the tall, skinny man. "You arrived barely an hour ago and you've been under our protection the whole time. How could you possibly have broken the law?"

"That's right," said Bill. "Then why are you holding me? Why the interrogation? I don't understand."

"Bill, Bill don't you see?" said the tall, skinny man sympathetically. "We ask the questions. You're here only to give answers — the right answers. Your questions are most improper."

"For Chrissakes, this is absolute madness."

"Madness? Well, well."

"Godamnit, I can tell you now you'll get nothing out of me. Nothing, nothing," Bill screamed.

"Come, come, my friend, calm yourself. Just give me the right answers and everything will be fine."

"What if I don't?" asked Bill with a leer. "What'll happen then? Torture?"

"Those are questions again, Bill. Most definitely not the right answers. Be advised that we're prepared to stay here indefinitely—perhaps forever. You must know that our patience has no end."

The tall, skinny man gazed at the squat, fat man, whose eyes were suddenly teary with deep sorrow.

"Tell me what to say," Bill said, "and I'll say it."

"Tell you what to say?" The tall, skinny man and the squat, fat man burst into laughter again, the squat, fat man uncontrollably. "If I told you to say that you despise your mother, would you say it?"

"That's absurd," said Bill.

"Exactly. If I told you to say that you raped your daughter and wished your wife dead, would you say it?"

"Certainly not."

"Then you can see how ridiculous your request is."

The squat, fat man giggled with satisfaction over the tall, skinny man's argument.

Bill decided to try a different strategy. He'd play their game.

"Actually, I can say anything. It doesn't matter, does it?"

The interrogators smiled at each other and nodded. "That was partly a question, my friend," said the tall, skinny man. "But you're catching on."

"I don't think you like what you're doing. That's my answer."

"And what is that? What do you think we're doing?"

"Well, victimizing people, controlling them, belittling them."

The squat, fat man and the tall, skinny man rose from their chairs, stared in consternation at each other, and left the room.

Ah, I struck a chord, thought Bill. After a few minutes the interrogators returned and sat facing him, forming a closed triangle.

"You must understand, my friend, that we're simply doing our job, nothing more," said the tall, skinny man.

"I realize that," said Bill. "But I don't think you believe in your job. You don't beat me or torture me the way professionals do."

The squat, fat man screeched with laughter and rolled on the floor.

"We have our principles," said the tall, skinny man. "Our ethics."

"I understand, and that's all you have. But you have no core belief, no belief in — in yourselves. You do what you're told to do, like everybody else."

"You're very clever," said the tall, skinny man as the squat, fat man stopped laughing, got up off the floor and sat on his chair. He cast his eyes on the dusty, bare hardwood floor.

"I don't believe there are any right answers," said Bill confidently.

The tall, skinny man joined the squat, fat man staring at the dusty, bare hardwood floor.

"Isn't that right?"

"That's a question," said the tall, skinny man.

"Damn right it's a question. Now it's my turn." Bill reached for the tall, skinny man's chin and raised his head so that their eyes met. The tall, skinny man's eyes were filled with pain — pain from his sawdust soul. Then Bill struck the tall, skinny man's face with the flat of his hand. "Now it's my turn, you bastard." The squat, fat man remained motionless, staring at the floor. "So, now tell me. What are the right answers?"

"But you don't believe there are any. You just said so," the tall, skinny man said meekly.

"What in hell has that got to do with it? What I believe has nothing to do with it." Bill stared at the squat, fat man with contempt. "You sonofabitch." The squat, fat man was unresponsive. "You're a coward, a weak, good-for-nothing coward. That's all you are." Striking the squat, fat man on the side of the head with the flat of his hand, Bill felled him to the dusty bare floor. There he lay whimpering, his body as slack as a pile of sawdust.

Turning to the tall, skinny man, Bill said, "Okay let's have it—the right answer."

"Now you're just like one of us."

"What do you mean?" Bill asked, suddenly frightened.

"Now you're one of us, but worse. You resort to profanity and physical punishment."

"No, no, no, no, no, no, no—" Bill screamed. The sound came from deep within. He writhed and beat his pillow and began whimpering. His pajamas were soaked with sweat and stuck to his skin.

"It's all right, Bill. It's all right," his wife said as she stroked his damp hair.

"There's no right answer," Bill said. "Is there?" He pulled away from her, avoiding her touch. They hadn't made love in months.

"To what, Bill?" his wife asked. "What are you talking about?"

Bill laughed with relief. "For God's sake, I haven't the vaguest idea." But he knew the right answer. And the question? He knew the right question, too. It was, do I have the courage to look into myself and find the key to my sawdust soul? And the answer was, yes, I do now.

CHILDHOOD AND YOUTH

The Mechanical Cop

"Hi there, Barney, you old sonofabitch," yelled Officer Tanzer from his traffic box at Commercial Square as my old man and I whizzed by in a black Model A Ford. Its rumble seat made into a small wooden truck body, the Model A was used for hauling furniture to and from my father's upholstery shop. Seeing the three-piece parlor suite stacked onto it ready to topple, Officer Tanzer stopped traffic from all directions and motioned my father to proceed alone as if he were a star act entering a circus ring.

"Hi, Hank," my father shouted, waving and grinning so wide it lasted for five minutes.

To get to my father's shop you had to pass through the square, which was known as the city's worst nightmare. Why? Picture an intersection with eight streets entering, five of which have heavy traffic, two of them on steep grades. Awful, right? Wait, a railroad track crosses through the heart of the square. Imagine what happens when the gates drop, cutting the square in two, to make way for a hundred-car freight train. Remember, back in the thirties, rail being the favored mode of carrying freight, mile-long trains were common and frequent; they crossed Commercial Square two or three times a day. Since the intersection was at one end of downtown, the city would be in gridlock for miles around.

After about a half hour of going no place, drivers would become irate. Officer Tanzer knew how to calm them down by walking among the cars, cracking jokes and telling the drivers "keep your hats on," even talking politics and religion. No matter what the complaint, Officer Tanzer was on their side, so that soon most everybody felt soothed and happy and forgot they were in a hurry.

Officer Tanzer was famous around town for the way he directed traffic. His motions were mechanical, like a robot's. A big robot, at that, for he was a good six-foot-five with a large long face and a big blue nose that matched his blue uniform. When he flung his arm up indicating stop, it seemed to spring and vibrate. When he waved cars to go, his arm moved from his elbow toward his chest like the lever of a machine. You'd think he was gathering the cars up into himself. As he was moving his arms, all the while pirouetting in a small circle in his silvery box sizing up the situation on all eight streets that entered the square, he shouted greetings to his friends. Most everybody was "buddy" except close friends, who were "sons of bitches."

Unlike other cops on the traffic force, Officer Tanzer didn't use a whistle. He didn't have to because he had a better natural whistle, his lips, which produced a piercing trill that so startled any half-asleep driver that he'd practically rear out of control when he first stepped on the gas. Well, Officer Tanzer's motions and his shrill lip whistle always made people smile. I daresay he may have been partly the cause of the frequent traffic jams at the square because people went out of their way to pass through just for the entertainment.

My father and Officer Tanzer were uncommonly compatible; they always agreed on things and had enormous respect for each other. I was proud of my father for having such a prestigious friend and for being chosen by undoubtedly the most colorful, best known, most appreciated personality in the city.

I was seven or eight at the time and determined to be a cop like Officer Tanzer when I grew up, although I kept my ambition a secret. Now that I'm grown up and not a cop, I still admire the old show-off for the fun and joy he brought to so many in those rough times. The only difference is that I don't believe in heroes anymore and it's Officer Tanzer's fault.

He and his wife, May, who ran a dress shop downtown, were our landlords, owning the three decker we lived in. They occupied the top floor apartment, and we the first floor. The middle floor, commanding the highest rent, was mostly vacant. The Tanzers didn't go much for kids—they kind of tolerated my kid brother and me—but they were crazy about my father and mother, who often had them down for breakfast of freshly ground coffee, just-delivered hot bagels, and an egg or two. The smell of coffee permeated our apartment, wafting upstairs to the third floor like a floating engraved invitation.

Indeed the egg man and the bread man, drawn by the delicious fragrance in the rear hallway, would on occasion join them for coffee and they would have hot political discussions. My father and Officer Tanzer, resplendent in his uniform, which I couldn't resist touching in awe, were great Roosevelt men, and the egg man and bread man were rabid, stiff-lipped Republicans. Roosevelt was definitely my father's hero. Sometimes the egg man or the bread man would leave in a tiff, but when in a few days they came back to deliver again, they acted as friendly as ever over a new cup of coffee.

Officer Tanzer's gun was imposingly present those mornings. Only its shiny brown handle showed from the holster, which, with its belt wound around it, lay on the table through breakfast. The gun enhanced officer Tanzer in my esteem, endowing him with special power and, more important, enormous responsibility.

One New Year's Eve both apartments were opened to the front hallway so that the celebrants could ply between them at will throughout the evening. Lying in my bed I heard the couples shouting and reveling from the distant second floor or the hallway or from our own kitchen. As the evening progressed they grew drunker and louder, especially Officer Tanzer. I heard May yelling at him to lay off, that he had enough booze.

In the morning I found Officer Tanzer and my father asleep, snoring on the living room rug under a single blanket. After they awoke my mother and May served them coffee to ease their hangovers, and May reminded her husband that he had duty that New Year's Day and should get ready to report to the station.

"I ain't working today. I'm sick," Officer Tanzer said in a surly voice.

"You'll get over it, dearie," May said.

"Like hell I will. I ain't going to work no more. I'm through. I quit."

May shrugged and laughed, maybe a bit nervously. She called the station and told them her husband was sick. I was alarmed at what Officer Tanzer said, for I couldn't imagine that he didn't like his job, the most important job in the entire city. But I saw that he meant it because each day for the rest of the week he didn't report to work.

Meanwhile Commercial Square was, as always, jammed, a mess. After two days the cop directing traffic at the square begged to be let off the hook. No matter who was assigned to the job, the confusion continued. Three cops later the lead article on the first page of the only city newspaper prayed that Officer Tanzer would quickly recover from his illness and return to duty to "bring order to the worst intersection conceived by man." On reading this my father suspected that the police department hadn't leveled with the paper about Officer Tanzer having actually quit.

The fact was that the department wouldn't let him quit. They called him at home every day, told him how important he was "to the general welfare, the very sanity of the city." Refusing to change his mind, Officer Tanzer suggested they go to hell. Of course they were already there, only it was called Commercial Square.

Well, finally the police chief decided to take charge of the matter directly, face to face. On Saturday morning he appeared in front of our house in his gussied-up black Oldsmobile police car with the number plate that read PCHIEF. With him were three lieutenants with gold badges on their tailored blues. They went up the wide front porch and rang the bell and stood waiting. Soon May, who saw the chief's car parked in front, stuck her balloon shaped head out the parlor window and yelled down that they should stand on the front lawn and state their business.

"Where's Hank?" the chief bellowed.

"He's here, Chief, in the kitchen, cleaning his gun."

"I'm asking Hank as a personal favor to report to work, May," the chief shouted back.

"It won't do no good, dearie," May said. "He's made up his mind." She sighed.

"I'd like to know what his complaint is. I'll come up and talk with him."

"Better not, Chief. I'd strongly advise . . ."

The chief bounded to the porch, his men following. "Tell Hank I'm coming up, May."

My old man and my ma and my brother and I watched from our own parlor window, which looks out on the porch. So did the neighbors, gathered on their dandelion lawns. The chief pressed our doorbell and my father went to the front hallway door to let him in.

"Thank-you, sir," said the chief.

"Good luck," said my old man.

As soon as the four officers stormed upstairs, making a great racket, we heard a loud bang echo from the hallway, then another, and the sound of the officers scrambling down the stairs like rocks in a landslide.

"Holy jehosaphat, the sonofabitch is shooting at us," one of the lieutenants screamed.

The chief pounded on our door and, without waiting for anyone to respond, entered our parlor.

"You a friend of Hank's?" he asked my old man who nodded in the affirmative.

With half an eye out the window, I observed that several more police cars had accumulated on the street and a group of policemen had assembled on the lawn. Of course by now the whole neighborhood as well as passersby had been attracted and the crowd was beginning to block traffic. I was excited and troubled at the same time.

Then May came down to our parlor. Looking worried, she said, "He's never been like this — off his rocker — yes, he must be, I swear."

"We've got to get the gun, May," the chief said.

"Don't look at me, dearie. He said he'd shoot a bullet into his ear before he'd ever give up."

The chief dashed out to the lawn once more and yelled, "Listen, Hank. You don't have to report to work. I accept your resignation. Hear me, Hank? Just toss out the gun and we'll let bygones be bygones. Okay, Hank?"

A shot shattered the windshield of the chief's prized car.

"Sonofabitch. You sonofabitch, Hank. I'll have your badge for this!" the chief screeched.

"Barney!" Hank called from inside the open third floor window.

"What's that, Hank?" the chief shouted.

"Barney!"

"Barney who? Who's Barney, Hank?"

Returning to our parlor, the chief quickly found out who Barney was. Putting his arm over my old man's shoulder, the chief said, "You're our best hope, Barney. Are you willing to go up, talk to him, and get the gun?"

"Don't do it, Barney," my ma said.

"If you don't, somebody is liable to get hurt," the chief said.

"Hank wouldn't harm me," my father said. "He knows I'm his friend."

"Then you'll go?" asked the chief.

"It's me, Hank, it's Barney," my old man kept saying as he mounted the stairway without hesitation.

A long time passed, so it seemed, until my father called from the top of the stairs. "You can come up now, Chief."

Reaching over the bannister, he let six harmless bullets rain down the stairwell onto the floor at our feet.

The chief and his men clambered up the stairs and in only a few minutes came down with Officer Tanzer handcuffed, hanging his head like a beaten lion, keeping his eyes stuck to the floor. Then just as he reached the front door to the porch he turned to my old man and said: "S'long Barney, you sonofabitch."

The Mechanical Cop

You can take that two ways, I thought, and looking at my old man's expression I saw he couldn't decide which. Neither could I. Should I be proud of my old man? I mean, did he deceive his good friend into giving up the gun? Or did he tell him the way it was honestly and talk him into it for his own sake? I never found out. I was also confused about Officer Tanzer himself. How could such an admired and gifted man just go off his rocker like that? May said she thought he cracked under the pressure of keeping Commercial Square running smoothly day in and day out for years. In her opinion the department itself was responsible for his destruction.

On passing through the city of my youth after I retired fifty-eight years later, I visited Commercial Square. The train tracks were gone, having been rerouted through a tunnel under the square. Some streets that once led into the square were dead-ended or diverted. Others were made one way. The whole complex was now smoothly controlled by several coordinated sets of traffic lights. Indeed, the scene wasn't recognizable. And what do you know, the square had been renamed; it is now called Tanzer Square. I wonder how many are left who remember why.

The Coffee Break

$\mathbf{B}$ack in the late thirties my father had a small custom upholstery shop on the edge of downtown in Worcester. Next door an Armenian named Johnny operated a combination luncheonette and convenience market, which my father visited twice a day for coffee break. Whenever the two men got together they would put on an impromptu comedy show.

No matter what my father was doing, at 10:00 A.M. and 3:00 P.M. sharp he would stray over to Johnny's.

"If anyone calls, tell them I'm not here," he'd say to my mother, who answered the phone and did the books. The coffee break must not be interrupted under any circumstances.

Despite my father's parting words, my mother, who lived according to her own compulsive agenda, would rush next door to tell him that he had a phone call, which would inevitably lead to an unpleasant scene.

"Bernie, (my father's real name was Benjamin, but everyone called him Barney except my mother who called him Bernie). Bernie, it's the federal tax bureau," my mother shouted through the doorway of the luncheonette one afternoon. Clearly she feared the government more than my father's wrath. My father was seated on his favorite stool at the long counter, which was lined with customers.

"I don't care if it's Roosevelt himself. Leave me alone," he said, turning his back on her.

"What if it was the Pope, Barney?" Johnny piped up, standing behind the counter holding a pot of coffee.

The patrons, mostly men and women office workers from the huge building supply company across the street, joined Johnny in awaiting my old man's reply.

My father, who was Jewish, grinned. "If it's the Pope, I'd tell her to hang up on him."

"Bernie," my mother warned, "this is no time for joking. You don't fool around with the government."

The Coffee Break

Johnny chuckled, eyeing his patrons seated at the counter to make sure he had their attention. "Tell me this, Barney, what if it was Jesus Christ Almighty Himself."

My old man thought a minute and feigning seriousness, said, "If it was Jesus Christ Almighty" — he hesitated as everyone waited — "I'd take the call."

The crowd gasped, expecting that my father would reject Jesus even more than the Pope.

"You would? Why is that?" Johnny said. "You're not a believer."

Johnny was a Catholic and a closet Communist. My father, though a labor sympathizer, was a committed capitalist. Their bond of friendship overrode their political differences.

Johnny loved to shock his customers. He continued: "To tell the truth, I wouldn't take that call myself, so why would you?"

The crowd turned to my father.

"You ask why? Have you forgotten, Johnny? He's one of our boys," my father replied, triumphant.

There was an uproar. "Good going, Barney!" some shouted. "You win this one Barney." "Chalk one up for Barney." "'One of his boys,' that's a good one."

Even my mother laughed, and for the moment stopped nagging my father.

Johnny and my father were about the same age — early fifties. My father was barely five-six and chunky. Johnny was tall and thin, and had an Armenian accent that sometimes rendered his English impenetrable. He always looked as if he had just awakened from a nap. About once an hour he'd disappear into the back room to take a nip of whisky.

On occasion the two men also performed unrehearsed skits for the benefit of the patrons. After a while they developed a repertoire such as Laurel and Hardy and Abbott and Costello routines. But the Jack Benny skit was the biggest hit of all.

Wearing his hat at a jaunty angle, my father would sit at the counter and put on a tough demeanor—an imitation of Dillinger or Pretty Boy Floyd, the most popular criminals of the time. Johnny would then ask in a normal tone, "What can I do for you today, sir?"

"Gimme a cup of coffee," my father would say in a surly manner.

"Anything with it, sir?" Johnny would ask.

"Yeah," my father would reply, withdrawing a water pistol from his pocket. "Your money."

By then, the crowd knew the act had begun. Of course any stranger present would be alarmed, until a regular patron would let him in on it.

"My money?" Johnny would say, suspending an empty coffee cup and saucer in his hand.

"Yeah, your money or your life."

At this point Johnny would keep silent, trying to suppress a giggle—not part of the act. The crowd would be motionless. The only sound came from the coffee cup rattling in its saucer.

"You heard me, your money or your life," my father would say again.

Any stranger would expect Johnny to reply with Jack Benny's punch line—"Wait a minute, I'm thinking"—but the patrons were never sure how he'd respond. Sometimes Johnny followed the regular routine; sometimes he'd introduce a brilliant variant. And no one knew how my father would react to that, least of all Johnny himself.

"Go ahead, shoot," he'd say, for instance. "I'll keep the money." Whereupon, my father would then pepper him with spurts from his water pistol.

Well, the crowd would rock with laughter. Then Johnny would treat everyone to a free cup of coffee, and he and my father would congratulate each other for a successful performance.

One day the usual crowd was there at coffee break. Johnny, who was reeking from a recent nip, had taken my

The Coffee Break

father aside, as he often did, to proselytize the benefits of communism.

A stranger, wearing a broad-brimmed gangster-style hat, entered and sat at the counter.

Johnny attended to the stranger. "What would you like, sir?"

"Gimme your cash," the stranger demanded, flashing a gun. "Don't anybody make a move or he gets it."

Everyone realized this was the real thing. My father was right there, and the stranger certainly wasn't Jack Benny.

Johnny remained motionless.

"I said gimme your cash," the stranger repeated.

"And if I don't?" Johnny said. "You'll take my life, is that it?"

"What the hell is this?" said the stranger. "I said, gimme your cash. Open the register."

"Go ahead, shoot," Johnny said as cool as soda pop.

"For Christ's sake, Johnny, give him the money," my father shouted.

"Oh sure, Barney, you'd take his side," Johnny said feigning hurt.

"This ain't funny," my father said. "That's no water pistol he's holding."

A murmur of agreement rose from the crowd. The stranger, his eyes darting from the register to Johnny and back, was growing nervous. He lurched off the stool and headed around the end of the counter to the register. Johnny, blocking his way, began grappling with him. A shot rang out. Johnny fell as the stranger bolted out the door—empty handed. My old man rushed to his wounded friend.

"Godammit, Johnny, to hell with the money," my father said as he held him. "You knew this was no act."

"Barney, for me it never was."

Johnny's wound was not fatal. "It was above the waist. That's all that matters," he told everybody later.

From then on Johnny and my father chose not to do the Jack Benny routine again. Instead they did a version of the

Abbott and Costello baseball bit. They made an exception a few months later when the noted pitcher Lefty Grove stopped by as he was passing through town. Lefty laughed so much that Johnny treated him to a bottomless cup of coffee and two pieces of homemade apple pie.

A couple of years later Johnny passed away. After that, life and my father were never the same. My father never again exhibited his old high spirited humor. He took to staying in his shop and having coffee from a thermos my mother prepared.

Eventually both the luncheonette and the upholstery shop were bulldozed to the ground to make way for an urban renewal project. All that's left of the way it was is this story.

This Land Is Mine
A Child's Story

"You can't plant there, boy," Mr. Barker said after Seth had loosened a few scoops of earth with his pitchfork. Mr. Barker was angry, squinting his eyes the way Seth's ma does before she gives him the strap.

"Why not, Mr. Barker?" Seth asked, feeling hurt and afraid. Mr. Barker never acted this way before. What's so bad about what he's doing? Just digging up the ground to plant some flowers. Mr. Barker had always been kind to him. Always. This spring he let him help dig in his big vegetable garden in the field behind his house. Together they planted corn seed which Mr. Barker said would grow twice as tall as he, taller even than Mr. Barker. Just think. And he promised Seth he could pick some when the time came.

"It's my property," Mr. Barker said, as if God gave it to him.

Seth lived here too, next door. He was only taking a narrow strip of dirt beside the driveway between their houses. The dirt was good, rich and dark brown. Only weeds and dandelions grew in it now. Seth chose the spot so his father would see the flowers when he drives his black Model T Ford up their weed-dotted gravel driveway. The flowers would cheer him up. He'd make colorful bouquets for his mother that would smell like her perfume. Seth couldn't wait for the flowers to begin sprouting. He could picture them, their blossoms in more colors than his crayons. Just think.

"This is my garden, Mr. Barker," Seth said.

"It's my land," Mr. Barker shouted angrily.

"You have your garden," Seth said, trembling, ready to cry.

"You can't have one on my land," Mr. Barker said grabbing the pitchfork from Seth's hands.

Well, Seth was so mad he began crying and stomping his feet in the damp dirt, trying to get the pitchfork that Mr. Barker raised high above his head.

Doesn't the world belong to everyone? Don't the birds fly anywhere they wish? Don't dogs and cats roam across everybody's yard? Why can't people? What does Mr. Barker mean by saying the land is his? Seth only wanted to grow beautiful plants that drink the rain and bend in the breeze and bring bees that make honey. He didn't understand Mr. Barker.

"I'm going to tell my father on you," Seth said as he started for the back door of his house, howling as if he had just fallen down and hurt himself.

Mr. Barker stabbed the pitchfork into the earth and smiled a little. Seth didn't think that what he had just said was funny.

"That ain't necessary, boy," Mr. Barker said, motioning Seth to come toward him. "I believe we can settle this between ourselves."

With tears still pouring down his cheeks, Seth said, "I thought we were friends."

"We are, son, we are," Mr. Barker responded, looking serious and placing his hands on Seth's shoulders. "I'm trying to teach you a lesson, that's all. Y'understand?"

Seth nodded even though he didn't really.

"You can't dig anywhere you want. Land belongs to people. The world ain't free, son."

"But I only want to make it more beautiful. Is that wrong?"

"It ain't wrong, boy."

Seth could see that Mr. Barker was puzzled, maybe troubled a little.

"The world sure needs all the beauty it can get, but you can't beautify it in a place that ain't yours."

Well, Seth began crying again, quietly this time, from a bigger sadness than before, from disappointment in the way the world was.

"Tell you what," Mr. Barker said after thinking. "You can make your garden here, but you gotta remember it's my property."

"Gee, Mr. Barker," Seth said, laughing and hugging his legs, his tears gone. "But the flowers are mine, aren't they?"

"Sure, son, sure, they're all yours."

Mr. Barker gathered Seth's skinny body into his strong, sun-bronzed arms. "Friends again, are we?"

Seth giggled from Mr. Barker's tickling, happy once more. The world may not have been his, but he could use it—for a while anyway.

OLD AGE

Sailing Free

The sail shook and danced, tore off to starboard, pulling most of the mainsheet over the water, and fluttered limply. Watching the antics, the aging sailor bounced to the cuddy deck and released the painter. As the sail filled, the boat moved off. There was no getting tangled in the floating mooring lines or the dinghy painter, not this time. Great take off, he thought. If only my son could be here; he'd appreciate the smoothness.

The bay was angry, its dark blue waves foaming and howling like mad dogs. The man reached the red buoy at the beginning of the marked channel that guided the way behind the barrier beach down the five-mile narrow corridor to Monomoy and the treacherous opening to the ocean.

He hadn't left the main part of the bay in any substantial way for several summers. Once last year on a sweltering Sunday afternoon, he had sailed lazily as far as the Chatham light, fighting the crazy parade of stinkpots whose wakes rocked him silly. Finding the trip boring, he returned home feeling unfulfilled. Not since he sailed with his son five or six years ago in his previous boat, a light 17-foot sloop, to the north island of Monomoy had he had any real adventure. They had beached, had lunch, swum in the chilly water, and explored. His son had wanted to go further, visit the south island, round its tip, and sail up the back side, but he nixed the idea.

"It's too dangerous," he said. "Those are real ocean waves coming in. They could swamp us."

"But the boat rides them pretty good, Dad," his son said. "It would be fun."

"I don't think so. We can't take a chance. If we capsized in this cold water, I don't think we'd last long."

"We'd just climb on the boat bottom and sit in the sun until someone spots us," his son said.

"Forget it," he said with finality.

He hadn't forgotten that day with his son, a day of adventure and exploring. Ever since, he had kept to the bay, never venturing into the unknown again.

The strong but steady southwest breeze and an enormous unblemished blue sky made the day ideal for a Monomoy trip again. What a shame his son wasn't with him. The tide was low, still on the ebb according to the slant of the buoys. It was bound to be coming in for the trip back. As for the weather, no storm would develop over the next four or five hours in that clean sky. Go for it, fella, go for it. Pleased at having reefed the sail, which made him ready for any wind, he headed down the jagged line of buoys to the edge of the world.

After slipping on leather gloves to protect his hands against rope burns, he tightened sail and glided near to the wind on a firm beat. South of Strong Island, where the expanse is uninterrupted and the ocean elements take over, the air was wild. The sail went into frequent spasm, flapping crazily as it tried to break free from his control. But he held to course riding high and securely above the seething chop as the boat heeled. The *Sweetwind* was a marvel, as if sharing his pleasure. He was sailing free, as free as he'd ever been in his life.

His wife should have been there to see how nicely he was handling things. Three summers ago when he replaced his old sloop with the *Sweetwind* and sought ideas for a name, his wife suggested calling it the CRISIS. Although she intended it in jest, he knew better. She had stopped going on the boat, saying he made her a nervous wreck. All that unnecessary tension. His son also made excuses not to go sailing with him. Yet his son didn't hesitate to take the boat out alone. His son was a good sailor, always cool. The man was willing to admit now that his son was a damn better sailor than he ever would be.

Through the blear he spotted a 19-foot sloop. He found comfort in not being alone. Gaining on her, he made it a contest. Suddenly he felt an overwhelming urge to urinate, typical of his sixty-year-old plumbing.

Usually urinating was no problem. Finding a private boatless stretch of the bay, he would loosen sail, let the tiller go on a reach, duck under the cuddy, and, kneeling, release his stream into a faded plastic sand pail. Now he hesitated because of the madness around him. The sloop was making distance. He kept the *Sweetwind* on the move.

Securing the mainsheet, he rushed under the cuddy, knelt, pulled the sand pail to his crotch, fumbled to open his fly, struggled to withdraw his penis through the hidden slot in his undershorts, and began voiding. The *Sweetwind* gyrated and slipped sharply on its side, taking water over the port gunwhale. He scrambled back to the tiller while the boat slowly headed into the wind. Loosening the mainsheet from its cleat, he brought the *Sweetwind* back to a safe beat again. Seeing his extremity hanging free, he laughed. Soaked and cold, looking like a pornographic idiot, he was nevertheless happy. Let it all go, he thought, releasing what remained in his bladder into the sloshing cockpit. No crisis was ever this much fun.

With water heavy in the bilge, the boat lost speed. The race with the sloop was futile. Still he kept her in sight, curious to see how near she would go toward the edge of the world.

He sailed down the narrow funnel of the bay, tacking every few hundred yards to avoid the barely two-foot-deep shoals that bordered the underwater channel. He played games with the shallows, racing to see how closely he could approach them without running aground. "Hard a'lee," he shouted into the air as away he rammed the tiller again and again.

They were a glorious team, he and the *Sweetwind*. Slicing the tossing waves with impunity, she responded like a trained show horse. A mystical mutuality seemed to prevail between boat and man. Of course, it was all within himself. Although now alone, he was in no sense lonely. How remarkable it was to find such joy in a simple sail. He hadn't known it was possible.

His life had always been too conservative. He had the choice of leaving the company gracefully (they called it voluntary early retirement) or being kicked upstairs into useless oblivion with an empty title. No longer in the mainstream, he was now only an observer. But after a year of painful obsolescence he realized he wasn't ready to withdraw. He planned to start a new career, become a consultant in his field.

Coming abreast of the limit of the barrier beach, he watched the sloop lower its sail in a sheltered cove. It had opted not to venture beyond the edge of the world after all. To his right was a low sand spit comprising the north island of Monomoy. It was separated by a shallow channel from the mainland, the most southeasterly point of Cape Cod. A string of buoys zigzagged toward Monomoy, heading for a cut to open sea where the surf was moaning among hidden sandbars.

Trailing a swarm of sea gulls above its wake like a billowing parachute, a fishing boat was coming in from its long morning's work. Gulls dropped like a shower of squealing snowflakes around him. The passing vessel's great wash temporarily interrupted his steady tack.

Sailing beyond the channel and the place where he and his son had reached so long ago, he was isolated among perpetual mounds of ocean. They diminished him as they lifted and dropped him into shiny valleys below crests that seemed higher than his mast top. The *Sweetwind* was hardly more than sixteen feet long, weighing less than a thousand pounds. Ah, the danger, danger he had never known, danger he had spent a lifetime avoiding. He was unafraid as the boat mounted each surge, leaving a white rudder trail streaking behind. Her sail close-hauled, she clung to the very brink of doom. They were winning; the mastery, the sheer exhilaration of it all. The Cape mainland was barely a distant silhouette. Ahead was the tip of Monomoy, the edge of the world. He had reached a psychological point of no return.

The rest was suddenly easy. He felt free and light. All sense of danger evaporated. In his small way he was conquering the mindless sea. But also something else. His fear of risk. His self-doubt. His suffocating caution. His self-imprisonment.

At last, late in the afternoon, he rounded the south island and began a run up the back side. He hadn't taken lunch, hadn't eaten since breakfast, but he wasn't hungry. No need to bother with mundane physical needs; no time anyway. Concentrate on the experience, ponder the victory, and enjoy a quiet voyage home.

He found himself caught in insidious shallows. Despite raising the centerboard, the rudder eventually scraped the sandy bottom. He moved forward to the cuddy deck to counterbalance the weight aft. Aided by a strong following wind (which had risen to twenty knots or more during the afternoon), the rudder cut a swath through the bottom sand and the *Sweetwind* broke into deep water. Such small success was still a pleasurable anticlimax.

His return trip was easy, swift, and sure. At early dusk he reached the mooring at the corner of "big" Pleasant Bay. Happy and relaxed, he calmly secured the *Sweetwind,* rowed the dinghy to shore, laid it bottom up in the marsh grass, and stood looking at his boat, feeling satisfied.

Back home he called his son, now a young architect in Chicago.

"I did Monomoy today—rounded the tip of the south island and came up the back side," he said.

"You're kidding. You mean you did it alone?"

"Alone. All by myself."

"Wasn't it kind of dangerous? I mean, the *Sweetwind* isn't exactly oceangoing."

"She handled the sea like a dream. Don't you remember you wanted to do it six years ago?"

"I was a lot younger then," his son laughed.

"I'm a lot younger now," he said. "Next time we'll do it together. Okay?"

Through a window he could see Monomoy low on the faint horizon. After he hung up he watched it fade into the evening. It was sure one hell of a beautiful day.

Old Hands Don't Need Motors

I dialed the phone number listed in the advertisement. A man with a gruff voice answered. "I'm calling regarding the sailboat . . ." I began.

"When do you want to see her?" he interrupted.

"Well," I said, pausing to consider a convenient time.

"How about two this afternoon?" he suggested.

"I suppose . . ."

He cut me off again. "She's in the water, y'know. Maybe you'd like to try her out." And he told me where the boat was moored.

"Sure," I said. "Your name, sir?"

"The Doc," he replied. "By the way, you got good hands?"

"Good hands?"

"Yeah, they strong?"

"I suppose so."

"Good," he said. Before I had a chance to inquire the asking price, he hung up.

The boat sounded as though it was exactly what I had been looking for without success during the previous winter and spring: "23-foot Sea Sprite. Excellent condition. Reasonable," read the ad in the local paper. Good used Sea Sprites were hard to come by. I couldn't afford a new one, although my sixteen-year-old son and I would frequently drive down to the nearest dealer on Cape Cod and look them over longingly. Two had stood in their cradles in the marina, and one sat shiny in the water. We examined and reexamined every detail, as if each vessel were a finely cut gem. "Nice lines," I'd say.

"We can sail to Nantucket on her, can't we Dad?" Andy would ask.

"Sure, someday," I would say.

For a half dozen summers we'd been sailing a 17-foot Day Sailer in Pleasant Bay. But each year the bay seemed more and more confining. The surf roared on the barrier beach that separated the bay from the exciting open ocean. It was like a siren call luring me to play in the vaster, more challenging world. The Sea Sprite was known to have sailed around the globe. Not that I was that ambitious. But it would be gratifying to know that I had a boat with unlimited possibilities.

As we drove to the harbor where the vessel was moored, Andy and I began to dream out loud of already owning the boat we hadn't yet seen. We were ripe to buy. If the price was anywhere near right, we'd take her.

After parking the car, we stood searching the harbor for the familiar outline of a Sea Sprite and found one bobbing lustily in the gusts. "That's got to be the one," I said.

Andy grinned. "She's a beauty."

As we walked toward the harbormaster's hut, we passed a silver-haired man seated behind the steering wheel of a big, late-model Lincoln Continental. He was staring into space. At the hut I asked the man on duty for the Doc.

"That's him," he said, pointing to the Lincoln. "Better knock on the window, or he won't know you're here." The young man's manner suggested this was an oft-repeated routine.

After I awakened the Doc from his reverie, he slowly opened the car door then pulled himself up from the seat by grabbing the car roof. "This your son?" he asked.

"Yes, this is Andy," I responded.

"When my son was your age," he said to Andy, "we used to have great times on her. There she is, out there." With great effort he pointed a gnarled and twisted hand toward the scores of sailboats. "See, there, just behind that gray powerboat." Andy's eyes met mine; it was the one we had identified a few minutes before.

We clambered into the launch waiting beside the pier. Almost falling as he boarded, the Doc collapsed beside me on the seat. "You okay, Doc?" the young launch driver inquired.

"Sure, sure, I'm fine," the Doc said impatiently, waving him on. We took off, heading into the wind.

"How old is she?" I asked.

"Bought her new eight years ago," the Doc replied.

The spray beat coldly against our faces. Andy and I zipped up our windbreakers, but the Doc, in shorts and a short-sleeved shirt, ignored the spray and was getting soaked. "Oh, it's one of the early models," I commented.

"Yeah, when they made them real sturdy," he said. "She's good for another ten years, maybe more. I wish to hell I could keep her." Drawing closer to the boat, I made out her name: *Brainstorm.*

As we pulled alongside her badly sea-stained hull, Andy climbed into the cockpit and fastened the launch's bow and stern lines at the young man's directions. "Give me a hand, son," the Doc said, reaching out his arm. With tremendous effort, Andy pulled him, and the young man pushed his buttocks from behind. The Doc bellowed like a cow. It took three tries. The Doc wasn't a large man, and he wasn't old—in his late fifties, I judged. But his every motion seemed to cause agony and require more strength than he could muster. As I climbed from the launch, the young man said softly, "If I were you, I'd keep an eye on him."

The Doc, in rising frustration, fumbled through his pockets for a key to the hatch cover panel padlock. "Must have left it at home," he said, pointing to a lid in the cockpit seat. "Gimme the hammer in the toolbox under there." I became oddly uneasy. Grasping the tool near its head, he struck the lock with a series of weak blows, often missing and denting the panel.

"Don't you think you should go back to your house for the key? We can wait," I said.

"I think I lost it," he grumbled as he continued hammering. Then trying another approach, he slipped the claw under the hasp and, in a burst of strength, ripped it from its mounting, leaving a portion of the panel in splinters.

"Follow me. I'll show you the cabin," he said, groaning as he stepped down the ladder.

When he disappeared, Andy whispered, "Dad, some of the cleats near the bow have been ripped out and the holes filled in."

We followed the Doc belowdecks. The cabin, stinking with mustiness, was a shambles. Torn cushions were strewn on the floor, damp to the touch, and the interior walls and portholes were slick with moisture. Water was sloshing across the cabin sole from the bilge. "Haven't had a chance to clean her up," the Doc said, "but I'll take care of it. Don't you worry."

Once back in the cockpit, the Doc tackled the motor. He lowered it on its bracket, but it refused to stay down. "It's supposed to catch on a gizmo down there," he said, bending across the transom and reaching into the water. I grasped him by his belt to prevent him from falling overboard. As I pulled him back upright, he said gloomily, "Maybe it'll stay down if we take it easy."

Then he attacked the starting cord. After pulling it a half-dozen times, the motor remained unresponsive. He cursed, staring at his hands. Andy then took a turn, and after two tries the motor coughed into action. "Good lad," the Doc said. "My son used to be pretty good at pitching in like that, too. Okay, lad, go forward and loosen her from the mooring." He seemed reinvigorated as he stood by the tiller giving Andy the order.

Wending our way toward the outer harbor among the closely moored vessels, we fell silent, observing each boat as we passed. I always leave a mooring expecting adventure; every departure is a voyage into the unknown. Judging from the eagerness I saw in Andy's eyes, and in the Doc's, too, we all shared the same sense. What will the sea really be like? How strong are the gusts? How will the boat handle? And, I thought, especially after what had already happened, will anything go wrong?

"Take the halyards, son, and let's raise sail," crooned the Doc. Up went the main and then the genoa. "Ya got a swell boy there," the Doc shouted as the main clapped and filled. "Reminds me of my son. Sure does. We had great times aboard, great times." Then the Doc shut off the motor; we ran marvelously quiet and free, hearing only the whish of the bow wave curling along the hull and the whistle of the wind across the sails. "Take over, son," the Doc said as he left the tiller for Andy.

Andy led the boat through a complete trial, seeing how close to the wind she'd beat, how dependably she'd come about, how fast she'd sail on a reach, how steady she handled in a following wind. Meanwhile the Doc and I relaxed and talked. "I'm in no hurry to get back," he said. "If you'd like to stay out for a while, it's okay with me." I suspected he hadn't been out for some time.

"We can't stay too long," I replied apologetically. "I told my wife we'd be home in a few hours. And you know how wives worry."

"Sure, sure," he said, "they're all the same. Hell, mine goes into panic when I tell her I'm going to the harbor. You see, I can't singlehand the boat any more. Trouble is, I got this damned arthritis, so I promised her I wouldn't go out alone. The most I can do these days is sit out here in the cockpit and dream." He sighed. "If only I had my son. Great sailor, my son, just like your Andy. But sons grow up very fast, y'know."

Taking a turn at the tiller, I repeated Andy's trials. The boat handled well; she was what I had hoped she would be. But clearly the boat had also been abused. As I stood at the helm, my eyes fell on one disturbing item after another. Some of the rigging had been repaired jury-fashion. There were gouges in the teak combing and deep scratches in the transom fiberglass. As we had stood by in the launch, I hadn't failed to notice several bruises in the hull and areas that appeared to have been poorly patched. The price would have to be right; even then I wasn't so sure.

The Doc's voice interrupted my thoughts. "Any time you'd like to go sailing with me, Andy, be my guest. I can always use a first class helmsman." Had the Doc forgotten that he was trying to sell the boat?

"I think we've seen all we need to," I finally said. "Let's head back." Andy relieved me at the helm. It was time to talk business, which the Doc deliberately seemed to be avoiding. "Doc, what are you asking for her?"

The Doc shifted on the cockpit cushion. Without looking me in the eye, he said, "You can take her for twelve thousand." I was thunderstruck; his price was absurd, especially since a new Sea Sprite sells for about $15,000, which he must have known. And I knew that used ones in fairly good condition sold for about $8,000.

"Don't you think that's a bit steep?" I asked, indicating the going price of a new boat and other used boats. Ignoring my argument, he changed the subject. Where was I from? he asked. What did I do? Where did I sail?

And what about him? I asked. He was a brain surgeon. "These hands used to be magical, the best in the field. But I don't operate any more," he said resignedly.

As we approached the inner harbor he took the tiller from Andy. "Not that I doubt your ability, son," he said. "But I'm an old hand at taking her in. Just get ready to snag the mooring when I say so."

"Don't you want to start the motor?" I asked apprehensively.

"Old hands don't need motors," he shot back defiantly.

"I don't think he can do it, Dad," Andy whispered. I shrugged. This being the peak of the season, the boats were densely packed. But the wind was behind us and no tacking was necessary, so perhaps the Doc could pull it off.

Andy stationed himself at the bow, ready to grab the mooring buoy. I stood in the cockpit, watching the often precariously close distance between us and the moored boats as we slid too swiftly by them. Our boom scraped the shroud of a neighboring boat, causing no apparent damage.

"It's okay, it's okay," the Doc assured us. Still, it was a signal that he might not be in total control. Under pressure of a strong following wind with our genoa and main flying wing-and-wing, there was no way he could restrict the boat's speed. We were approaching our mooring in the crowded anchorage too fast to allow for error. The Doc would have to slip beyond the buoy and come up quickly into the wind at precisely the right moment for us to reach the mooring.

The Doc delayed too long. I knew immediately after we passed the buoy that he had gone too far to make it back. At the appropriate second I wanted to shout, "Turn, turn, damnit," but foolishly I feared offending him. Andy threw up his hands in exasperation. At last the Doc turned, but about ten feet short of the mooring the boat stalled. The Doc, confused, stood beside the tiller immobile. Andy raced back to the motor as we began to drift backward, then sideways. Frantically, he pulled the starting cord over and over. Seeing that we were headed for a sure collision with an immaculate sixty-footer, I stood by to try to fend her off.

The odor of gasoline fumes filled the cockpit; the motor had flooded. We bounced off the beautiful boat, causing a section of her polished hull to break into a cobweb of cracks. The Sea Sprite continued to be blown downwind, a menace to any boat in her wild path. Feeling helpless, I was appalled at what was happening.

Then, like a white knight, the young man in the launch came to our rescue. "Throw a line," he shouted. The Doc tossed him one from the cockpit. "Damnit, not from there, Doc." Andy ran forward and flung him a line from the bow. The Sea Sprite steadied. We were under control at the end of a tether.

"I'm afraid I'm out of practice," the Doc apologized on the trip back to the pier. "I used to be pretty good. Always came in under sail without a mishap. Right, fella?"

"Yup, you were one of the best, Doc," said the young man. Then he added as we pulled up to the pier, "But I hope you don't try it again."

"You can relax, fella. This is it," the Doc said confidently. "I'm selling the boat to these people. I'm going to give them the boat bargain of the century."

The Doc and the young man went into a huddle in the hut while Andy and I waited. Through the walls of the hut I could hear the young man say, "They're going to be awfully angry, Doc, awfully angry." The Doc replied, "Don't worry, fella, I'll make good on the damage."

When the Doc returned, he was shaken and struggling to control his equanimity. "I'm willing to let her go for eight thousand," he said right off. "That's dropping the price fifty percent. She's a top-notch boat. Y'know one of these sailed around the world. I hope you don't blame the accident on her. It was all my fault."

"Of course, I understand. But I've got to think it over," I said. "The price is still out of line."

"Well," he responded, "I'm not much for sailing anymore, so I'll tell you what. I'll consider your best offer."

Andy and I excused ourselves and consulted. I had almost decided against a deal at any price.

"She's in pretty bad shape, Dad. Did you see the new gouges in her hull after the accident?"

"Yeah, it's going to take a lot to fix her up."

We returned to the Doc. "We're not sure this is the right boat for us," I said.

"Y'know," he said, "while I was watching Andy handle her, I said to myself: It's the perfect boat for this man and his son. So I'm going to give you the boat bargain of the century. Give me two thousand, and she's yours."

"I think you can get more from somebody else, Doc," I said, embarrassed for him.

"Course I can. But I don't care about the money."

"We'll have to think about it," I said awkwardly.

He shook his head and kicked the wooden planks of the pier. "You shouldn't blame the boat for what happened," he said. "Well, remember to call me if you're interested." There was defeat in his voice.

"I'll be in touch," I said. We shook hands and headed for our respective cars.

I turned on the ignition. As we drove off the pier, we turned our gaze to the Doc sitting in his car. He was just as we found him, staring ahead through the windshield as if in a trance. As if he had no place in the world to go.

Fear of Life

When Roger sailed his 16-foot catboat through the cut from Stage Harbor into foam-flecked Nantucket Sound, he had no idea where he would head. It didn't matter. He simply wanted to be in touch with the sea and wind and sun and sky. Sailing always cleared his mind and heart.

Eighteen months ago when he retired, his wife, Julie, asked, "Won't you be bored?"

"Bored? Hell, no," he said.

"You've been so active, having people report to you, making decisions, all that excitement. I mean, after all, you've been chief honcho."

"I'll do all the things I've wanted to do all my life."

"Such as?"

"I plan to make furniture, for one thing."

"Well, yes, you've said that before. But it's only a hobby. Will it be enough?"

"There's the gardening. You know how much I love working in the soil—since I was a kid. Maybe I can make our place into the dream spot I envisioned when we bought it."

"But you can't garden in the winter."

"And I'll do a lot of sailing. I'll take the *Sea Swallow* to the islands. Something I've been wanting to do for years."

"Over my dead body."

"For God's sake, the boat can handle it."

"But I can't," she said.

A large, muscular man, Roger maneuvered easily against the brisk October breeze. But being master of his boat didn't ease his inner chaos. He had left Julie barely a week ago, an act undreamed of the day he retired.

Ahead and stretching in the distance lay Monomoy, a littoral strand of rust-colored dunes. He bore southeast toward the broad opening between their southern end and Nantucket. The sea was busy but manageable. His thoughts drifted.

He had spent long hours making furniture in the shop in his cellar. The house was full of his tables and small chairs and chests of drawers. But it wasn't enough. Julie was right.

"I told you you'd miss the excitement, the challenge," she said.

What was missing? Not the business. He had had his fill of that.

Here on the ocean was excitement. Here he must be alert to hidden shallows and wind changes and keeping to course. This was challenge. Whether a good sail or a business deal, the satisfaction was the same. And here he'd find answers he would never find ashore.

"We'll travel," Julie said. "There's nothing to tie us down. The kids are on their own now. We're free as birds."

"Right," he said.

"Well, you don't sound very enthusiastic."

"Sure I am. I agree. We'll do some traveling. But within reason."

"What do you mean, within reason?"

"I mean I've traveled a lot on business, so it doesn't necessarily turn me on."

"Well, I've been cooped up for years raising kids," Julie barked.

The breeze flung a chilling spray over the bow as the *Sea Swallow* plunged into steepening billows. It was a lot different from the warm water in the British Virgins, where last February he and Julie had chartered a forty-two-foot sailboat and cruised. It was the fulfillment of a dream for him. Julie went along out of wifely duty.

Their cabin had two bunks. He had awakened in the middle of the night surprised at finding Julie next to him.

"Let's make love," she whispered.

He couldn't remember the last time she had taken the initiative.

"I'll try."

He wasn't sure he could. He had lost the habit.

She merged her small, frail body with his as he softened and kissed her forehead, then her face, her neck, her lips. How deeply he loved her. He abandoned himself. How rare a moment, how brief and how dangerous.

Last May the choice was Julie's: Paris. Right after the war when she was in college she had visited the city and had dreamed of returning.

Roger had no desire to see Europe. Someday he'd go, he figured, because that's what comfortable retired Americans did. He agreed to go for Julie's sake; it would even up her sacrifice on the trip to the Virgins.

His two weeks in Paris were miserable; he felt imprisoned. They had a blowup in the Louvre. Weary, their backs and feet aching, they searched for the exit in the maze of galleries.

"This way," Roger said as he strode down a high-windowed corridor.

Julie, taking two steps to his one, had trouble keeping up. After awhile Roger paused.

"I don't remember this place. There's an arrow. Where in hell are the signs? *Sortie*, I think that means exit."

He headed towards a flight of wide marble stairs.

"You don't know where you're going," Julie said. "You're just rushing without thinking, the way you always do."

"I know exactly where I'm going," he said. "These stairs lead to a *sortie*."

They emptied into a long, low corridor, at the end of which he and Julie took a moment to view the white marble statue of Venus de Milo.

"We should go back to the Mona Lisa and start over," Julie said. They backtracked and began again, ending up at the same staircase.

"Let's go back and try again," Julie said.

"No, let's go down the other corridor. It'll lead to an exit."

"How do you know?"

"Well, it has to. Can't you see the other way takes us to Venus?"

"Please, let's begin at the Mona Lisa or find a guard and ask," Julie pleaded.

"I know this corridor goes to an exit. It's only logical," Roger insisted.

"Let's look for a guard, Roger. I'm not following you," she shouted.

"You've followed me for thirty fucking years," Roger yelled.

"That's my mistake," she screeched.

"I've made you a goddamn rich woman. What in hell do you want? Go. You don't need me. You've got your own mind. Go back to your fucking Mona Lisa and find your own way out."

They cared little that a group of astonished onlookers had gathered.

Angry and miserable, Roger walked off. Julie ran after him, confused and fearful. She knew she'd follow him to the ends of the earth.

The waves were fuller now and foaming at their crests. They contained the force of open ocean. He held to a southeasterly course, passing Nantucket faintly to his right. The catboat scaled the watery peaks and slid down them easily. The ocean drew him on.

The summer after Paris had gone smoothly. Roger laid a brick walk, planted a boxwood hedge, and weeded the perennials. Julie frequently joined him planting vegetables in a plot he had prepared. He enjoyed having her work by his side at such times. They were at peace with each other but not always.

They had gone out to dinner with another couple, meeting them at the restaurant. During the conversation Julie said, "Roger never lifted a finger when our children were babies. All he ever did when they cried at night was yell at me. 'Shut them up,' he'd say. He had to have his sleep. He never helped. Not once."

Roger's blood rose. "She's never forgiven me for the sins of her father," he said, controlled. "He left her mother for another woman. She's down on men."

On the drive home he tore at her. "Don't ever do that again. Don't ever criticize me to our friends, in a public place where I can't defend myself. If you have a complaint, tell me to my face." His arms flailed the air, leaving the steering wheel free. She was terrified. Tears poured down her cheeks. He floored the accelerator.

"It was the truth—you never lifted a finger," she said.

"I was working my balls off, struggling to make it. What in hell did you expect of me?"

"They're your kids too," she said between sobs.

"And you're still carrying it after all these years. You're still carrying it."

"I remember everything, every detail. Our marriage is my whole life. You could have helped."

"I'll leave you if you do that again," he seethed.

She stared stonily through the windshield into the blackness. There was only blackness.

The waves rolled on, lifting and lowering the boat rhythmically. Nothing lasts in the sea. In an hour he could be in an ocean at war. The farther he sailed, the greater the risk. Still, he stayed on course into the emptiness.

Because she was a poor swimmer and feared the water, Julie rarely went sailing. But occasionally when the wind was gentle, she would go with him on the bay, wearing a life preserver. One mild afternoon in August they went for a brief sail. Within an hour an unexpected blow developed, churning the sea into whitecaps. Pleading with Roger to return to shore, Julie clung white-knuckled to the combing as the boat heeled. Since their destination was windward, he had to tack back and forth. Her fright worried him.

"We're safe. It looks worse than it is," he assured her.

"But we're going away from land. Why are you doing this to me?"

"Please, Julie, I told you. We can't sail into the wind. Don't worry, we'll get there."

He prepared to tack. "Ready to come about," he shouted. "Hard a'lee." But Julie refused to release her grip and change sides as she was supposed to. Water poured into the cockpit. "Move, move to the other side!" Roger screamed. Julie had been standing and fell backward into the waves. Tossing a flotation cushion overboard, Roger attempted to come about to rescue her, but the tiller had become tangled in the mainsheet. The boat heeled sharply, taking on more water and finally capsizing. In only a few minutes it went down.

Hearing her shout, he swam to her. "Everything will be all right," he said calmly. "We're sure to drift to shore."

"I love you, Roger," she said, reaching for him. "I love you more than my own life."

"And I love you," he said embracing her.

Land was no longer in sight. His course was steady, due east out to sea. Sailing always helped him think straight. He must try to understand what happened.

Understand? What about his infidelity? Julie never let him forget it.

"I believe in monogamy," she said after they had seen a movie in which the hero had a mistress.

"So do I," he said.

"No you don't. You're no different than he is."

"For crissakes, that was fifteen years ago. Can't you give it up? You said you forgave me when I dropped her."

"And I have."

"Doesn't sound like it to me. You're still bitter."

"I just don't trust you anymore. Forgiving and trusting are different things. I would never be unfaithful to you; I couldn't."

"I told you it was lousy. I didn't plan it. Feelings take over. I wasn't sorry when it ended."

"Then why did you do it? I don't understand. You are my whole life. Why? Don't I mean anything to you?"

He had no answer and he'd been asking the question of himself ever since.

Alone on the sea he'd find the answer. On the watery hills, under the limitless sky, he'd find the truth. He loved her. Why was he unfaithful? And why did he have to leave her?

Thirty years ago they had planned to spend their honeymoon on Prince Edward Island, but they had gotten no farther than Boothbay Harbor. Ever since, Julie had talked of visiting the island, as if completing the journey would set things right. At last a driving trip was planned for late September.

All summer Julie had checked with Roger to ensure his promise they'd make the trip. She advised the children and friends of their plans. She made arrangements with the post office, the newspaper delivery boy, and the kennel to take care of their cat.

However, she was troubled as she watched her husband gradually retreating into an imaginary cage. He refused to dine out with friends or make their customary day trips to Boston or Provincetown. Somehow he seemed lost.

"You're bored. You miss the business," she told him. "Do something. You're driving me crazy."

As they lay in bed the night before they were supposed to leave, Roger announced he couldn't make the trip.

"I really want to stay home and do my own thing."

"Which is?"

"You know, working in the shop, gardening, sailing. Anyway, this is the best time of year on the Cape. The summer people are gone, the weather is ideal."

"You're going," Julie demanded. "You promised me."

"I'm sorry. I can't."

"You're deliberately being a bastard."

"No, Julie. I'm not against you."

"Then what is it?"

"I'm comfortable here."

"You're a zombie here. I don't know you."

"Go by yourself or with a friend if you've got your heart set."

"No, you're going with me, you're going, you're going," she shrieked.

"I haven't worked and reached this stage of my life to have someone tell me what I can and cannot do. I'm not going."

He turned out the bed lamp and they lay back to back as he listened to her sob.

The waves had changed. Now and then a swell slammed the boat sideways, making it shudder. High cirrus clouds appeared. Before he had set out, the weather bureau had forecast a storm by evening and issued small craft warnings. He had expected to return long before the storm struck, but now it was too late to make land in time to avoid it.

"I'm moving out, Julie," he said the next morning.

"You're leaving me?"

"Yes."

She fell silent. When he returned that afternoon to pick up a few personal items he had forgotten, he found her in a trance. It made him anxious.

For three days, except to go out to eat, he stayed in a motel room watching television. He was overwhelmed with loneliness. It was a loneliness that had been aching inside him all his life. No one could assuage it, least of all Julie, the one he loved. On the evening of the fourth day, the phone rang.

He heard Julie wailing at the other end. Her words were almost unintelligible. He could make out only, "Help me."

"Do you want me to come?"

Her wail persisted. He repeated himself several times until he thought she said "yes."

He found her sitting in the bedroom rocking and keening the way Irish women do at a wake. Her voice was animal-like. It seemed to come from the well of her being. He slid to his knees, embraced her, and stroked her hair.

"My heart is broken, my heart is broken, my heart is broken," she moaned.

He held her for a long while, perhaps an hour. Gradually she calmed herself.

"I'm so sorry, so sorry, I can't help it, I've got to go through with it," he said.

"I know. We're miserable together. You're doing the right thing, the only thing you can do."

Her change of attitude startled him.

"I'm okay," she said. "We do what we have to do. Go. I'm okay."

That night Julie overdosed on sleeping pills and ended her unbearable pain.

Fear of Life

Flecks of cold spray pelted Roger's face. Astern was the formidable black storm approaching. Ahead lay the mindless, restless sea. He would perform his final act of love. This was the truth. He held to an easterly course into the vastness, never more certain of where he was going.

Change

"Won't you stay awhile at the hacienda before returning to the States?" she asked as we drove from the cemetery in the limousine. "Of all the friends we have, none knew Barry like you."

I saw that she needed me, just as I needed my sons nearby after my wife's death barely a year ago. Yes, we are always alone, but never more so than when finally alone.

"Of course, Nina. I'll stay as long as you want. I have three months off from the university."

"It's just like you, Hal, you're always so generous."

"Your wish is no less than mine," I responded.

How unbelievably nostalgic it was to see the Santos hacienda again. I had often romanticized the place. Old people do that. But the reality—the house now shining, white, and clean, tropical flower gardens everywhere—surpassed my imagining.

"Nina," I said. "You've created a—a vision, a beautiful dream."

"Would you like your old room?" she asked as if it had been saved for me as her guest in the Philippines just as I had left it forty years before.

She led me through old familiar rooms, once bare and forbidding, now hardly recognizable with their Oriental rugs which softened the cold, white marble floor. The once-barren great room with the eye-high fireplace, over which Nina's father's portrait had hung before the occupation, was now furnished with deep, soft comfortable sofas and chairs, antique tables and elaborate chests from dynastic China. I walked among these treasures, touching everything.

In the evening we dined at the same table, sat on the same hard chairs, as we had during my last sojourn, when we were both young and the countryside was in shambles. Had time stopped in this exalted house? Nina, sitting across from

—240—

Change

me, was now wrinkled and white and I, well— Her eyes still sparkled and her voice was spirited, and remnants of her beauty lingered like a sunset.

"How good to have you here. How comforting it is," she remarked after the servants cleared the table and we sat sipping tea.

"Yes," I said. "I spent one of the happiest months of my life in this house, and now . . . somehow nothing really changes, Nina."

"And everything changes," she said.

"And for the worse," I added.

"Without Barry, my Barry," she said sighing.

My "old room" still had the same bed, but now there was a thick blue Chinese carpet on the native mahogany floor, an antique chest of drawers, and a fine teakwood desk. I awoke in the middle of each night, a symptom of my age. I needed very little sleep really. Sitting at the desk, I gazed through the open window across the peaceful rice fields in which I had once labored. Yes, nothing had changed—and everything had changed. I began writing. I wrote Barry Fortune's story, continuing almost until dawn when, finally weary, I lay on the hard floor beside the rich carpet and fell asleep.

Most mornings I arose late and walked the grounds among the flowers, and out along the paths through the paddies, and sometimes down the hard white highway where I used to walk with Anita—lovely Anita. I walked then the few miles to the barrio, to Lugao. At first nothing seemed changed. The path was the same, the thatched houses the same. But the church: The shell holes in its walls were filled, the bullet holes gone. Everything had changed. I was a stranger to the barrio people who stared at this American.

Nina and I usually lunched together.

"And how did you sleep last night?" she asked.

"I didn't—until the morning."

"Oh, I'm sorry. Is it the bed?"

"No, no. My mind won't stop. I've been writing about Barry, and what it was like for all of us in the war—what it was like here when we were young."

"What a wonderful idea. May I read it?"

"If you'd like—but only to the point at which you appear," I said playfully.

"I'll write the second volume about what it was like after the war," she said laughing for the first time since the funeral, "about Barry after you went home and forgot about us."

"Never, Nina. Life takes over: marriage, career, family. Old friends take a back seat—but not for good. I'm here now."

"It was never dull, never for a moment, and I confess it was often exhausting. He had boundless energy." Her eyes grew distant.

"I could never keep up with him," I chortled. "He was, well, a master juggler."

"Yes," she said, "he always had to have a dozen deals going all at once. I've always been sorry that you didn't accept his offer after the war. He never found anyone to replace you. You were more than a friend. You were his alter ego, his conscience. There was no one like you to tell him what he didn't want to hear, no one honest like you. He wanted to make you rich with him. Why didn't you join him, Hal?"

"Frankly, Nina, I didn't approve of his cutting down precious virgin rainforests. I couldn't bear doing it when we were Seabees together. Least of all, could I do it for the money."

"You were always the young idealist. That's why he needed you."

"Still the idealist, Nina. That hasn't changed."

"You know, Hal, Barry and I were never happier than when we lived in the shack together, before the money. How wonderful was our illicit love. He had to steal off from the camp in the middle of the night to be with me and steal back at the faint call of reveille. I had him all to myself then. No distractions. No business deals. It was bliss."

She was radiant, as she used to be. Then suddenly she sobbed. I sat beside her and reached my arm across her heaving shoulders. She buried her face in my chest as her warm tears soaked through my shirt. When she lifted her head, she smiled, composing herself.

"I needed that," she said.

"I've been to Lugao," I said, "and I saw no one I knew. What has happened to my old friends, Nina? Where have they gone?"

"Reverend Mr. Corum died a long time ago. Of course, he was old when you knew him."

"Of course, of course. But Hando?"

"He was a Communist, you know."

"Yes, yes, I knew."

"The government soldiers killed him some years ago in an anti-Communist drive."

"And Anita's father, Lucio?" I asked leading up to the question most on my mind.

"He died about ten years ago, but her mother—"

"Possibly I didn't recognize Anita yesterday, nor she me. Did she marry?"

"I have no idea. You see, she left the barrio to live in Manila shortly after you returned to the States."

"Left Lugao? But why? She said she would never leave the barrio."

"I'm not sure. Some say she had to leave because she was with child. You know, the shame. Her mother went with her."

"No, no. That can't be true," I said, getting up and pacing.

"Maybe it was only talk."

"I'm sure she would have let me know," I said distressed.

"I see. Can I assume it would have been yours?"

I nodded imperceptibly.

That night, unable to write or sleep, I lay on the floor agonizing over what I had learned about Anita. At sunrise, I dressed and walked along the quiet level highway where we used to walk together when we were young, and by the sluggish stream where Anita and I had made love in the cool, tall grass. I knew this was business I had yet to finish.

In the weeks that followed, all my inquiries on trips to Manila led to dead ends.

I had come to the hacienda for renewal. After all, I had found it here once before, during the war. But how elusive it is. I should realize that the past in its essence is never repeatable. So why do I insist on the illusion? Why do I hunger for those months that I once spent here? To escape what? My beloved America? The hills and canyons of my beautiful Southern California sliced into endless subdivisions? The enormous fouled air? The denuded hillsides? The abandoned pits dotting the land? The nondescript buildings and miles of poverty? The desecration of the countryside? To escape the immense scale of things? The smallness I feel?

Each night I wrote, each day I walked, and each evening Nina and I talked or played cards or listened to Bach or read. We spent the weeks of the monsoon in temperate Baguio at Nina's isolated mountain retreat.

But the hacienda soon beckoned. An old song, old when we sang it together in the rice fields forty years ago, fluttered across my mind:

> Planting rice is never fun;
> Bent from morn till set of sun;
> Cannot stand and cannot sit;
> Cannot rest for a little bit.

I tried once more to help the field hands (no longer tenant farmers) plant seedlings in the flooded rice paddies. The cool mud oozing between my toes felt good, but the work was too hard, too painful. I had to lie down on the Oriental carpet before dinnertime to relieve the ache. Nina's legs astride my buttocks, she massaged my weary muscles. I was free to love her. We had become like a married couple. At night she would lie on the floor beside me, and we would fall asleep curled against each other.

Change

It had been almost three months and I now missed home. My sabbatical was over. I yearned to teach again. My story about Barry and our lives during the war was finished.

"Please stay," Nina begged. "Help me manage the hacienda."

"I'm not competent in such matters, Nina. I have my teaching. I want to see my sons,"

"But they no longer need you," she said, and I understood that she was telling me that she did.

"I need them. Look, come with me to the States."

"Then will we come back here?"

"Only for a visit."

"But you love the hacienda," she said, holding my hand.

"It's not the same. I can't live in this country, not the way it is. Nothing has changed—the corruption, the cronyism. No one is better off than they were forty years ago—maybe worse off. I miss the freedom back home. I hadn't realized how free I felt there. There's a vibrancy about America. It's part of me. Come home with me. You'll see what I'm talking about."

"At my age, leave the hacienda?" she said with a wave of her hand. "I would never adjust to a strange place at this late stage. No, this is where I belong, where I wish to die."

"Will you drive me to Manila tomorrow?"

"Of course. But when may I read your story?" she asked.

"I'll leave it with you."

"Good. I'll make a copy and send the original to you."

"You needn't bother."

"Don't you wish to have it published?"

"I needed only to write it, Nina. That you'll read it is a bonus."

I felt as anxious and excited as I did long ago when Barry drove me to the aircraft carrier that was bound home for America. Tomorrow I would say my second and perhaps last good-bye to Nina.

ADDENDUM

From Adversity Comes Wisdom
A True Short Story Concerning the Publication of "Old Hands Don't Need Motors"

To my daughter Betsy upon her college graduation

Many true stories have a quality of perfection rarely attained in fiction. Their message is a clear melody. This true story, hardly perfect but clear, begins when my daughter Betsy joined the staff of *SAIL* magazine as a part-time intern while in her sophomore year at college. It ends — almost — with a phone call from my old friend Roy. Let me begin at the ending.

Roy called to say, "My son was reading an account in May's *SAIL* of a man and his young son looking to buy a used boat and he was surprised to find your name as the author."

"No kidding. Whaddya know," I said. "They finally published it." I was guardedly delighted. Having sold the story originally entitled "Old Hands Don't Need Motors" to the magazine almost two years earlier, I entertained the idea of buying it back so I could send it elsewhere to ensure its survival. If published, it would be my first short story in a national magazine.

"What did they call it?" I asked, knowing the magazine had been displeased with my title.

"Why, I don't know," Roy replied, perhaps puzzled that I didn't know the name of my own story.

"How did your son like it?"

"Very much. A lot."

I sighed, relieved, even though I suspect insincerity of anyone — especially a friend or the son of a friend — who tells me he or she likes what I've written.

An hour later Hoyt, another friend and sailor, phoned. Knowing he was a subscriber to *SAIL*, I blurted the good news. He hadn't seen the latest copy but he promised to get back to me with all the details.

Two days later I found the following message on my phone answering tape: "This is Hoyt. I don't know why you have an unlisted number. (He is audibly annoyed.) Anyway, I just finished the *SAIL* magazine article. It's on page 106B and it's entitled 'I'll Let Her Go' dot, dot, dot, quote, unquote. (And in an obviously pleased voice.) And, uh, I thought it was pretty good. Uh, anyway, congratulations on getting it in."

After a few days, Hoyt called again to inform me that he would temporarily lend me the magazine, which had not yet appeared on the stands. He would also deliver the next day a photocopy of the story on his way by my door. He kept his promise, as true friends do.

Now I go back nearly two years to the beginning of the story when Betsy began her internship at the magazine. I had mentioned to her then that I had a story in mind that might appeal to the editors of *SAIL.*

"Of course, Dad, you understand I can't help you," she had warned. "I mean I have no influence. The story would have to sell itself."

In fact the story had not been born. It was little more than a weak series of electrical impulses whirring crazily through the synapses of the right side of my brain.

"Certainly. I'd want it no other way," I said firmly. "But couldn't you see that it got to the proper editor and not end up in the slush pile or read by some lightweight?"

Suggesting that I mail it in routinely, she promised that she would bring my manuscript to the attention of the proper person, again emphasizing her nonpolitical position.

A month later, after a reading by both willing and unwilling members of my family, the completed story received no strongly negative comments. From one's family, especially from one's wife, this is nothing short of having rave notices. I sent the story to the magazine and alerted Betsy.

Here is *SAIL*'s surprisingly prompt verdict:

[The editor-in-chief] passed your piece "Old Hands" to me because it seemed best suited to the side feature section,

which I edit. You have a nice twist to the "buying a boat" story, and I would like to buy first-time North American serial rights to it, for use as a side feature, for $200, payable on acceptance.

The story does still need a bit of work to make it work for SAIL. [The editor-in-chief], Betsy, and I have discussed what we think is needed. Normally, I would type out suggestions to you, but we thought that Betsy, as part of her training, could pass the comments on and deal with the author's reactions. She also will be the editor of record for the piece.

If the editing process and the sum are agreeable to you, please let me know. I will also need your social security number in order to start the accounting department's wheels, and Betsy will need a short author's bio statement so she can craft the one- or two-sentence note that goes at a story's end.

I look forward to hearing from you.

Best,
Catherine
Copy/Production Editor

Thirty seconds after reading the above, I wrote,

Thank you for accepting "Old Hands." I accept your terms and hold my breath that the changes you wish to make will not alter the essence of the story, which, as no doubt you realize, has less to do with buying a boat than revealing the universal tragedy of aging.

In any case, I am touched by your generosity of spirit in having Betsy participate in the process. Her input can only be tremendously gratifying to both of us. What father could have a more delightful mentor than his own daughter?

My social security number is . . . I shall be in touch with Betsy, who really knows more about the author than I, to give her the biographical information she needs.

Again thank you for your interest and your kindness.
Most cordially yours,
Hugh Aaron

Two days later I received a letter from a middle-aged lady acquaintance whom I had met on the beach during her vacation and on whom I had foisted "Old Hands."

Your story, "Old Hands Don't Need Motors" is a wonderful tale. Thank you for so thoughtfully sharing this endearing piece with us before it is published. I'm sure the subscribers to SAILing (her title) Magazine will identify with the love of sailing found in the three men and will appreciate this very sensitive story.
Please keep writing! We will look forward to reading more from you in the future.

In the meantime Betsy had sent me a three-page tome called imposingly, SPECIFICATIONS FOR ARTICLES AND PHOTOGRAPHS IN SAIL MAGAZINE. She also sent me an official *SAIL* memo demanding: "Take out specifics such as Sea Sprite and City Hospital, etc. Change ending—stop at $8000—instead have father and son in the story go home and think about buying the boat. Make it so there's no change in Doc's fantasy—less Mother stuff."
Crammed in the left-hand corner of the returned manuscript Betsy had also written: "Pop—these are all suggestions—change them as you like within the limitations, Betsy."

I was outraged. What does she mean "change ending"? Is she out of her mind? What does she mean, "Change them as you like WITHIN LIMITATIONS"? Sure as shooting she's gone loco.
By the time we met I had cooled off and with superhuman restraint penned the following, in part, to *SAIL*.

From Adversity Comes Wisdom

During her visit home this weekend, Betsy gave me an indication of the changes you will require in my story "Old Hands Don't Need Motors," in order to make it more suitable for publication in SAIL. While I do not wish to appear recalcitrant, I feel compelled to offer a rebuttal.

The story is intended to be a fully integrated "work of art," albeit far from a perfect one. Each part was included to explain motivation, build mood, and advance the story's principal theme: the human tragedy of aging. While I see no harm in minor changes that do not detract from the basic meaning of the story, I fear some of the recommended changes, especially in the ending, will do just that.

May I . . . suggest that this tale, mostly as it is, will find a ready and understanding audience among your readers, that they will appreciate the circumstances of the story, identify with one or the other of the characters, and be moved by the message?. . . To alter either circumstances, characters or message will damage the effectiveness of the whole. . . .

As I now reread this letter, written almost two years ago, I say to myself: What chutzpah. My god, the editor must be an Everest of patience. For damned sure, in her shoes, I would have told me to go to hell. Here, in part, is her letter written two days later.

From considerable experience both as an editor and writer, I can say that I know of no writer who enjoys every minute of being critiqued. Invariably there are elements a writer is particularly fond of that do not strike an editor as entirely appropriate — and vice versa — and which in turn cause stabs of regret in the writer. The hope is, of course, that neither is blinded by particular fondnesses.

. . . At times the piece tends toward the melodramatic; choosing to pare down some descriptions and do away with others altogether will, in our opinion as professionals with

bundreds of articles and several books in our pasts,
strengthen the piece by forcing the reader to concentrate on
the principal dynamics of the relationships. . . .

Both [the editor-in-chief] and I liked the general thrust
of your piece, the overall organization and the basic clarity.
Some of the changes we are suggesting are designed to make
the particulars of the drama less particular in order to
protect the real Doc. Doing so will not affect the power of the
story. . . .

At this point, I see three options. You could re-work the
piece yourself, taking into account our suggestions. This is
the option I prefer. We could simply edit it ourselves into a
final piece. Or you could submit it elsewhere.

I await your reactions. . . .

Catherine

Bless you. That's what I call "laying it on the line." It's
true. I'm a melodramatic guy.

Betsy having been provided copies on all
correspondence between Catherine and myself, of course,
was kept up to the minute on the matter. As "editor-of-
record" she must understandably put in her two cents worth.
A day after Catherine's letter arrived, I received Betsy's
irresistible masterpiece on *SAIL* stationery.

Hi Pop! Thanks for the birthday [her 20th] lunch and
everything yesterday—I love the Paris paintings. . . . But
actually this isn't a real thank-you note—I mean Official
Business. Something came up yesterday that as a
professional intern I feel is necessary to talk to you about.
(ouch)

I know that you said you don't care really whether you
get published or not—that is for this story—if SAIL wants to
change the ending then forget it. Well, as I said before, I
think you're making a mistake. Perhaps not one that you'll
regret, but one that brings up the question you brought up in
your article you sent to Modern Maturity. Who are you now?

From Adversity Comes Wisdom

Well, I talked to Catherine and she made the dilemma I was having about your article (story) a little clearer.

You wrote the article (story) with the intention of getting SAIL to publish it. They agreed, but wanted to make changes. Then you said it's a piece of art, it shouldn't be changed. Catherine said there are two kinds of writers. One who writes with the intention of selling for a certain market and one who writes for artistic value, not to live on but for pleasure. You wrote this article for a market and you should expect it to be treated as it would in a market — a process of going through editors and possibly being changed. That's why I don't think you should withdraw the story. I don't really think it's fair to the people here who have taken the time out to offer suggestions to better your story for the market.

Isn't one of the joys of writing having as many people as possible read your stuff so they too can enjoy it and discuss it and have their eyes opened to new experiences?

Plus I think you're drivin' Ma wacko by complaining about not being published. Now that you have the opportunity, get published and she might not spend so much time in the basement painting!!!!

Let me know what you think. We'll talk soon.

Love,

Betsy

Your daughter/ Editorial Intern

After pondering Betsy's letter, which followed on the heels of Catherine's, my tendency towards paranoia asserted itself. I was convinced *SAIL* not only wished to remold the offspring of my imagination, the product of my soul, but it also had brainwashed my daughter against me. Feeling under siege, I attacked.

Dear Catherine, Perhaps from now on we should be on a first name basis, because, I hope, despite this letter, after you have read it we can still be friends. I have tried as best I could, as well as my sense of personal integrity will allow, to comply with your wishes. The words in my story are not sacred, nor is the story's architecture. But my meaning is, because once I've lost that, the story becomes a mere shell and so do I.

Now for the ending. This is where we are on a collision course. . . . His (Doc's) inability to sell his boat is merely the continuation of a string of failures he has endured after a life of supreme success. It is a story about the universal tragedy of becoming old. Anything upbeat here would be false.

Ah yes. Could it be our real collision is between your professionalism and my innocence? I acknowledge your superior expertise; what you know about the craft I have yet to learn. Please forget the magazine for a minute, and think about the future course of your life. How will you think and feel at age 55 or 60? Hard to know, to imagine, isn't it? Well, you see, Catherine, that's my advantage. I know what it's like, and that's what I've tried to capture. Because, after all, I'm the real, the true Doc.

With all respect and warmest regards,
Hugh Aaron

P.S. If, because I'm giving you so much trouble, you feel it isn't worth it, I'll understand. I lose patience with nuts like me too.

P.P.S. Please note new title: "Boat Bargain of the Century." Hope you like it.

Clearly, I fired all salvos at hand. I thought my pulling rank with respect to age and experience particularly ingenious. How on earth could a vibrant woman editor in her thirties one-up me on that?

Two days passed while I mulled over a proper reply to Betsy, toward whom I felt a twin responsibility: that of father as well as collaborator. The following letter in part, I believe, amply blended both roles.

From Adversity Comes Wisdom

My dear Betsy, Your warm and winning letter is extremely helpful for it does "clear the air" not only by giving me a perspective on my present conflict with SAIL, but also on how I should look at my work. So your talk with Catherine is beneficial all around, and I hope you will tell her so.

"Old Hands" had been sloshing around inside me for a long time . . . long before you joined SAIL. As I recall, I indicated that I had a story in mind that MIGHT BE useful to the magazine. The fact that you were on the staff provided me the impetus to put it down on paper. But I did not write it explicitly for SAIL. Indeed I had doubts that they'd go for it, especially after reading some of the material in the magazines you left with me. I saw that SAIL's stories, unlike mine, are rich in incident and drama. And they often give practical information. That the editors like "Old Hands" didn't surprise me because it reveals a truth that touches everyone. But when they expressed an interest in publishing it, I was floored. I honestly felt my submission was a long shot.

I should have researched SAIL's style more thoroughly before sending in "Old Hands." That is my mistake and I feel awful that this could lead to your embarrassment. But I'm proud of you for taking their point of view because as a burgeoning professional, you must.

Since it is now clear my goal is to offer deeper meanings to my readers in a literary way, then SAIL and I should call it quits, friendly quits.

Yes, I'd like to be published (although I hadn't realized I was driving your mother wacky about it) exactly for the reasons you suggest in your letter. But I wish my audience to . . . comprehend what I mean to say, not what someone else thinks I ought to say to suit their purposes. I refuse to allow the "truth" I express to be diluted or demeaned. Whether it's an oppressive government or the mediocrity of the marketplace that promulgates compromise, the result is the same: the cheapening of truth and human dignity. Dearest

Betsy, you can see I'm impossible. I'll bide my time. I have faith that someday I'll find the right publication for my material. And best of all, now I know who and what I am (in retirement) and you've helped me find out.

This entire experience, which on the surface appears so troubling, has really been most salutary for me. It's the old story: From adversity comes wisdom. I hope you have come up with similar results.

With all my love and gratitude,
Dad

For the next three weeks Betsy and I held a silent truce, avoiding mention of our collaboration. Then the subject of "Old Hands" surfaced again in the form of a startling letter from Catherine.

Dear Hugh, Your rewrite of "Old Hands/Boat Bargain" is a much improved version, in my opinion. You have pruned superfluous drama, and the ambiguity at the end is right (and despite what you think I'd do, I would indeed keep the final paragraph). . . . If you can agree to my editing the piece, we're on for my buying it on the terms I mentioned in my first letter.

I look forward to hearing from you.
Sincerely,
Catherine
Assistant Managing Editor

Redeemed, victorious, and blindly failing to acknowledge that Catherine had received a promotion, I replied immediately as follows.

Dear Catherine, OK. You may go with what's-its-name (Old Hands or Boat Bargain) in the manner you suggest . . . and on the terms of your prior letter. Only one request: when you perform the surgery please leave no scars.

From Adversity Comes Wisdom

Thanks for your patience.
Most cordially yours,
Hugh Aaron

So that ended it. As time went on — eighteen months — and when nothing happened, I assumed Catherine had decided to bury their story (it was no longer mine) in a pauper's grave. After all, didn't it now belong to *SAIL* to do with what they wished? Hadn't I signed away my rights? I felt strangely like a mother who, having given up her infant for adoption, found herself suffering pangs of regret. In the meantime more than twenty of my short stories of mixed quality were written and rejected by a variety of commercial and literary magazines.

A few months ago, when paying a social visit to the offices of *SAIL*, Betsy learned the story was at the typesetters, and so informed me. Containing myself, I was skeptical. Still unpublished, I was reconciled to becoming a posthumous author. No — nearer the truth — I was looking forward to it. Once published, I would be subjected to criticism.

When my long-time friend Roy phoned to tell me that *SAIL* had finally come through, I was forced to drastically adjust my thinking. I can't say I was unhappy, but I wished I could have been more enthusiastic. It just proves that some people are never satisfied.

I promptly read the published story through a microscope and found hardly any scars. Thank God, my message, all that mattered, was intact.

In a phone discussion with Betsy about the story's publication, she asked how I liked what the editors had done to it.

"Well, they retained 90 percent — no 95 percent — of the original," I said. "They cut out some of the drama, made it more restrained in places, but it's not so bad. Actually I like some of the things they did, things that I would do myself were I to rewrite the story today. I guess I've made some progress as a writer over the past two years.

"But the title they chose is something else — it's for the birds. I think they should have kept 'Old Hands Don't Need Motors.' It isn't really quite the same story without it."

Yesterday Betsy phoned to say: "Guess what, Dad. *The Atlantic Monthly* called offering me a job after graduation. I'll not be doing exactly what I want but I think it's a start, at least a foot in the door."

"Take it. Take it," I urged. A wonderful vision presented itself. Wouldn't it be great to have one of my stories published by the prestigious *Atlantic*? Betsy certainly would see that it got to the proper editor. You know, not end up in the slush pile or read by some lightweight. I can taste it already.